E.E. Bertram

November Fox – Book 1. Following Joy

A Metaphysical Visionary Fable

First published by Conscious Fiction in 2016.

Second Edition.

ISBN: 978-0-9953813-1-5

This book was professionally typeset on Reedsy.
Find out more at reedsy.com

Contents

Introduction

Things aren't always as they seem, do we wake or do we dream? Are we dreaming life or living the dream?

The answer may be we do both.

*****

A letter from me, to you. The dawn is near.

How delightful. This being my first ever letter, I must apologise, as it may be on the long side as far as letters are concerned. My Father always said, *if you are going to do something, do it properly, or not at all.* They call me The Architect. I am much more accustomed to construction and landscaping, which is worlds away from writing language on a page. Although of late, I seem to be doing far more observing than designing. Never could I have imagined I would become an observer and a letter-writer. Funny thing, life; how it sneaks up on you like that. Your World of Form fascinates me so—curious, busy people, always *doing, doing, doing.*

I must admit that I tend to be the same myself, although in a different way, as you will come to witness. *Perhaps you and I shared some things in common?* (It is, of course, no coincidence that you found my message.) I sense that you have spent some tick-tocks, or at least a few moments, wondering *who you are? What is this life all about? How did we get here? Where are we going?* I myself cannot give you any fixed answers to these questions, yet I can perhaps share with you another perspective on this wondrous ride we call life. My observations of one fascinating young lady—who you will soon know as November Fox—may also shed some light. In writing you this letter, I intend to show you a glimpse behind the curtain. This is a world not seen by anyone in your sphere, until

i

now.

Before we get started, I must say I am rather joyous to meet you here, in this peculiar part of the universe. This invisible space; the distance of approximately 46cm or 18 inches that the black letters of these words travel to your eyes, which then absorb, filter, and process them. Yes, this is *indeed* a rather fascinating location, out of all the possible places to connect. This unique space is one where we can both float free in a dialogue of sorts, sharing this moment. *Although perhaps reading this, you may think I existed in the past, writing this letter?*

Maybe you believe you are here, now, alone, scanning words I left behind for you to find? Is this the case? Let me say that the universe is far more mysterious than you have ever imagined. *Are you open to the possibility that it may only be you travelling down linear tick-tock?* I do hope so, because the truth is, I float here with you in this moment. Hello, (insert me shaking your hand and smiling,) I am delighted to make your acquaintance in this curious part of the cosmos.

My Father always called me a dreamer He was right about that. Dreamers are also important; I realise that now. As a young Architect, I spent any spare moment I could, stretched out across my magic flying carpet, Charlie, staring into the heavens and wondering how everything came into being. I shall tell you more about Charlie a little bit later. I still wonder why my Father displayed a notably more negative tone than his default persecutory edge when he called me a dreamer. *Perhaps dreams and those bestowed with the job to explore them, are not so simple to understand; perhaps even frightening?* I am rather sure, as one of the ones with my head in another dimension, that it is not always easy to be a dreamer. You will need to trust me on that, unless you are a dreamer yourself. *Are you?*

Oscar Wilde, the fine chap he is (or perhaps was, from your perspective), once said, *A dreamer is one who can only find his way by moonlight, and his punishment is that he sees the dawn before the rest of the world.* How true that is, and how punished I have been because of my dreaming. I say this with heartfelt sincerity; life can be a double-edged sword of tranquillity and loneliness, when living in the solitude of shadows. Yet I am not writing to dwell on such dark affairs. Today the precious dawn is soon to arrive, and I just cannot contain my excitement anymore. I can sense change in my bones; although, to be clear, I carry no skeletons as such. My TMD machine (I will also explain him later) is doing his utmost to translate, and "Bones" is the best the poor fellow could come up with. Anyway, the sun is near, my dear friend! So let this letter-writing business commence.

Have you ever had an exceptionally strong sense of something or a gigantic idea? One so immense that you are unsure your small body or mind can contain the complex monstrosity. You feel you may crack open when you allow it to push your edges too far. Well, the moment is here to let you in on *my* little secret.

There comes—or came—a period (depending on where you reside on linear tick-tock) when dreams and ideas began to grow at a faster rate than humans could contain them. I recognised a gap in the market to build my cities—cities of dreams—to house the overflow; and I did, starting with one prototype.

It was quite some moons ago when I constructed my first little city. She was not the cosmopolitan environment I am more often commissioned to design. This beauty was an experimental side project I started to create in my rare time off. My boss, who was my Father, the absolute slave-driver, *NEVER* let me take a holiday. The moments needed to establish the foundations of my secret, urban venture, were hard to arrange. He had assigned me to New York, a massive undertaking, still unfinished in the year 2020, yet I persisted with my little city whenever possible. Brick by brick, park by park, building by building, I built her from the ground up without a soul knowing. Eventually, my labour of love began to take form, and a lovely creation emerged—a unique imagined landscape. I named her Lucitopia; the first city not requiring people to keep her alive. I had created a concept reservoir. A place ignited and fuelled by idea energy, to turn her many cogs. All the big dreams and thoughts, too large to fit in your World of

Form, could reside in Lucitopia. Here, they await their ideal moment to cross over to your side through the underground water canals of the collective mind.

Well, when I had gained enough confidence in the initial model of Lucitopia's design, I showed my colleagues, and then (insert deep breath of angst for emotive effect), my Father. I stood, knees trembling, before the Ogre and his dark-brown desk as a sheepish defendant, breathless, awaiting the verdict. He paused in contemplative thought for eons while my legs rattled. Finally, he cracked his neck from side to side and responded by promoting me to run the whole Architectural department! Actions were his words; Father strikes again! He made only one rule: no screens. I saw beyond the permanent look of disapproval scarred across his overworked face, that he was proud. Now, thanks to me, every living soul has their own Lucitopia, although not all are yet filled with life, the frameworks are prepared. There is even one for you. *Were you aware of that?* (Insert me smiling.) The Empire is now massive and contains the entire dream and idea collection from all people of the World of Form. That is everyone who has or will ever live. *Can you imagine what would have happened if all the small, football-sized heads of humans had to house all those tremendous concepts?* They would literally explode like watermelons. Not a lovely sight.

I am still bamboozled to think it is I, The Architect, in this moment, writing to you, and I mean *you* specifically. For, as I have said, it is not a matter of chance that this letter is especially for *you*. Hello. (Insert me waving to you.) Right now is indeed an exciting period of tick-tock—almost too much to bear.

Together, we have crossed the final frontier; space, the space between you and me. Bravo to those mystical 46cm or 18 inches here in front of you, where magic is possible. Just you wait and observe, although perhaps you will not perceive it as such, the wonder happens between the words and space. It may just arrive as a feeling.

I do, however, have three doubts: 1. Are my calculations correct? 2.

Will this message reach you? 3. Can my TMDM translate without error, allowing this letter to travel between dimensions without losing its integrity? As I think you say in your World of Form, tick-tock will tell. Despite my insecurities, I heed the call to contact you and share some of the curious things I have seen in one of the first Lucitopias I created. May the universe conspire to allow you to receive this letter, which your soul has requested.

Back in the 1980s (my comparative version), I experimented in one Lucitopia by furnishing one of the city's penthouse apartments. Crazy, I know, considering no people live there. I was just playing, like you would with a model house, creating a home away from my cocoon. Charlie also enjoyed it, as he had a comfortable floor to have a rest upon. Two rather peculiar things happened. One was with the mirror. The other was the television. *Sorry, Father.* The looking glass made me so incredibly dizzy. *Have you ever looked into a mirror with another one behind you at the precise angle to create never-ending reflections? Perplexing, is it not? Where does the tunnel end? What is down that rabbit hole of infinite recursion?* I took that bizarre, reflecting glass down.

The TV was even more fascinating. I installed a little television set on the corner table. I cannot say that I was the most obedient of Architects. I had to build him from scratch in complete secrecy, so my Father would not discover the betrayal of his *no screens* rule. Fortunately, I find electronics very easy to understand. Well, you can imagine my amazement when I turned on the little device, and it had instant reception.

We have no TVs over here, although we learn about them at school in our World of Form culture classes; yet we have never seen one for real. They are absolutely forbidden, making them even more exciting for me. I did not respect his ridiculous rule. *Tell me, what is the point in knowing about something riveting without being able to experience the glory of its existence?* Anyway, I am quite sure mine was the first screen activated on our side. Pride outweighed the terror of potential consequence, enabling me to complete building it. Mesmerised by the colours and images on my new TV, I sat my jittery self down on the sofa, mouth and eyes wide open. A farmer peered out of his red, wooden farmhouse to see a small fox looking in at him from the frosty garden. This was the moment I decided observing was much more enthralling than designing. I was more delinquent than usual that day and skipped work to stay in the cosy, rooftop apartment; eyes glued to the screen, to watch what unfolded. Sadly, I neglected the Cincinnati Subway project and left it incomplete.

As I mentioned, the passage of tick-tock does not happen the same way over here as it does for you on your side. You travel in a linear way—past and future all stretched out along a long ruler. Where I reside, we live in a bend of sorts, in the space-tick-tock continuum. Let us call it a type of non-tick-tock. Perhaps more on that later. So while I am sorry, Cincinnati residents, for my diversion, to this day, I do not regret the decision.

Anyway, *where was I?* Ah yes, tucked up under a purple cover in my rooftop apartment, watching...

The curious farmer followed the fox to a towering, mustard tree across some fields. He was shocked to find a little, frosty baby wrapped in a purple, gypsy blanket, wailing to the high heavens. The iced grass crunched beneath his feet, as he walked over and picked up the distressed tear-machine in his rough worker's hands. He looked over at the young fox, who pointed with her nose at a small, music box lying at his feet. After staring for some time, the small, orange fox suddenly disappeared into the nearby forest. The nervous man, in his red-and-black checked shirt and torn gardening trousers, held the young one at quite a distance from him. It was quite evident that he did not know what to do with a tearful little bag of arms and legs.

My watching was then interrupted as I was summoned to the office by Mr. Slave-Driver himself. He was a brute, who disliked laziness more than anything, so I anticipated being put on trial for my disobedient behaviour; a trial that could be long and treacherous—perhaps even fatal. I prayed he did not discover the TV, for that could mean the end of it all.

So Charlie and I flew slowly back to work headquarters, a one-hundred-storey, pointed skyscraper made entirely of glass. After leaving Charlie with the magic carpets concierge downstairs, I took the elevator to level 100. With a shaking hand, I opened his office door. The glare of a tiger about to catch his prey, pierced my quivering shell.

"That's it son! I have had it with you and your rebellion!" He boomed, smashing his fists on the desk with such force, the building shuddered. I retreated, shielding myself behind the translucent door, leaving it slightly ajar to hear the rest of my sentence.

"I banish you to the other side!" He thundered.

My heart skipped a beat, for he has been known to send people to the far end of the universe. "Other side of what, Father?" I murmured just loud enough for him to hear. I did not think he meant the World of Form. Beings from our side had yet to go there, except, perhaps, my Mother, although I am yet to confirm. (More on her later.)

"The Earth, you fool!" I stood in silence and sighed a *phew*, internally. With such a punishment, the TV was still safe—for the moment.

"You will design Canberra and not return until I believe you have acquired the discipline needed to complete projects and not skip work!" Hammering his fist on the desk once more, his mottled face screamed, "Now get out of my sight!"

Accustomed as I was to his shouting, it still made me shudder. Head bowed, and shoulders caved, I gazed at the reflective floor of his office, noticing a trail of blood spots leading to his desk. I left, shooting a quick glance back at him as the glass door closed behind me. He was rubbing his leg. Never had I seen my Father with an injury. Both pity and pleasure circled my heart. For too long I, alone, had carried all the wounds. I scurried away, sensing a change in the ether, of a kind I found hard to identify.

Thinking of the punishment he had served, I smiled to myself and chuckled. Again, I could show off my talent for architecture. I would make an elegant design of this city, and prove my Father wrong. I also quite fancied the idea of taking off on an adventure across the world, far away from him and normal life. Although, before the banishment commenced, Charlie and I returned in a flash to the penthouse. I realised my actions were devious, yet I knew I would be leaving soon and guessed Father would be tied up fixing his leg. I had done my work for the day, and he had punished me already; *so what would it matter?*

So I switched on the TV and jumped back under the blanket, eager to find out what was happening in this strange, other- worldly tale.

The farmer now had the baby in a cardboard box, secured with a seatbelt in his battered, old truck. They were passing through a town. I spotted a sign above a bank, *Rockfield Credit Union. Rockfield?* My nose wrinkled as I leaned towards the television. I am one of the most prolific Architects, yet this Rockfield place remained a mystery. *Who designed it?* I kept my eyes glued to the TV.

The unlikely pair arrived at a big, weather-torn castle, dressed in shadows with tiny windows, dully alight. *Kaboom*, a bolt of lightning shot down, and rain began to fall like lead bullets as they pulled onto the crunching gravel of the drive. The farmer tucked the baby under one arm, using his other as a rain shield as the gloomy structure gobbled them up. A stumpy, silver-haired human, who wore a rope-shaped scar around her neck, greeted them from behind her desk. She looked more like an entity from the underworld than a creature I would call a woman. She had liquorice-black pupils and a scrunched-up, vicious expression that screamed silently, "No one ever loved me, so I hate every single one of you!"

"No admissions. We're full!" She hissed from under the curve of her hunched back.

"But I... I... I-" The farmer stopped in his tracks, shocked, I think, both at the thought of raising the child himself and the beast standing before him.

"Cat got ya tongue? You, farmers, are all the same—all hands, nothing upstairs," She snarled, with a curled lip and the glare of a raven.

"I… I have money," the farmer stuttered, as his trembling hand fumbled with a pouch of cash and coins, eventually depositing it on the desk.

The haggard woman's beady eyes ignited as she hobbled closer to inspect the offering, rummaging through it with her face only inches above the sack. She began mumbling under her breath as she snatched the pouch and put it in the pocket of her oversized, grey, raggedy gown.

"Huh, the last thing we need is another one." She growled, as she pulled out the logbook and whacked it down hard on the counter.

The farmer jumped back, covering the baby's ears.

"Name?"

"Tom Meadows."

"Not you, stupid. That wretched thing in your arms!"

The farmer's mouth fell open. "Oh, um, no name," he replied, peering down at the small child.

"Mother died in labour?" Her dry voice asked without a hint of empathy.

"No, I found her under a tree."

"In November? The frost should have taken her."

The farmer's eyes widened. "Mmm, I was surprised to find her alive. Thankfully, a fox led me to her," he said, smiling at the infant.

"A fox?" The woman stared at the baby in disbelief. "How that dirty, little, mud basket survived both the frost and the fox, is a tale to be told." She reached over and roughly brushed the soiled blanket with her bony, scaled hands.

The farmer pulled the newborn closer to his chest. The hag retreated to pick up her feathered pen.

"Well then. We shall call it *November Fox*," she said as she logged the arrival, hunching over the leather-bound book, her nose almost touching the page.

The farmer looked down at the peaceful, sleeping baby with her soft, orange hair. "November Fox," he whispered, caressing her cheek with the side of his weathered finger.

"You know Hartwall Orphanage has a strict no-returns rule. You give us that thing today; you walk away forever. NO RETURNS. Understood?" She snapped.

"That thing," he murmured to himself, taking a slow step back from the desk, clutching to his heart the precious life he had found. After some moments, the farmer sighed dejectedly and shook his head. "I have no choice; my wife died two years ago. There is no way I can raise this baby." He gave the infant a sad smile and stroked her soft hair gently. "As much as I would like to."

"Ok then, give it here." The gnarly beast reached over and snatched up baby November like a sea eagle catching a mullet.

The TV screen went blank.

I felt sure my eyes betrayed me. I shook the TV vigorously and pressed all the buttons like a madman. Nothing. I paced up and down the apartment, biting my nails and knowing my hair would be going greyer by the second if I had any. *What would become of this poor baby?* I so wanted to dive into the television and pull her through to our side, *although how?* I did not know. The television showed no signs of life. I rattled it with all my might again, just in case. Nothing. I wondered whether I had imagined the whole story. Perhaps my Father was right about me: *Had I dreamt up the entire tale?*

After hours of fiddling with the electronics to no avail, I covered the TV with the purple blanket and signalled to Charlie, to return us home, to our cocoon in the sky. The heavens murmured with broody, dark storm-clouds, as melancholia drenched me from mind to mud. On the flight home, I racked my brain for ideas on how to power the TV. I had no answer. As we flew up the black, circular stairway, I noticed a message tucked under the doormat. It read, almost as if written in blood. "You are an Architect. Remember that." My soul trembled. It was from my Father. *How did he know? Why a letter? Was it only a warning?* I would not dare disobey such a direct order about my life's duty. I did once, and let me just say that I will not be doing that again. The note meant not taking many more trips back to the rooftop apartment—maybe none at all—unless I was ready to risk the end; the end of it all. I wondered when I would ever see baby November Fox again. My head ached at my careless installation of the television in the first place. Now I had a direct connection to the other side—yet without being allowed an open channel. It is such a terrible situation to get a taste for something and be kept from having more. That in itself was perhaps a worse punishment than my temporary exile to the other side of the world.

I wondered about this tale of November Fox and how it mirrored my situation; she without a family, and the hole in her heart and me with an absent mother and a tyrant of a father. It made me wonder if this little TV screen was something of a dream-machine reflecting back to me, in its distorted manner, a story that called for me to plunge into my own depths. The universe, as I know only too well, is a very mysterious place, and I would not put the possibility beyond the Master Designer of it all.

Well, after that day, many of your World of Form Earth-years passed, while I was busy drafting and designing Ancient Rome, Paris, the Grand Canyon, and the Lake District. Yet I never stopped thinking about poor baby November.

I did manage to pop in once a few years ago and discovered nearly all the buildings in November Fox's Lucitopia, destroyed. I wailed to the roof of the sky. The entirety of my work *ruined!* I flew through the abandoned streets of shattered remains, with rivers of tears streaming down my face, drenching poor Charlie, and raining on the devastation. *How had this happened?* I wondered if my Father had demolished my beloved Lucitopia because of the betrayal of his no-screen rule. I cracked my knuckles and clenched my teeth. I would make him pay if he were responsible! For the first time, I felt no fear of him, Arriving where the rooftop apartment had been, the adrenaline flooding my system screamed, *VENGEANCE!* Then, I spotted the old television set, lying on a street corner, and the internal roar diminished. I willed Charlie to speed down. The TV's screen was cracked. I prayed the circuits would still work. I brushed away the jagged rubble that littered the curb, badly cutting my fingers in the process, and set the TV upright. I checked that the internal cabling was still intact then switched it on.

After flickering a bit, amazingly, the screen lit up. When sweet November Fox appeared, I clapped and cried with joy. My excitement was short-lived; however, she was now a small child, and she was crying helplessly.

"Shut up and sleep, you selfish maggot!" Bellowed the liquorice-eyed creature, even greyer and limping more heavily than ever.

Poor tear-soaked November, in her number-five bed, covered her face with her hands as she sniffed and sobbed, quieting herself as best she could. All forty beds—or should I say blanket scraps on the floor—had red, wooden numbers attached to the end of them with rusty safety pins. November's bed was by the window. You may think this was a blessing. Unfortunately, this window was too high up to peer out of and too out of reach to close properly. The sharp winter's air pierced its way through, accompanying November, like an evil teddy bear, into her dreams and nightmares each night. I knew this implicitly. This was the turning point; when my observation escalated to another level. I was not only seeing her; I could feel her pain—and more than the sensations I had experienced when I last saw her as a baby. I heard her thoughts as if they were my own. I remembered my earlier speculation about her story mirroring something within me—our connection had strengthened. In that moment, the emptiness inside her heart grew to an intolerable level.

She clutched at her chest, fearing that she might accidentally fall into herself and disappear, forever.

Mysteriously, I sensed that I could follow her. She ached with incredible aloneness. *Did I not also?* I yearned for her to know she was not alone. I whispered for her to pick up her music box and gasped when she retrieved her precious music maker and turned the handle. *Had she heard my words?* The melody of *Somewhere Over the Rainbow* filled the room as all the other children slept, and her tears began to subside. The notes travelled directly into her heart.

The music gave her the inspiration to survive, even though the hopeful light was only a tiny spark. It was just enough, however, to block the inner vacuum of the black cavern inside her. My heart broke in half, right there and then, as I knew it would be suicide to stay with her any longer. If I did, I feared I would fall down the same emotional black hole.

My personal slave-driver had burdened me with so many other commitments that demanded my focused attention, I was sure he would be keeping a strict eye on me. I sighed with deep regret, knowing the situation was impossible—*or was this an easy way out for me? I wondered.* Part of me wished I could take the TV with me; another was relieved I could not. I dreaded that Father would find out and would even punish November, somehow. He was such a mighty force, with powers far beyond my knowledge, so I did not dare risk too much devious behaviour. I had to walk away for both November's sake and mine, and maybe for my peace of mind, but to this day I regret that impossible choice.

When I left and waved my final goodbye, my fury had subsided. Once again depression and tremors overcame me at the mere thought of my cruel master. I was not yet ready to confront him or the wounds from my time as a small Architect. I realised I must wait for the right moment for both—a moment yet to arrive.

I prayed the music box would be enough for November. Every opportunity I had, without my dominator knowing, I set about re-building November's Lucitopia. Many years have passed in making version two. I still possess the scars on my fingers from that terrible day. They have been an ongoing reminder to continue my mission. Now, this very evening, I have finished rebuilding her city, and I rejoice to say I am far ahead of schedule. Focus has been easier since my Father has been unable to check up on me.

I kept a close eye on November through the broken TV screen and began to understand what makes her so unique. Last week, I inherited my Father's job. How I came to receive the promotion is for another moment. The main news is that I now have the freedom to install as many TVs as I like. I spent all of last Luna week placing screens throughout one quadrant of November's Lucitopia. I also replaced the glass on the little penthouse TV. Now I can observe her whenever and wherever I wish. My plan is to cover the whole city with viewing stations. For the moment, however, I must focus on this letter.

Living alone in the ever-moonlit Lucitopia Empire has not been easy. Many a night, I lay upon Charlie and gazed up at Luna, my dear moon friend in the sky, hoping she did not mind that I let myself go. I could not see the point, in keeping up appearances. The deep pain of isolation was only tempered by my project work and the discovery of November Fox, my saving grace. Yes, I know what you think. I am going a little mad perhaps and need to address these issues, particularly my segregation from others.

Charlie has been with me, yet I suppose in your World of Form, rugs do not count. Allow me to tell you briefly about him, and perhaps you might consider him an exception.

Charlie is my rather conservative Persian, flying carpet and my number one companion.

Every newly-stamped Architect receives a rug at their Sterling Service event. I shall never forget mine. In an elaborate ceremony, with fireworks lighting the sky as grand as the Milky Way, and the elders guzzled cosmic wine in waterfall quantities, lovely rolled-up Charlie was presented to me. We were both quite small back then. *Did you know flying carpets grow as their owners do?* Although I try not to think of myself as owning him. We are more like equal friends, despite me being the rider and he being the ridden.

I must admit he is a rather sensitive and often moody little carpet. I cannot imagine why, since he has a fabulous life. I am proud to say Charlie is the most honest carpet I know, and he has no fear of speaking his mind. He cannot talk. Instead, we have an empathetic connection and can feel each other's state of being and wishes. That is how he knows where I want to fly. Alas, I digress. It is an unspoken law that all carpets must obey their Architect, so Charlie complies, yet I always know when he is upset as he wrinkles his fabric. He has never been a naughty carpet and flung me off, although I have experienced a few bumpy rides.

As long as I avoid exposing him to too much moonlight, comb his fringe, clean up any spills immediately and vacuum him with a gentle hand, we get along just fine.

Anyway, where was I, where was I? Ah yes. I ask myself, is November Fox a distraction or will she someday lead me to fertile ground? She has at least kept me company during the past years, and I thank her for that, even though she does not realise I exist. I hope that I can tell her someday soon. I still cannot quite see the dawn, yet I can feel the change. A spring of sorts is soon to arrive. I am certain it is, and I am quite sure you sense something, too. That is why I write to you. (Insert me smiling at you and doing a few airborne loop-de-loops in the 46cm or 18 inch space between us.) When I switched on the new screens for the first time last night, I was thrilled to fly through the city, watching their peculiar blossoming.

This pre-dawn even inspired me to design more cities to contain the overflow, *although I do wonder if that is possible anymore.* I think November Fox's Lucitopia is now my home, although I cannot complain; I do love life here. If only Father were able to witness me at this moment.

Perhaps he can?

Erica's Note

Three days ago, my phone rang at 6:03 in the morning. Everyone knows not to call me before 10, unless... It seemed the dreaded *unless* had found me. Ripped from a tsunami nightmare in which escape seemed futile, I was momentarily relieved to find myself in the safety of my bed. Safe that is, until those nasty red digits pierced my barely focused eyes. Sitting up and brushing hair tangles from my face, I fumbled to answer the call. A voice, which I recognised, although it was distinctly missing its regular, upbeat, Australian pitch, wobbled down the long-distance line.

"Erica, it's Kath," It was Steven's auntie; her voice full of pain. "I'm so sorry to have to tell you this, but Steven was killed in a car crash today..."

That's all I can remember before everything went blank. I must have collapsed with shock and hit my head on the bedpost. On waking, I wished I'd hit my head harder.

Steven was my dearest long-time friend. Perhaps even my soul-mate, but I guess I'll never know now, I'll never know. Growing up in various foster homes, he was my one constant. I hadn't seen him in two years, yet a stake pierced my heart with the devastating news, which just added to my devastation. If only he hadn't loved his Noble M600 sports car more than anything else. But I guess if you are going to pass on, you may as well go doing the thing you love most. *Yet why now?* He was too young at only twenty-five. Time seemed frozen when I awoke. It was the kind of chill, with its agonising bite, that no amount of clothing can remedy.

I sobbed. *Why hadn't I called him for over a month?* I felt sick to my core, wrapping my arms around myself. *What did we last talk about? Did I tell him I loved him?* I reached for my phone to check my saved voice messages. All gone. "Nooooo," I wailed, remembering deleting them in the café yesterday. Tears streamed down my face, as I sat staring blankly at my white wall, clasping my phone; knowing he would never call again. Life didn't seem real. This must be a nightmare... oh, how I wished to wake up. We take people and experiences for granted like they will never end. Everything ends. Steven had ended. *Why?*

I had to get out of London. Maybe if I ran fast enough, I could get ahead of this woeful, dark cloud that was threatening to enshroud me. Without even packing a bag, I headed straight down to Brighton. I needed the seaside. To be honest, I think I wished the tsunami from my dream, would be waiting for me. It was an hour on the train to get there. I usually love trains, but on this journey, I thought I might never love anything again.

I walked down to the stony beach, strewn with pebbles that were as varied as the weird, eclectic mix of passers-by, meandering along its shore. I would usually get caught up in people-watching, but not today. My terrible loss pushed me further into my igloo of isolation. I was now entirely alone in a sea of strangers, most of whom appeared to be on cloud nine, enjoying themselves, on a rare (for England) 26 degree day; all oblivious to my bereavement and the dark hole in my heart. I began to throw a few rocks at a pile of pebbles. In the past, I have made profound discoveries, when surrendering to the graceful art of selecting rocks, aiming, and letting them go; but today, all I saw was destruction. Things fall apart. The law of entropy wins, again and again, breaking forms down into smaller and smaller pieces in its wake. We are all food for worms. I sighed. Steven and I used to play this pebble game as children. The tears continued; my new constant, now that my best friend was gone, forever.

I was watching the gentle waves, sparkling in the sunlight, caressing the shore, when my eye caught a ruby-coloured glint. I was amazed to see a red, glimmering bottle, washed up on the beach. It had the beautiful form of an Egyptian, hand-blown, perfume bottle but was as large as a wine bottle.

Why weren't the people walking past it, stopping to inspect it?

Distracted from my grief, I went over to examine it. I stood, staring at its mysterious beauty. The bottle looked even more exquisite up close, with gold trims and beautiful detail. I hesitated, before picking it up. Something this precious must belong to someone? I glanced around, but everyone seemed unaware of its presence.

I took the smooth, semi-translucent bottle back to my fallen, stone towers, and sat down to inspect it. Inside its weathered glass was a wad of tightly rolled-up pages. After a struggle to remove the stopper and extract the pages, I began to read. The story it told, about an architect, kept me captivated until a passing dog started barking at some children throwing a Frisbee. I looked up and saw that the sun was low in the sky; it was time to head back to London. I picked up the bottle, noticing more pages had magically appeared in it. Or maybe I hadn't fished them all out? I wasn't sure, as I was feeling a little delirious.

I couldn't wait to read the next instalment, so I jumped onto the train and on the way home, read what I had in my hands.

Note to Reader

At the time of publication, there are augmented reality layers in this book. These are accessed through the illustrations, and can be activated by downloading the Layar app, and scanning the inner pictures, the ones in the middle of the carpet, with your phone or tablet. Here you will discover more layers to the tale as well as access the connected November Fox music. You can also read it as a stand-alone book without these additions, as the story is not dependent on them. As we are living in a time of rapid technological advancement, should this method be made redundant, you will find updated information here: www.eebertram.com/bookupdates

1

A New Day

Yesterday (my comparative version), I had such a frustrating and annoying day of work. You know, even we Architects must do such mundane tasks as filing for approval when starting and ending new projects, and more often than not, our requests are rejected. Ah, bureaucracy! If only I were independent and able to live outside this hierarchical system. Anyway, when I had battled through it all, I rushed back, tingling all over in anticipation of what I would find in November Fox's Lucitopia—after my installation of the screens. The city lit up with sound and colour when I turned them on. 'She lives.' I sounded like Dr Frankenstein as I flew to the closest plasma.

"Get it together, Fox," November mumbled, disentangling herself from the soft, brown bedding on her king-sized bed. The cosy, new carpet snuggled the soles of her feet, as she stood upright; a little shaky. She rubbed her eyes, blinded by the bright light of day. The morning newspaper lay at the foot of her bed, which was strange. Honey, her dog, had stopped the sunrise-paper-fetching routine some years ago when arthritis set in.

"*Honey?*" No response. She swiped the newspaper open to the entertainment section and read the headline. "November Fox – Final Show of a Sell-Out World Tour". She was smiling until she read the first line of the article. "Ironically, the vegan rock icon, November Fox, sure knows how to *milk* the old hits." *I knew we needed new material for our home show.*" she sighed.

November wondered if she was still suited to the fast-paced entertainment world. This was not the first time she had considered whether her intense performing life was a healthy choice. It seemed to pull her outwards into endlessly jumping through other people's hoops, leaving little time for herself. During the last few months of this latest tour, she had questioned the record labels' instruction to only play the old hits. "That's what the people want!" Frustration, at these imposed limits, was beginning to surface. November felt that the shows were more like fancy karaoke nights, lacking passion. She wanted to be so much more than a puppet with a play button. Creativity was her lifeblood, as was her need to make a difference in the world. Her current melodies and lyrics were becoming tiresome. She so yearned for a deeper life purpose and a more balanced existence.

Clapping her hands twice, her favourite Lamb song, *Gorecki*, played loudly through the house, and she started to dance off the newspaper's sour review—not wanting to start the day under a shadow.

A peculiar, chilling breeze skimmed her cheeks. She noticed the window was closed, and that her fox dog, Honey, was not in her bed.

"*Honey*" she called out again.

Honey was a stray, although she may have followed November to Hartwall Orphanage from the farm. I cannot be sure. As soon as November was old enough to escape the crowd inside Hartwall, she spent as much time as she could, outside, in the courtyard. That's when she met Honey. Every night November would sneak down to the yard and feed the meat she had refused to eat at dinner to Honey through the fence. They have been inseparable since then. November even brought Honey along on the recent world tour, despite her ageing bones. The hotel elevator would often open with November and Honey exiting to eat breakfast or attend a function. Being allowed to keep her dog with her, was just one of the many benefits of being a modern rock star. She loves that smart dog more than anyone in the world, and she is the closest thing to family November has ever known.

"Where are you, dog dog?" November called, pulling her fingers through her tangled hair, as she continued her dance down the hall.

She stopped at the top of the stairs, peering at the carpet. The grape-juice stain she had left on the carpet last night had vanished like a drawing in the sand after an early-morning tide. *How?*

She continued her dance, accompanied by the music that filled the house, down the stairs and into the living room. It was a peaceful space with its Japanese-inspired, minimalist décor.

"Good morning, plants. Oh, what a deliciously, simple life you live." The deep-green, heart-shaped leaves of two Philodendron vines, covered most of the light-yellow walls of the spacious living room. She ran her hands over the strings of her guitar that hung on the wall. "Hello, Guitar; singing is enough for you, isn't it?" She laughed, as it vibrated its six- stringed response. November interrupted her dance, when she reached down to the table in the corner, to turn on her laptop. "Good morning, computer. Your purpose is clear, and I so love you for it."

November continued her freestyle promenade, revelling in this space where she could be free, with no one to question her antics. Suddenly realising that Honey was not downstairs, she clapped twice to shut off the music.

Three metres from the front door, she stopped in her tracks, noticing the clock had disappeared as well. *What's going on?* She squinted at the blank wall, then opened the front door, surprised to find it unlocked "Oh, door, I'm certain I locked you last night, didn't I?" She mumbled, patting it a few times as if it were a pet. She was forced to shield her eyes with her hands, as bright, blinding light flooded in.

"*Honey,*" she called, like a blind woman seeking her guide. No response. She stepped onto the porch. Morning birds sang their summer song. Fresh air, laced with sunbeams and cut -grass aromas, tickled her exposed skin and filled her lungs. Her reverie ended abruptly at the sight of a white box lying at her feet. It was about the size of a hat-box with a small gift tag attached. She glanced around, wondering who had left it. A warm, tingling sensation spread down her limbs, and her knees weakened slightly. Excited, she crouched down to inspect it more closely.

"Well, good morning, lovely white present; where did you come from?" She reached out to pick it up, noticing her hands were pulsing with energy, seeping out like gloves made from rainbows.

She shook her hands. "Huh?" She said as she counted her fingers.

First, there were six on one hand and seven on the other. Again, she shook them. "Phew," she sighed, as her hands returned to their proper starfish shapes.

She picked up the gift. It was almost weightless. The chilled, smooth texture caressed her skin, and she wondered how it had remained cold in the morning sun.

The gift tag read: "For the attention of November Fox." Her eyes widened. *Is it today? November had no idea when her birthday was, but maybe somebody did.*

She revelled in the anticipation of what comes next more than the moment itself and loved to prolong that in-between, butterflies-in-the-stomach time.

This was one of those moments.

"No, Fox, we are a master of our self-control, aren't we?" She was doing her best to not rip the package open with the impatience of a five-year-old. Forgetting about finding Honey, she went inside to the kitchen.

She set the present on the breakfast bench and sat beside it on a kitchen stool to read the tiny writing on the back of the card.

"You are cordially invited to commence the initiation period to become a member of the LOTNE (Leaders of the New Earth). I hereby install you as an official Keeper of The Cube. Pass Level One, and you will be part of the Collective forever more. The time has come for the next generation of Wayshowers to help shape the destiny of Earth, through first saving themselves.

We offer the cube to only a select few. You are the ones who have the key within yourselves to unlock the mysteries of Form. Your cube is your doorway. *In feeling the way, in thinking the way, in sensing the way, in creating the way, in developing the way, in facing the way, you will BE the way.* May the force of you be WITHIN you." No signature

"P.S. Your cube's name is Joy. DOB. 1st of November 2010."

No signature was actually written on the note. Why they bothered to write that, I do not know. I patted Charlie. "Well, what do you make of that, my flying friend?"

2

Opening the Box

With sweaty palms and trembling hands, November stood for an extended moment staring at the message, somehow knowing her life was soon to change dramatically. The last time she had such a strong intuition, was before she received a letter confirming she had a full scholarship to study music at BIM (The Brighton Institute of Music). She had only a few days to mentally prepare for a whole new life beyond the oppressive walls of Hartwall. The day she left, Honey jumped into the bus that collected November and sat on the seat next to her. She often remembers this parting, and how it seemed so natural for Honey to go with her. She has always had an unspoken understanding with Honey. It did, however, take some convincing before the bus driver would drive with a fox dog on board.

Anyway, I digress. After being invited to the music institute, her life changed in a big way. I was busy designing the Eiffel Tower at the time—beautiful creature, he is. *Have you ever been to the top?* You will understand my enthusiasm if you have. He was one of my favourite projects. I sincerely regret that I was unable to witness that period of November's life first-hand. I only know it through viewing her memories of those early years.

In her first year at the school, she wrote a hit song entitled, *Reset*. As well as giving expression to her childhood pain, it made her an overnight star. And, although fame and fortune have since helped to comfort her inner longing, that black hole has yet to be filled and sealed.

Standing now, with the note in her hands, she sensed answers may be nearer than ever. She took the present and went upstairs to the bathroom.

As November reached over to turn the bath water on, she caught a glimpse of herself in the mirror. She frowned, confused; she was already dressed for the day, apart from her bare feet. She couldn't remember putting on her clothes. *Maybe I fell asleep like this, tired after last night's show?* Time stretched as she glanced around the spotless bathroom, having no memory of the past evening. She looked back at the box and soon forgot about getting herself ready. As she lifted her hand to open the gift, the mood ring she wore on her right middle finger, caught her eye.

Instantly, her mind flooded with the memory of her first world tour, which was when her band manager, Hamish, had presented her with the ring as a gift.

It was in the park next to the hotel in Tokyo, under the pink froth of cherry-blossom trees that a moment occurred that she would never forget. It was here she realised, despite being ill at ease with the concept, that there may be some truth in the saying, *no risk, no gain.* Her caution had led her to miss a great opportunity and she felt sick with regret.

November sat, brooding, on an old, wooden bench as a gentle early-morning breeze cooled her cheeks. She gazed over the pond to a light-yellow teahouse, set in a perfectly manicured, landscaped garden. Coloured hydrangeas followed the contours of the winding path around the water, which reflected the stillness of the sky at sunrise. The graceful morning mist wafted in patches along the surface of the mirrored pond, and the scent of freshly-ground coffee, from a passing street vendor, drifted up her nose. The yin-yang juxtaposition of opposing forces around her distracted her from her woes; Tokyo's modern technology, flashing billboards and gadgets, mingled with the ancient traditions of the country, like the teahouse and its ceremonies. The future and the past were briefly eclipsed, leaving her spellbound and momentarily free from the shackles of actions and their consequences.

She sat very still; at home in the tranquillity of the present. Her gaze landed on three people doing tai chi. Taken by the austere discipline and its orchestrated refinement, she wished that she were Japanese, or at least would be one day. It was then she made a pledge to come back to Japan; to understand this mysterious intuition of hers and maybe remedy her error of judgement.

She sighed with anguish, remembering the previous night. She had refused to go to the other side of the city after the show. Their host said it was to play a practical joke on a record label executive. November detested such pranks and opted for bed and a movie.

Later, Hamish came to tell her that it was a surprise party for her. Apparently, the record label, the biggest in Japan and run by an impulsive billionaire, was set to offer her a three-album contract with a ridiculously high advance, after being so impressed with that night's concert. When November did not attend, it had offended the hot-headed owner, and he rescinded the offer immediately, declaring publicly that November Fox was an ungrateful foreigner. Little did he know, and nor did anyone tell him, her good reasons for not coming.

"Mate, I got ya somethin'," Hamish said in his broad Australian accent as he approached with the shimmery ring.

"Hamey, I think I should be alone. I'm so stupid. We could've been set up for life, had I not been such a paranoid freak," she stared at a Mandarin Duck gliding across the pond.

"For mood stabilisation, and having trust in the unknown," he continued, ignoring her protests. "The gypsy lady said when you look at the ring, and the colour shows stress or fear, ya just need to wait a bit."

"For what?"

9

"So you can separate from negative thoughts and unnecessary anxiety. Just watch the stone until the hue changes, and then you'll be right as rain."

November engaged his pale blue eyes, weakly returning his smile and wondering why he wasn't angrier with her.

"Thanks, Hamey, you're so good to me. But you do realise a ring can't control my emotions or change the past." She put it on and peered into its surface. It reminded her of the pond in front of them.

"I know, mate, but it'll remind ya that these mad feelings don't last long, and you'll have proof right there on ya finger."

"Thank you. You're sweet to try to help me, Hamey, and thank you for not being upset with me about the lost contract."

"No worries, mate. Next time, just remember; no risk, no gain."

November sat, spinning the ring around her finger. As it spun, she once again found herself in her bathroom, standing before the mysterious box.

Peering into the oval ring, she half smiled at the stone, which shone a bluish colour. 'No risk, no gain." She whispered, carefully lifting the lid.

A cube shot up out of the box and hovered in the air above the opened box. It had nine small squares on each of its six differently-coloured sides.

It was similar to the Rubik's cube she had played with at the orphanage as a young child. She had only seen that cube suspended once when little Stevie Dunn hit grumpy Agnes Witherbottom on the head with it, by mistake. Stevie Dunn suffered the same fate when Agnes grabbed him by the collar and suspended him in mid-air.

Her skin tingled as she passed her arm through the air under the cube to check if it were somehow connected to the box.

She paced around the floating form, wondering what to do next, so wishing to hold the mysterious thing in her hands, yet resisting. It could be dangerous. *This must be a trick. You've come back and set it up as payback, haven't you?* She muttered, as her eyes darted around the room, looking for her childhood nemesis.

I am sad to report that November learnt the lesson of actions and their repercussions the hard way, when one of her choices had terrible consequences that haunt her to this day. Despite being a natural-born adventurer, and many years having passed since the incident, she remains uncomfortable with uncertainty and surprise. I was working on the M23 motorway south of London at the actual time of the event, and ever since my return to her Lucitopia; I have been bombarded nightly with her extreme regret.

Before November could take hold of the cube, she had another flashback.

Her face paled, as images of the death of Rebmevon filled her mind, reminding her of that awful time when her actions produced a hideous reaction, leaving her with constant internal grief.

I did not wish to live through the horror in picture form, so I flew on to the next screen.

3

The Death of Rebmevon

I had no luck evading November's emotions. Not that I believe in luck. "Luck is when preparation meets opportunity!" My father's voice still echoes with conviction in my mind. Hence my dedication to groundwork. Architecture is all about the artful and pragmatic execution of preparation in its highest form. And when done with precision, the results are indeed fantastic opportunities. The miracle of being able to witness November on these massive plasmas is worth all the planning and hard work. I must say, however, that not having the ability to edit out the obstacles is quite frustrating. When November tunes into her innermost feelings, the daily emotional onslaught is intensified by this shocking event from her past.

Ever since arriving back in her Lucitopia and starting the rebuild, I wished I could figure out a way to communicate with her. I longed to remind her that it was not her fault. I sense she can feel me watching somehow, but she has no conscious awareness of it. Not yet, anyway. I saw no escape as I arrived at the screen. She had completely regressed into reliving her second deepest painful experience, the first being her childhood abandonment.

Back at the orphanage, November shivered under her blanket pile. The rain hammered the windows like relentless rounds of ammunition from a machine gun. The raging, howling wind, mirroring the inner rage of her soul; a soul that she felt was battling to escape her.

The daughter of the orphanage director, Mr Russell, was a little girl with piercing, forest-green eyes, named Rebmevon. November always wondered how such a beautiful-looking creation, with her raven-black hair framing a porcelain doll face, could contain such a horrible child. Despite being opposites in character, the two girls were of similar age, of similar slim build, and both of them loved Rebmevon's father. November concluded that jealousy had eaten Rebmevon's heart away. Mr Russell gave so much of his attention to all of the children under his care at Hartwall Orphanage that he had unintentionally turned his only offspring into a nasty, jealous piece of work.

Only once did November remember Rebmevon being kind. She had told November that she had given Honey some meat. November panicked, assuming Rebmevon must have poisoned Honey, but later discovered she had not. She still wondered if the little monster had tried.

November both feared and slightly admired Rebmevon's two faces. One face epitomised malicious intent, and the other was the perfect daughter, incapable of any misconduct—a face she only showed to her kind father. November often marvelled that both sides of Rebmevon seemed completely authentic and she half-respected the girl's ability to manipulate so effortlessly, not that she condoned her behaviour. Eventually, the moment arrived when November reached boiling point. On this tragic day, the dynamic between the future orphan star and the two-faced beauty, changed forever.

It happened the evening after Rebmevon cut November's hair for the tenth time while she slept. No one ever believed November's claim, as the wild, orange mess atop her head looked like a bird's nest most of the time. With the low ratio of hairbrushes to children at Hartwall, keeping it under control was nearly impossible, and it grew faster than weeds. Nevertheless, November knew when she had any strands missing.

Rebmevon followed Mr Russell around everywhere and always stood behind him. Whenever he showed kindness to November, like arranging additional music tuition or complimenting her, Rebmevon would glare at November. Her cold, envious stares made November shudder. Sometimes the girl would even bare her teeth and hiss like an angry cat.

The worst abuse of all happened three weeks before the fatal incident, when Rebmevon stole November's music box. The girl stood glowering, with nostrils flared, at the end of November's bed, the music box tucked under her arm and waving a bread knife, threateningly. November scrambled to hide under her red blanket. "If you dare tell father another thing, I will crush your music box to pieces with his sledgehammer," she sneered.

November clutched her blanket, deterred from retrieving her music maker, by the large knife and its wicked bearer.

"Now, I'm taking this for a while. Don't try to get it back, or I'll return with a better utensil to show you whose house this *really* is."

This nasty, vengeful act almost killed November. She tolerated physical threats more easily than psychological violations, and the idea of losing her music box was debilitating. For three weeks, November didn't think she could live another day. She skipped meals, stayed in bed, and cried into the wee hours, unable to tell a soul why she was so unwell, at the risk of losing the music box forever. The small melody-making contraption was the last thread linking her to her past, her lifeboat of hope, and her Achilles heel.

Eventually, she found her beloved music box under her bed's wooden number, at the bottom of her blanket pile. Rebmevon must have returned it while she slept. She clutched it with all her might and whispered to its spinning components, "Oh, box, thank goodness you're back. Don't ever leave me again."

Rebmevon had been tormenting November every single week for years until the incident when November snapped. It was while sitting, shivering, on her blanket pile, looking at her freshly butchered hair, that she became enraged. Rebmevon would never show this nasty side to her father, so in this moment, November decided to be the silent disciplinarian.

Her blood was now boiling, "Enough is enough!" She declared, with fists clenched, and her face growing redder.

Her chance arrived the day Mr Russell and Rebmevon were out on a family outing together. "Perfect," she whispered, spotting Joe Wishbone's toy spider by his pile of blankets in the shadowy hall, an hour after lights-out. Her vengeance-filled mind quickly formed a plan to frighten the little demon. Rebmevon was terrified of spiders.

With her window of opportunity closing, she gathered her courage, tiptoed to Joe Wishbone's bed and shoved his spider up her pyjama shirt. Then, still fuelled by anger, she light-footed her way down the stairs, towards the office.

November clasped the pointed corner of the entrance hall wall, carefully edging her head around. Old Mrs Witherbottom sat in the reception under the glow of a small desk light, humming *Amazing Grace*. November retreated back around the wall and squatted on the floor with her hand over her mouth, as she let out a sigh of relief.

Mrs Lucy Witherbottom was the slightly kinder, younger sister of that grey-haired monster of an office woman, angry Agnes Witherbottom. Had it been Agnes on early evening duty, the revenge mission would not have been worth the risk. Agnes was the beastly woman, who had reluctantly accepted November from the farmer, years earlier, and had never let November forget what an inconvenience that had been.

When she noticed the time on the clock behind Lucy Witherbottom, her heart pounded; 8:17. November realised that she would have to act quickly, as angry Agnes would soon be here for the late night-shift. Also, Mr Russell and Rebmevon would be returning from their day trip any time. Her chest tightened as she waited in the draughty, dark hall for old Mrs Witherbottom to go to the toilet. Her plan was to steal the keys to the Russell's residence.

After almost an hour of waiting, she had her chance. November dashed into the office and grabbed the key. Just then the door hinge creaked and Mrs Witherbottom returned to the desk for her handbag. November jumped under the desk to hide, banging her head hard as she went.

"Oww!"

"November Fox? Is that you?"

November clasped the key behind her back and emerged, rubbing her bumped head with the other hand.

"Goodness gracious, child, what on earth are you doing here at this hour?"

November had to think quickly. "I- I- I have a headache."

"What?" She leant over with one hand cupping her ear.

"A headache," November said, raising her voice to be understood by the half-deaf woman.

"Go back to bed. It is just air pressure from the storm. Off with you, and go fast. Agnes will be here any minute, and she'd wring your neck to find you out of bed," she said, waving her away.

November decided that having come this far; she would continue with her plan; she'd just have to be quick about it.

The storm surged with more intensity. The lightning and thunder made walking on the squeaky floorboards of the residence above the office, marginally less audible. This was the only time November had ever visited the Russell's home. She opened the apartment door with a trembling hand. Despite her best efforts, it squeaked like a tortured rat. She crept down the hall, wincing at every creak of the worn floorboards. "I hope this makes you scream, you mean, nasty thing," November whispered, as she popped her head into two of the rooms. Neither looked like Rebmevon's bedroom.

Then it occurred to her. *Demon-girl probably shares the same room as her father. She does tend to follow him around like a dog, worried its owner will disappear.* With this thought, her toe stubbed hard on a raised floorboard. "Oww!" She hopped a few steps, clasping her toe and her mouth at the same time. "Instant Karma," she sighed. Mr Russell had taught all of the children about the law of Karma-actions

17

causing reactions—just that week. With this new knowledge, November understood her negative thought about Rebmevon, resulted in hurting herself, but unfortunately, this realisation was not enough to deter her from her current plan.

At the end of the hall was the only door she had yet to try. She hobbled towards it and peeked inside. "Got it," she whispered. Mr Russell's bedroom was quite sparse with only a bed, a bowl of fruit on a table and a sofa by the window. *That's where she must sleep.* November dashed across the room with adrenalin pumping through her veins, no longer aware of the pain in her toe. She placed Joe Wishbone's spider on the sofa and got out of there, running.

She yanked the keys out of the front door and darted down the stairs. From behind the wall, she caught her breath, awaiting the old woman's next wash-room visit, to return the key. The office phone rang. November saw her chance. Mrs Witherbottom picked up the receiver with her back to the key hooks. November scrambled on all fours into the room and leapt up to return the key just as Mrs Witherbottom said hello to her caller. She dashed out as fast as her legs could carry her and hurried back up the stairs. November thanked the next loud thunder clap as she scurried past the forty sleeping children, and returned, undetected, to her number-five blanket pile.

She buried herself under her red cover, puffing with nervous energy. *Thank goodness that's over*, she thought, at the same time hearing something crunch under her pillow. She fished it out. It was a small piece of paper all crumpled up. She unwrapped it and squinted to make out the words in the dark hall. When the moon popped out from behind a storm cloud, there was just enough light to see the scribbly writing.

"I am sorry. For everything." November darted her eyes around the dark sleeping hall, but the only person she imagined it could be from was Rebmevon. Maybe the promise of a full day of attention from her father was enough to make her realise how mean she's been acting. November felt guilty, but there was no way she could make it back to retrieve the spider without being caught. *Well, she probably deserves at least a little of her own medicine,* she thought, pulling her knees closer to her chest and wishing she were able to turn back time. November lay wide-awake with the storm now in full frenzy. She snuggled deeper into her covers and watched the rain pelt against the glass up above, sensing disappointment and anger from the weather gods. A shot of lightning whipped past the window, followed by a giant rumbling, shaking the old window frame. Her bravado gone, she ached with anguish. *Why did I do that?*

As the rain began to subside, the full moon popped out again from behind a drifting storm cloud and lit up the hall. *Are they back yet? Has Rebmevon discovered the spider? Why can't I turn time back?* She rubbed her eyes with her blanket, feeling both proud of executing her plan and sorry for her actions. Yet the worst was still to come.

A primal scream, like that of a tortured animal, filled the air, "*Wwwwaaaahhhhh.*" Seconds later, she heard the sound of a window smashing and then a dull thud that jolted November out of her blanket scraps. She leapt from her bed and dragged a wooden chair over to the window and climbed up. No other child stirred. She pressed her forehead against the icy, dust-coated glass and peered down into the courtyard. The wet and shadowy night was not black enough to mask the horrible sight, forever now etched in her mind.

Her hands lifted to her face, covering her nose and mouth. Down below, lay a vision of pure terribleness; almost too ghastly to witness. Rebmevon's body lay awkwardly; broken, and destroyed. Her long, white nightgown striped with scarlet red that snaked its way over her jagged contours. November grabbed her chest. *Oh my god, what have I done?*

She scrambled back and hid under her covers, heart pounding and breathing fast, in a state of pure panic.

The following weeks were horrendous. November's emotions paralysed her to the point where her body was unable to leave her bed. Even her music box provided no comfort, as a nurse sat by her bed spinning its handle, trying to encourage November to get up. Nothing worked.

November couldn't hear anyone. It was as if she were stuck inside a black box, bobbing on an ocean of contrition, trapped and alone. The orphanage then sent her to a special hospital, where they gave her such strong medicine her head spun like an endless merry-go-round, but it didn't take away the massive guilt, or the torment of Rebmevon's frequent visits to her dreams, turning them into nightmares.

The death of Rebmevon was the last time November took revenge on anyone, even as a joke or a prank. Last week I watched her in a supermarket in Helsinki and detected evidence of her guilt. She and another girl reached for the last jar of peanut butter at the same time. When the other girl selfishly snatched it up first, November simply bit her bottom lip, and said calmly, "You can have it." She now seems to believe the world has a magical way of rewarding and punishing people, so she chooses to step out of the way of this process. I often witness her calculating risk probabilities and sensing what feels right, before she acts. That is why, in Japan, there was not a chance in the world that she was going to that practical joke, surprise party.

The flashback ended. I sighed and shook myself, attempting to expel the memory.

November remained hunched over, staring at the cube, her colour slowly returning to her face. I flew to the next screen.

Erica's Note

I finished the chapter just as the train pulled into London Victoria. I left the carriage, carrying the bottle like a precious infant, entered the station, found my trajectory amidst the 5 p.m. bustle of city legs and headed towards the circle line.

Both joy and sorrow swirled around my heart as November's inner curse reminded me of my own weakness: a tendency to run away when things got tough. I thought about the ghosts that still chase me. We share that misery. I wondered how the past can still be with me, when *now is now*; a long time and halfway across the world from when and where my bad childhood experiences occurred.

Now with the loss of Steven, the fact was etched into my mind that space and time are deceptive. They seem like conduits that you can travel through, and away from people and places, but as my friend, Hans, says, "Wherever you go, there you are." From the positive or the negative, escape is impossible. Old shadows can find us anywhere, and deep loves will be with us forever. I yearn for freedom from the ties that are holding me back. I somehow need to clean out my heart, *but how?*

Just when I was wondering if it might be time to stop running away from my life, another peculiar thing happened. A tall man in a jet-black suit stepped right in front of me, stopping me in my tracks. He seemed to come from nowhere.

"Excuse me," he said in a deep, smooth tone as I glanced up into his brown, almond eyes. He paused, staring at the bottle in my arms. I found this curious, since he was the first person to notice it, apart from me.

He looked me in the eyes and said, "To be full of wonder is wonderful, just as having the ability to respond is a responsibility."

Someone then tapped me on my shoulder. I turned around, but there wasn't anyone there. When I turned back, the man in the black suit had also disappeared.

It was very strange indeed. I thought about his message. *Had he read my mind? Was it time for me to take responsibility and somehow replace the dark spirits lurking around and within me, filling myself with wonder instead?*

I looked down at my mysterious bottle, now filled with new pages, and realised I had entered a strange magical world by acquiring it, and needed to expect the unexpected.

I boarded the underground and continued to read.

4

The Turning of the Cube

I arrived at the next screen as November stood tall, eyes aglow, scrutinising the cube. She rubbed the stone of her mood ring with her thumb and looked to its colour as if searching for permission to move forward into this unknowable journey. It shone with a vibrant, green hue. *Green for go?*

After one last deep breath, she reached out for the cube. "Ok, here we go," were her last words before everything flashed bright, and she found herself sitting in a white, tranquil room.

Its sheer luminance made opening her eyes difficult. She did manage to make out the curved walls, which reminded her of a space module. *What is this place?*

She could just make out the sound of very faint music drifting down the hall. The melody was intriguingly familiar. She couldn't quite remember the song, but it reassured her that she was in the right place.

With all her might, she raised the cube in her hand. It felt like she was lifting a tonne of weight. She thought perhaps the air contained glue, or maybe she was half-paralysed from the dislocation caused by this inexplicable jump.

She tried turning the cube, but it wouldn't budge. The green squares were aglow like little glow worms. She pressed one, wondering if maybe they had significance. Nothing happened.

As if under a massive pile of sand, she pushed with all her might, and finally managed to stand up and mobility became easier. She took a step. A colossal *boooboom* came from above as she instinctively dropped to the floor, ducking for cover.

The sound of what seemed to be a whopping heartbeat shuddered through the room like an amplified stethoscope echoing an elephant's heartbeat. She lifted her leg almost twice as quickly as the last effort and placed it down with care. *Boooboom.* The pulsation boomed again as her widening eyes darted around. Her ability to move freely had returned. She ran across the bright space just to feel the joy of running. The beating quickened. When she stopped, it stopped. She sprang up again, gallivanting around the place, turning the heartbeat into a hip-hop rhythm.

November peered down at the cube and watched the green squares surge in intensity as she moved rapidly, and dim when she slowed. Again she tried to turn the square. It still wouldn't budge. "Stubborn, aren't you?" Something then caught her eye; a picture had appeared on one of the walls.

With hesitant steps, she approached the strange, new object. "Hello picture," she said with a giggle. She sensed her curious inner pixie winning over her innate cautiousness. When this inquisitive elf comes out, she experiences a sublime break from her enforced self-control. For better or for worse, she wears it like armour to protect her true essence as a free-flying spirit.

In moments like these, she could delve into full abandonment and shed her self-imposed shackles; the liberation was addictive for both of us. I share this trait with her; once the door of exploration is open, there is no turning back.

The image seemed almost as if it were a window, rather than a painting of a winding road, leading to a castle way off in the distance. The landscape appeared to be alive. She could see the grass on the hilltop moving in the breeze. She tentatively touched the surface. The sticky, chilled texture enveloped her fingertips as the light in the room started to strobe, accompanied by an underwater sound. The sensation reminded her of putting her fingers into the horrible green jelly at the orphanage, which was the only pleasure she received from that terrible-tasting muck.

Her hand disappeared further into the painting, and the flashing pulsated faster. Suddenly, a force sucked her whole body through. The music from down the hall seemed to follow her in, as she tumbled down a passage. I can only describe it as a rainbow vortex—a portal of light and colour. Every part of her body smiled with the incredible sensation of ultimate freedom as she hurtled along at high speed.

Ah! The bliss of true surrender, with no chance of negotiating with the force. What a phenomenal letting go. It was like being on a water slide in euphoria.

I felt a surge of vitality as I swooped around the corner in Lucitopia, hoping I would not miss any of her ride.

5

Meeting Klaus

The energy tunnel got me thinking that if November Fox could travel between dimensions, perhaps I could, too–*although how?* Even my narrow-minded carpet, Charlie, buckled a little underneath me at this prospect. He is such a traditionalist, always travelling along the known paths. You would think having magical powers and being able to fly would encourage him to think outside the box, yet sadly he does not. His fabric often wrinkles when I let my mind dream of other-worldly places. I cannot help myself. Ever since I was a fledgeling Architect, I have fantasised about venturing to your World of Form. It is one thing to design parts of it, but to *actually* go there, would be a dream come true. I remember once when I was little, asking my Father if we could go there for my birthday trip. I have never seen such a shade of red. *Can faces explode?* I did not dare ask again. Now that I am the boss, I have once again began pondering this possibility, much to Charlie's dismay. It may be time for me to make the journey; there must be a way. This letter is my first try; when or if it arrives safely, then perhaps a conduit will open. Anyway, you have my apologies; another digression. Let us get back to the story.

I looked up at the screen to witness November landing gently on the thick, lush grass of a hillside that overlooked a valley. She wondered how she had exited the wormhole so gracefully, considering the speed that she was travelling. Tussocks of grass, wild daisies and cow parsley waved in the gentlest of breezes. November scrunched her nose as the smell of freshly brewed, Earl Grey tea, wafted along the air currents, tickling her nostrils. In the distance, she spotted the castle she had seen in the picture.

She turned around to face the portal and the white building but saw only more of the undulating landscape. *"Oh no, what have I done now?"* she gasped.

Glancing at the cube, still clutched firmly in her hand, she noticed it appeared the same, jumbled-up, with green squares aglow. She again attempted to twist it, but it seemed fixed in its shape. "Come on, cube; please get me out of here." She paced up the hill in search of a way back into the portal or the white room. Nothing. The castle looked to be far away. She guessed it would take quite a few hours to walk there—perhaps even a full day. She sighed.

As she scanned the valley, she took in a deep breath of the fresh, tea-flavoured, country air. *"Mmmmm, well at least this place smells lovely."*

Something brushed past her cheek. A winged creature flapped right in front of her.

"Hello." The butterfly spoke in a high, sweet voice.

"Aaaa, umm, hello."

"I am destiny, and I have led someone to cross your path. Goodbye," she said and flew off, almost as quickly as she had arrived.

"Talking butterfly?" November said aloud, lightly slapping herself on the cheek. "It's now official. Hamey's right. I do have a few sheep loose in the top paddock after all." She began searching for bumps on her head, wondering if she had suffered a concussion during the tunnel trip.

Just moments after the butterfly disappeared, she heard someone whistling and coming closer.

"Guten Tag," A miniature elephant, about half a foot high, sat astride a flying, white cloud, "Wo ist der Schmetterlinge?"

November fell to the ground, gaping with astonishment.

"*Eeeeeeeee!*" The elephant squealed back at her, trembling on all fours. He continued screaming, "*Eeeeeeeeeeeeeeeeee!*"

November watched from behind her fingers, wondering how he could hold such a long note.

He stopped abruptly, cleared his throat, and then silently, held steady eye-contact with November for quite some time. November marvelled at the green sparkle of his eyes, like the colour of dew on a rainforest palm.

"Klaus, Klaus König."

"I'm sorry I frightened you; you startled me."

"Kein Problem, haben sie Kuchen?"

"Um, do you speak English?" She asked. "Am I really talking to a flying elephant?" She said aloud to herself, still unsure of her mental condition.

"Oh ja ja, English language is simple," he said nodding his head. "Have you cake?"

November perplexed, and more that a little taken aback, scratched her head to find that the flying elephant, not only spoke German but English, too. Her head swam in delirium. She decided she had no other choice than to step forward carefully into this strange new reality of magical tunnels and talking animals. *At least I'm not alone*, she reassured herself.

"Well, I am November–November Fox–pleased to meet you, Klaus König." She reached out to shake his tiny trunk, but he backed away, shaking his head.

"You have bent finger."

"I know," November said, quickly retracting her hand and looking down with a frown at her pinkie. She hadn't been able to straighten it since she was a young child, for reasons even I do not know, since she has blocked her memory of the injury.

"Und? Have you cake?" He asked again.

"Ah, no, sorry, I don't have any."

The elephant peered down at a tiny gold watch, hanging around his ankle on a fine chain, "Ok, this is time wasting," he said and flew off, without so much as a goodbye. "Schmetterling, wo bist du?" He called.

"Wait, please come back!" November pleaded. He paused and looked back.

"Have you cake?"

"No." November shook her head, and Klaus, the mini elephant continued flying away.

"I can help you find some!" November had no idea how, but she was running out of options and had to offer something more attractive than her company, which didn't appear to have any appeal.

Klaus stopped in his cloud tracks for a few seconds, still facing away from her.

November assumed he was considering her offer. "I'm very good at finding things. I once found a needle in a haystack; really, I did." She glanced over the valley, hoping that he would stay with her. As adventurous as she was, November didn't like the idea of exploring this strange land alone.

"Sewing or knitting?" He asked, turning his head around and squinting back at her.

"What do you mean?"

"Needle. Say the one."

"It was a quilting needle I think?"

"Betweens or Sharps?"

"*Huh?* It was sharp and between the floorboards under the haystack."

Klaus began to fly back. "These are two kinds of quilt ones, betweens and sharps! Tell the one."

"Oh, I'm not sure."

"Was it three size or five or ten size?"

"Um, small, like a needle; I don't know what size, about as long as your foot, I suppose?"

The elephant shook his head. "Details are mattering!" He snapped, stamping his little impatient foot on his cloud.

November felt like she was failing an intelligence test. "Well, what about me *finding* the needle in the first place? The haystack was ginormous, taller than me!"

"So six-foot pile and approximate six size needle?

"Yes, that sounds about right."

Klaus paused in contemplation. "Ok. This ratio is not *too* bad. Maybe you can be a good finder."

"Yes, I am. I will help you find cake."

With the mention of cake, Klaus' eyes appeared to double in size and his four legs straightened like newly-sharpened pencils. November gasped, worried he might pop out of himself.

"Do you know where we are, Klaus?" She asked, hoping to diffuse his inflation. It worked; his posture relaxed.

"No. Alles Kaputt. Today everything is not working. Klaus doesn't know this land, and Klaus can't find cake, and Klaus only found you!" He grumbled.

"Well, do you remember where you were earlier?" November smiled despite his obvious lack of interest in her as she found it sweet how serious he was, and cute the way he referred to himself in the third person like a two-year-old.

"The last part Klaus is remembering is flying through clouds; then Klaus is here. With you." He stared at her, obviously unconvinced.

"Where were the clouds?"

"Klaus' head is not so clear. There are three things Klaus only knows: 1. Klaus is Klaus, 2. Klaus wants cake, 3. You are November."

November grinned again; she had only known Klaus for a few minutes, and she had warmed to him already. "Well, Klaus, I'm very glad you're here," she said, rising to her feet and brushing the grass and twigs off her jeans.

"Ja, when you are a good cake finder, Klaus is happy too, except if you are hunting animals?" His eyes narrowed again.

November scrunched her face and shook her head, "no way! I love animals; I'm even vegan."

"So what, who here is not?"

November gulped without a reply.

Klaus sighed, "it is seeming Klaus has not many options, so Klaus comes with you." He peered at cube in her hand. "What is she?" He asked, pointing with his trunk.

"I'm not sure." November turned the six-sided form around. "Although I think she's the reason I'm here. I guess we'll soon find out."

"Ja, only if you *really* are a good finder."

November shrugged, hoping she could live up to the skills she'd offered. "When I got it, I was invited to be part of the LOTNE collective, if I pass the test. The letter said I have the key to unlocking the cube within myself."

"So then, it is clear, mach es so! Get x-ray, find key, and begin search to find Klaus cake!" His face beamed.

"Why an x-ray? I'm not broken. Not really, anyway."

"To find key inside yourself."

"Ha! You're funny, Klaus."

"Ja, and clever."

"LOTNE stands for Leaders of the New Earth, you know," her shoulders slumped, "the thing is, I am no leader. I can write and sing songs. That's about it." She stared at her ring. "I'm a jellyfish kite most of the time, wobbly and dreaming up in the sky, and I sometimes accidentally sting people if they come too close. I think whoever sent it made a mistake."

"Everything for a reason. Maybe someone is knowing more than you. It is quite possible."

November considered her new friend's perspective.

"You are the thing you believe," Klaus stated as a matter of fact.

November looked him in the eye. "Well, what do you believe you are?"

"Klaus is not believing. Believing is for ones who do not know."

November squinted at him.

"Then what do you *know* you are?"

"Klaus is knowing three things in this moment. 1. Klaus is Klaus, 2. Klaus wants cake, 3. You are November Fox, most times jellyfish without her sea, flying in the sky, good at finding, but not for details."

"Ha, yeah, there's some truth in that." November laughed as they both stared at the cube.

"What do you call her?"

"Her name is apparently, Joy,"

"So Joy finds cakes, you follow Joy, Klaus follows you, Klaus gets cake," he stated, as he clapped his two front feet together once, initiating the quest.

"Sounds like a plan, Klaus. Following Joy is what we shall do. Only, the trouble is, she is all jumbled up." She held up the cube. "But we can try. I do like fixing things."

"Flying and finding and fixing. Ok, Klaus comes with you, Jellyfish Kite."

"I thought you'd already decided you would?"

"Ja, there is no problem deciding things two times. Details are mattering."

"Ha. You're probably right. Can you smell tea? I'd love some tea?"

"Ja ja, Klaus ist immer Recht. Tea and cake is not ever mistake."

November laughed. "No, I guess not, unless you've had too much already."

Klaus lifted his left leg to peer into his small clock, "Keine Zeit Keine Zeit Keine Zeit," he blurted, jumping up and down on his cloud, wide-eyed, like he'd seen a ghost.

"What on earth is the matter?"

"No time!"

"No time for what?"

"Alles, everything. Timekeeper ist kaputt. Broken! Klaus said this day is terrible."

"It probably just needs a battery, Klaus. Don't worry."

"No timekeeper. No cake time for Klaus!"

"I'm sure you can still eat cake without your time-keeper—that's if we had cake."

"Nein nein nein nein nein!"

"Is nine o'clock cake time?"

"Nein! Mein Gott." He stamped his front foot down hard on his cloud.

"It's ok, let's head to the castle; they will most likely have a clock, so we can see when it's nine."

"Nein!" He protested.

"Goodness me! What is your obsession with nine? Come on, let's go," November started heading down the hill trying to ignore Klaus' vibe. "We will fix it. Let's first head to the castle. I'm sure we'll discover a solution along the way."

"*Neiiiiiiiiiinnnnn!*" Klaus didn't follow her.

She turned and walked back up the hill. "I *promise* I will help you mend your timekeeper and find cake." She reached out to stroke his back. "I will use my straight-fingered hand," noticing his look of alarm.

He flinched, shaking his head and looking away.

"What's the matter? Is my finger really so terrible?"

"All fingers straight or bent should stay away from Klaus."

November sighed, half relieved he didn't find her hand as disgusting as she had first imagined and glad that she wasn't the only one with issues. Although she felt slightly concerned that he was so uncomfortable with being touched.

"Ok, come on. Shall we go?"

"Ok. I guess there is no point staying." He nodded his head. "You know, when you help Klaus find cake, Klaus is not forgetting. Klaus is not forgetting all things."

"So it's true, elephants never forget." November smiled, pleased to be making some progress with her new friend.

They headed down the hill towards the valley. Klaus instantly resumed whistling, making November chuckle. She didn't realise elephants could whistle.

I remained floating in Lucitopia, watching the pair descend the hillside. I had never felt November connect with someone so fast. The isolation she was so used to feeling was one increment less. She trusted Klaus from the minute they met, which was a first for November. Who would have thought it would be a flying elephant that would make it across the vast and dangerous sea to the lonely island of her heart. Although I will have to admit, stranger things have happened, and some are yet to come.

6

Through the Black Forest

While the duo made their way through the valley, I went for an afternoon nap and had a peculiar dream. I was on a beach covered in stones. It was a place I had never been. Seagulls squawked as they fought over old potato chips, discarded on the shore. The aroma of salty air and the greasy, fried potato fingers with tomato sauce, was so intense that I could have sworn I was in the World of Form. For we do not have birds here, or sliced fried potatoes, or tomatoes for that matter. I have only learnt about them in culture class at school. My heart raced as a group of three girls proceeded to walk in my direction. It was unclear if they had seen me, yet they moved directly towards where I sat. As they drew nearer, they instinctively parted as if not to trample me. Two walked past my right and one past my left without even a glance. A ruby glint from the shoreline caught my eye, just before I awoke. Keen to check on November and Klaus, I rubbed my eyes and flew to the next screen, and saw that night was falling over the valley. The mist was gathering around the trees in the strange forest that rustled with peeps and scurries. The pair stood in front of the menacing wood.

As November stepped forward hesitantly, a wind chill snuck under her clothes. For a split-second, she could have sworn she saw Rebmevon floating in her long, white nightdress between the mist and the tree trunks. A shiver slithered down her spine like a red-bellied black snake.

"Ha ha, der Schwarzwald," announced Klaus with glee, causing November to jump.

"What? Did you say the Black Forest? Well then, we must be in Germany; thank goodness for that." November was temporarily relieved.

"Nein nein, this is not Germany Schwarzwald."

"Ah ha, nein means no, not the numeral nine." November was pleased it was her misunderstanding, and not that her friend was loopy.

"Ja ja," he replied.

"How do you know we're not in Germany?"

"The Christmas trees are a different green. Details are mattering."

"I'm happy we're together Klaus; this place gives me the creeps," she said, clutching Joy a little harder.

"*Reeeelax*, no-thing is lasting for always."

"Yes, but we still can't avoid going through it."

"Why fear? Everybody loves cake."

"What does cake have to do with this spooky woodland?"

"Cake comes from this forest."

"Huh? What do you mean?"

"Mumma told Klaus about der Schwarzwald a long time before."

"Where is your mother now?" Klaus didn't respond. November glanced over at him, and while she couldn't make out his expression in the misty shadows, she sensed his misery.

"Are you ok?"

After a few moments, he responded in a soft, slow voice. "She and Papa are gone."

"Where?"

Klaus didn't reply. His head hung low, lifting his foot, pretending to inspect his still-broken watch.

"What happened?" November sensed his pain and stopped walking to face him.

Klaus also stopped and then whispered, "Bad hunter got them and cut them up in pieces to get tusks for ivory. My baby sister was in Mumma's tummy. I saw her when Mumma's tummy was cut. She was small and not moving."

A surge of frigid cold swept through November's already-chilled body. She clenched Joy so hard, her fingers hurt. "Oh Klaus, that's so terrible. I'm sorry; humans can be so greedy and unconscious, sometimes. They don't realise animals have feelings." November leant over to stroke the curve of his small back. He flinched, and she pulled back. "You poor thing. You're an orphan, too, like me."

"Ja, Klaus ist allein. Klaus is alone."

"Oh Klaus, you're not anymore. I'm here with you." November very much wished to pat his smooth, leathery skin but knew it would take time for him to trust her to do that. "If your parents are gone, where do you live?"

"Some people found Klaus and took him far, far away to the zoo in Germany; now Klaus is locked und allein."

"Were you born in Africa and grew up in Germany?"

"Ja, Afrika was many years before. Deutschland ist Klaus's Heimat."

"How did you escape and get here?"

"There are three things Klaus only knows. 1. Klaus is Klaus, 2. Klaus wants cake, 3. You are Jellyfish Kite November."

November thought about her journey to this strange land and its inexplicable reality. "Are you sure you didn't come here through a rainbow portal in the sky?"

"Sounds fun. No. Klaus never had sky tunnel ride. Where can we make one?"

"I don't know," November said, shrugging her shoulders, enjoying the return of his good humour.

"So tell me about the cake."

"Ja, cake grows on tree here. We find cake."

"Ah, you must mean Black Forest Cake," November said, as they moved into the thick of the forest. "Your mother told you that they grow here when you were a baby elephant?"

"Ja."

November wondered whether to tell him there was no such thing as a cake tree, but she loved his optimism and didn't want to destroy his cake-tree dreammaybe later.

"Well, please find a vegan one for me."

"Ok, no problem," Klaus asserted.

They entered an even darker section of the forest. November found it hard to see more than a few steps in front of them and walked hesitantly. The cool mist chilled her skin. "This is a black forest, wherever we are." She listened to the strange, woodland noises.

The sound of small animals scampering off, so as to not be trodden on, and the eerie *hiss hiss* sound of swaying tree branches frightened her. Haunting owls *coo-cooed* in the distance—*a warning, she wondered?*

November saw an image in her mind of Rebmevon feeding worms to a pair of owls she kept in cages deep in the woods. She shook her head and rubbed the ring stone with her thumb. "Stop it!"

"Stop what?" Klaus asked.

"Oh, nothing. Don't worry," she sighed.

As the mist thickened, all she could see of Joy was her dim, green lights. She held the cube ahead of her, using what little light she emitted to illuminate the way.

The deeper they ventured, the louder the trees *hiss hiss hissed.* November wondered if they were talking to each other.

"Klaus," whispered November. "Can you please fly closer? I can't see you, and I'm scared." November felt the brush of his cloud, just above her left shoulder. "Thank you," she replied softly, only marginally reassured.

Klaus puffed up his chest. "Keine Angst, no fear. Klaus is master ninja," he said in all seriousness.

"Ha ha, and I'm Japanese," November laughed, imagining Klaus in a martial arts suit striking a pose. "No offence but I think *sometimes* size matters."

"Size is not mattering; it is only what you do with it! Details are mattering."

November chuckled and blew behind his ears.

The hissing of the branches and strange forest noises increased, the more the blackened woods enveloped them. November racked her brain for an alternative to proceeding, but found no option.

Another flash of white disappeared behind a tree. November gulped down her anxiety, hoping Rebmevon did not indeed lurk ahead. "Did you see that?"

"Klaus is seeing only trees, and none yet with cake." November was slightly worried she was hallucinating.

"Your cloud is glowing," There was a soft light pulsing by her shoulder.

Klaus raised his foot and the shine increased. "He goes, he goes!" He cheered. "Timekeeper keeps!"

"Hooray. What time is cake time?"

"Vier."

"Fear. Me too; it's *soooo* creepy in here."

"Nein Vier!"

"I know you're not afraid, *master ninja Klaus.*"

"Nein, vier. Cake time is vier. Four."

"Oh, I get it now. Well, what does Timekeeper say now?"

"Drei. Three."

"Oh, good, not long now."

The malicious whispering of the trees and the odour of decomposing foliage, increased November's reluctance to continue. Her bare feet were punished at every step, either by a sharp stick or a slimy caress. "Noveeeembeeeeer," sang a whispering voice, saddled on the hiss of the overhead timber. She stopped still, holding her breath. "Noveeeembeeeer, I can seeeeee you; you knoooow who I aaaaaaam." November shuddered to her core; the remaining air snatched from her frozen body. She knew exactly who it was, and so did I. Rebmevon.

Not again, I thought to myself. I was tempted to stop watching, yet for too many years I was unable to be by November's side, so I decided

41

to stay.

Without thinking, her inner survivor bolted.

November sprinted as fast as her legs could carry her, even though she couldn't see what was ahead. Recklessly, she ran into the darkness, adrenalin pulsing through her veins. *"Ahhhhhhhhhhh,"* November wailed, tripping over a rock and flying through the air. She somersaulted into the darkened woods and tumbled through forest brambles, smacking her knee hard along the way.

"Owwwww!" she screamed, clutching her knee. The forest was dead silent.

"Klaus, where are you?" She whimpered softly.

No reply. Only the *hiss hiss hissing* from above as she sat, shivering and crying.

Mr Russell's voice came back to her, telling her what to do when she was afraid. She tried to remember his words.

"Never forget your heritage, young November Fox. You are a survivor. The infant who beat a bitter frost and who fought for her rights to be heard, growing up here. Use the power of your brave heart to feel all the things that support you." She sat up and perched in a huddle. "Come on, Fox, pull it together," she urged herself on, thinking of yummy spaghetti meals and the joy of deliciousness. She thought of her favourite corner of the garden where the snowdrops grow, and the pleasure of sitting near them on a sunny day. She thought of singing to a crowd of enthusiastic fans. She remembered her good friend, Hermie, who she hadn't seen in a long time. She imagined eating pineapple, and finally, she thought of her new friend, Klaus. The positive memories were definitely working, when, suddenly, there came a delightful chiming from Joy: *Brrrringching.* Three of her green squares had lined up, and they were glowing even more brightly. November glanced up and saw a light ahead. The end of the forest was visible. *"Pheeeeew,"* she sighed, getting up, dusting herself off, and limping towards the light.

Exiting the woods, November turned around to bid good riddance to the most horrible cluster of trees she had ever passed through. The leaves above rustled malevolently in response.

"You may be leaving this forest, but you can't ever escape me," came a haunting whisper.

November forgot all about her painful knee and sprinted into the clearing.

7

Out of the Forest

I turned around to one of the screens on an opposing building, to see November step into an open space beyond the woods. Her heart filled with delight and relief as she spotted Klaus ahead of her.

"Hello." She noticed he had a cake floating along on a cloud behind him, attached like a trailer. He was sniffing up the icing with his trunk.

"Haaaaachooo!" He sneezed. "JFK, happy to see you again! Look, I caught her. I picked the best from high up in the trees."

"Wow, what a lovely cake. I'm amazed you found one in that scary, horrible place."

"Ja, ja, not black forest one. Vegan one that tastes of pineapple, for you."

November beamed. "I love pineapple; I eat it every day!"

"Where did you run?" Klaus flew closer.

"Didn't you hear the whispering voice calling my name?"

"Nein. You were just running and running, and Klaus lost you, so Klaus captured cake." He smiled victoriously.

"We have walked so far, my legs ache, I also hurt my knee. Let's have a picnic right here."

Klaus lifted his foot to inspect his timekeeper. "No, there are no plates and spoons; details are mattering."

"Yes, I guess that's fair enough. We're quite close to the castle now."

November ran her fingers through her messy, hair. Sticks and leaves fell out.

"Klaus, what is my hair doing? I tumbled in the forest."

"You are what you eat."

"What is that supposed to mean? You're a cake, and I'm a pineapple?"

Klaus just smiled in reply.

"Tell me. Is my hair really that bad?"

"Well, your hair is like November."

"You mean like a November storm? Can you fix it? I don't want it in a shambles for our visit to the castle."

"Reeeelax, no-thing is lasting for always."

November laughed at his philosophical attitude. "You are a clever Klaus."

"Klaus weis; Klaus knows."

"Although you are right that nothing lasts, sometimes we need to make changes along the way, so can you please fix my hair up?"

"Ok, ok, except I'm no hair expert."

"Oh, I guess not," she replied, looking at his shiny, bald, elephant head. She enjoyed the sensation of Klaus combing her hair with his trunk; it was the closest they had come to touching.

"I am so glad to be out of that forest. I hope we don't ever have to go back there!"

"Ja, except this cake is also not lasting always. No-thing is lasting for always."

"Come on; more cake will show up somewhere else. Let's not go back."

"Ok, ok," he huffed.

"Is your timekeeper still working?"

Klaus lifted up his foot and trumpeted vigorously, "*EeeeeRowrrh.* Thirty minutes after three," he proclaimed.

"Goodness, almost cake o'clock. We'd better get a move on." November thought about how Mr Russell's words had come back to her at the moment she needed them to escape the forest's clutches. Profound gratitude for him filled her up like a hot water spring. She glanced over to Klaus had now turned his whistle into a tune singing, "Klaus ist der Kuchen Jager der Kuchen Jager der Kuuuuchen."

From the German I studied in school in my World of Form languages class, this translates as "Klaus is the cake hunter the cake hunter the cake." November wondered how someone could be so silly and serious all in one tiny, flying, elephant package. She blew him a kiss. *Brrrringching*, Joy sang her song again. Three more green squares had lined up.

"Klaus!" She held up the cube.

"Ja, she works."

"Yes, but what does it mean?"

"Klaus weiß es nicht. Klaus does not know; Klaus knows only three things."

November interrupted. "I know. Let's get to the castle. Maybe answers await us there, and it's close to cake time."

"Caaaaaaaaakkkkkkeeeee!" Klaus cheered, as they headed down the road.

I rather fancied some cake, too. Alas, cake is another thing we know only as a concept over here. I wished again, more than ever, to dive through the screen so that I could join them for tea time. That got me thinking—now that I am the boss, perhaps I could remove cake from the strictly forbidden list, along with TV screens and hammocks. It is my sense that this new dawn approaching will take us out of the Age of Doing. My Father, appropriately, ruled this Age for many comparative tick-tocks. For soon we are entering the Age of Being, and with it comes all kinds of lovely delights—if I just had a cake recipe.

8

Arrival at the Fortress of Forgotten Fish

Hovering near the dark and shadowy screen was a challenge because my mind connection to Charlie was weak. When I am too indecisive, he ruffles in his carpet version of a *huff*, and has an autopilot setting to return me to my cocoon. I managed enough energy to get me to the rooftop apartment to rest for a while. I felt exhausted, despite having an afternoon nap. Napping is a new experience for me. I could not understand why I felt so tired until I saw November dragging her tired feet on the small TV and realised my energy levels reflected hers. She was the source of my lethargy. With slow steps, she was making her way through a stone tunnel towards the entrance of the castle. She was no longer limping, although her legs ached with fatigue.

The smooth, damp, ancient stones, underfoot, did not make the journey easier as everything seemed oversized for a human. November sighed, daunted by the staircase ahead. The steps appeared to be at least double the height of most regular stairs. Klaus flew along merrily, looking down at his timekeeper every few metres.

"Klaus, can you hear that music?"

"Ja."

Flowing music; single, long tones, gently over-lapping each other in strange harmonies, drifted down the tunnel. The pungent, spicy aroma of Earl Grey tea activated the reserves of November's energy. She began to climb the gigantic stairs up into the light. Hoisting herself up the last step, she arrived in a courtyard with Klaus at her side. November marvelled at a beautiful garden, full of flowers and lush with growth, enclosed by massive stone walls. The enchanting music filled the four-walled space, resonating in exquisite harmonics that escalated towards the heavens. November felt strangely renewed by the intense sensory input of the music and the smells in this serene place. The curving pathway continued through the green paradise, towards another ten steps that led to the castle door.

She stretched her arms and spun around like a ballerina, taking in the glory of this wonderland; her smile double-sized to match the increased sizes of everything around her. Abundant, lilac, trumpet flowers grew around the edges of the wall. These were also very large, causing November to wonder *if the plants were really that tall, or if she and Klaus had somehow shrunk?* Emerald moss patched the ancient, stone wall of grey, black and sandy-coloured limestone. One spot, in particular, reminded November of a big heart, shimmering with large dewdrops. Ivy ran rampant over most of walls and the weathered stone archway. Its tendrils extended in every direction, wriggling, almost as if it were growing before their eyes.

November marvelled at the somewhat surreal landscape, noticing, on the far side of the quadrant, the source of the fog and the music. There lay a pond with a harp-shaped fountain pulsing with sound and misty light. It seemed to be putting on a show just for their arrival. The instant she pointed it out to Klaus, the afternoon rays hit the mist at the precise angle required to create a beautiful rainbow.

November skipped over to the strange construction to inspect it more carefully.

"Goodness me, look at all those fish," she exclaimed, peering into the pond.

"I think they are the ones making the music."

"Ha ha," Klaus chuckled. "School of rock."

"Clever, Klaus," she giggled.

"What makes the difference between a piano and a fish?"

"I don't know, tell me." November sat down on the stone edge of the pond.

"You can tune a piano, except you can never tuna fish!"

"Ha ha, very funny. Those fish are playing beautifully; I bet they are singing about love." November watched their rainbow colours sparkling under the surface of the water.

"Thank goodness we've arrived. What a quest; we've been walking forever!"

"Welcome to the Fortress of Forgotten Fish," came a soft, soothing voice.

November jumped to her feet to find a graceful, giant lady in a princess dress, descending the stairs, like an angel from above.

"I am The High Priestess, Betty, daughter of King Hope, and I am humbled to welcome you to my castle. You are indeed November Fox, are you not?" The Priestess looked kindly into November's eyes, warming her heart.

"Yes, Your Highness, I am she."

The Priestess inspected Joy, still held tight in November's grip. "So then, you are now a Keeper of the Cube. All is in order," she said with a slight nod of her head. "Who, may I ask, is your delightful companion?"

"Klaus, Klaus *KÖNIG!*" Klaus replied, emphasising his royal surname, King.

"Well, I am exceptionally pleased that you are both here. Do come inside. Let us take tea together." November started to climb the oversized stairs, following the Priestess with Klaus and the cake close behind.

"May I ask Your Highness why your home is called The Fortress of Forgotten Fish? It is such an odd name for such a grand castle?"

The Priestess stopped and turned around. "Yes, my dear, I agree it appears rather bizarre at first mention, but it is more earnest than it may seem." She clasped one hand gently within the other. "Do you by chance remember Blounder, brother of Flounder? Or Milly, sister of Free Willy?"

November shook her head.

"Or perhaps, Toby Tick, uncle of Moby Dick?"

Again, November shook her head from side to side without saying a word.

"Or, surely you recall Remo cousin of Nemo? Or even sweet Dipper, great-grandfather of Flipper?"

"No," November replied. "I don't remember any of them?"

"That is exactly the point, my dear. All of these beloved fish and countless others are missing and forgotten by everyone; apart from me, of course. The Fortress is an orphanage for fish."

"Goodness, I've never heard of such a place."

"Yes. The situation is rather upsetting. Some have lost their family to show business in Hollywood, and for others, their schools are under threat from fishermen around the world, in search of fish finger material. My darling fish come here to find sanctuary."

"But, Your Highness," questioned November, "are they not remembered when your visitors arrive?"

"I do not receive guests. You two are the first since ..." She hesitated, "... ever since I decided to forsake human company, apart from you."

"My dear Highness, may I ask why?" November spoke gently, sensing it was a delicate subject.

The Priestess replied in a soft voice. "My dear child, was there a time you lost someone you loved more than you love the sun and the moon?"

November thought for a moment. "No, Your Highness; I never knew my parents. I love my dog, Honey, but I haven't misplaced her. I'm quite sure I've not yet experienced the kind of loss you talk about."

"Ok, let me re-phrase. Try to imagine two types of love. One is like the fountain over there. Imagine you are the fountain and your love is the emerging water. It flows from you to all who wish to bathe in its shores. You are free and rely on nobody. You give from an inner well

52

of strength."

"Ooooookay."

The High Priestess then pointed to the ivy-coated archway in the back of the garden. "Now imagine you are one-half of the arch, and the person you love is the other. The love can flow through the arc, but when one half leaves, you crumble and are nothing more than a pile of broken rocks. You require the other simply to have structural integrity." The Priestess gazed at the arch like a traveller at the harbour, realising the ferry that had just left the dock was the last one going home, ever.

"Well, my sweet child, I shall never be half of an arch again. The descent from the fall hurt more than breaking all of my bones. I also had to release two of the dearest things in the world to me." She turned her head towards the fountain.

"Now I choose to be a fountain of love. For that I need no one. My fish are perfect companions in the seas of my soul. You may understand this more when you are older, my dear." The Priestess kindly gazed into November's eyes. "Life is indeed a mirror ball, reflecting back all that resides within us." She caressed the side of November's face with her big, soft hand before turning to continue up the stairs. "Enough of this chitter-chatter; let us take tea now. I do hope you like Earl Grey tea, as that is all I keep."

November's eyes were wide with wonder. She turned around to Klaus, who had a big grin and a sparkle in his eye, which had nothing to do with The Priestess' words. He had just checked his timekeeper.

It was then I wondered to myself whether I was more a waterfall or an arch. I guess tick-tock will tell. *Did you know the central voussoir of an arch is called the keystone?* I have designed many an arch. *Perhaps that is what I am? A keystone. What are you?*

9

Inside the Fortress

I was mulling over some mystifying concepts as I flew out of my rooftop apartment window to a nearby hot-air balloon, *If I can see November, is there someone also watching me?* It reminded me of the mirror I had placed in the penthouse years earlier. *When would it end? Would there be someone watching my watcher? And another watcher watching their watcher? Perhaps the watcher's chain goes on forever? How is it only one-way? Why can November not see me? What if she were able to see me?*

I remembered learning at school about a concept called phase cancellation, where two of the same sound waves can cancel each other out. *If I can feel, hear, and observe November, at the point she could do the same to me, would we cease to exist? Phase- cancelling us both out of existence? Or, what if I only live because November does? And it is possible she only exists because I do. Does my observation of her summon her into reality?* Anyway, I better not rush the process of her knowing about me, just in case there is some adverse consequence. I decided I would not try to attempt official contact until after I had written you this letter.

When I successfully jump my first hurdle in crossing over, perhaps then I will investigate more communication options. The screen dangling from the hot-air balloon was lit up with a beautiful vision of the interior of the fortress, as the Priestess crossed the great hall to retrieve plates and cutlery.

"Cake time, cake time," Klaus sang, bouncing up and down on his cloud.

"*Shhhh,* Klaus, please be patient; remember no-thing is lasting always." November lowered her hand, signalling for him to relax and wait, as she looked around in awe at the big, royal room.

"Goodness, your castle is so lovely, Your Highness. You must sometimes get terribly lonely in such a fortress all by yourself?"

"Please sit, my dears."

November climbed onto the enormous, golden sofa, upholstered with thick, satin fabric and ran her hands along the smooth surface. It felt like silk of the highest weight. Klaus landed his cloud on a nearby chair; his legs began to tremble as his gaze fixed on the cake.

"Distraction," the Priestess sat, facing November. "Endless inter-ruptions fill this life we live, and other people are the main culprits." She paused for a moment. The mood in the room quickly changed from a light-hearted cake break to being as deep and reflective as a moonlit lake at midnight.

"When you stop and peer inside yourself, dear child, you will find the same depths as that of the cosmos."

November suddenly felt quite heavy and sank further into the sofa. The Priestess continued, "When we search the heavens with our eyes at night, we wonder at the infinite depth of space, but we are merely seeing that which is within us." She paused as November sat in silent contemplation. "Yet most people never even get a glimpse of this because of our relentless distraction."

November thought about the meaning of this wise insight and said, "isn't, *out there* just space and objects in space?"

"Precisely, and the expanse in both directions is incomprehensible. We are born with a choice of angles from which to observe it all. Many keep their blinkers on and choose not to see much at all." She took another sip of tea. "Ever since I lost my other half, and sacrificed keeping my most treasured creation, I vowed to explore the vastness of the self as far as I can reach." She paused for a moment and then smiled. "To boldly go where no one has gone before." She winked, as she quoted the *Star Trek* mantra, somehow aware of November's fondness for the show.

"And I must be alone to take on such a task."

November flushed, feeling bewildered contemplating these new ideas. After some moments, she asked, "What did you mean, when you said you sacrificed your most treasured creation?"

"Another time, my child." November nodded, not wanting to press her further on the subject, as the Priestess continued. "I have no wish for distraction. That is how I came to have and love my fish. They inspire further inner exploration, but demand nothing from me, and they give me space for my space." She gave her a warm smile.

Such concepts were new to November. She glanced at Klaus who was as focused as a queen's guard, staring at the cake.

"A cosmos living inside us," November wondered, clutching her waist.

The Priestess clapped her hands three times. "So, now must be cake time. Oh, how I do love a piece, and I had a sneaking suspicion you would also."

"Caaaakkkee!" Chorused Klaus, waking up from his trance. The Priestess glanced over to November with compassion, before standing up gracefully and moving across the room. "I shall fetch us more tea just as soon as I make a needed adjustment." The Priestess stood, still as a statue, concentrating intensely.

November wondered what the Priestess was contemplating, when, suddenly, lightning cracked like a cowgirl's whip, *Ka-boom*, and struck the cake at its centre. Sparkles of twinkling light began to rain down as the cake grew rapidly. Klaus, who had been trying hard to contain himself until that point, let out an excited *"EeeeeRowrrh,"* releasing his pent-up excitement.

November laughed at the delightful note, thinking it sounded like a bent out-of-tune trumpet. She welcomed the distraction, as she was not quite ready to dive into the unfamiliar depths of her own cosmos, and would leave such an exploration for another time. It was indeed cake time, and what a cake it was.

Inflated by her blissful feelings, I sailed down to the next screen.

10

The Doorway to Room Number One

After cruising down a long street in November Fox's Lucitopia, I was pleased to spot her with Klaus, and The Priestess, still sitting in the Great Hall of the Fortress of Forgotten Fish. The only difference being the cake was no longer a perfect cylinder. "Mmmmm, lovely," November murmured, sipping the last drop of tea from her, light-yellow, porcelain teacup.

"I could not help noticing, my dear." The Priestess nodded towards November's fingers.

November set down her cup and blushed, clasping her bent finger with her other hand. "I know, Your Highness. It isn't very nice, is it?"

"On the contrary child, it is a sign of royalty. You should be proud." November shyly took out her slightly deformed pinkie and smiled, giving it a stroke.

"You are only half human, my dear. Take a look." The Priestess handed November a large, intricately framed, antique mirror.

November needed both hands to hold up the looking glass.

"Examine your ears. You are part pixie from another world." November was not sure if The Priestess was serious. She rotated her face to inspect her ears. To her shock and bewilderment, she did indeed have one elf-shaped ear. She wondered why she'd never noticed it before. "But, what, how did you know?"

"The prophecy, child. Remember perfection is in imperfection." The Priestess stood up and signalled for them to follow. "The Cube Maker sent me a message through the fish. You can hear animal's thoughts, can you not?"

November glanced at Klaus and thought of Honey. "Um, yes, I suppose so. Not all but most. Can't everyone?"

"No, child. If they could, many more vegans like you and I would roam the Earth."

"I didn't realise you are also a vegan, Your Highness."

"Yes, there is much we share, yet we must press on. Time is unfolding."

November and Klaus stood up to follow The Priestess. She led them at a fast pace down an exceptionally long, labyrinthine hallway, passing many multi-coloured doorways along the way. Each door slammed shut as they neared it. November was just about to ask more questions when The Priestess stopped and faced her. "The instructions given to me said to show you behind the doorway to room Number One."

November wondered if this doorway had something to do with Joy's remaining three green squares. "Your Highness, have you met the Cube Maker? Do you know where did Joy came from?"

"Nobody knows the maker's true identity, and, my dear, you have Joy to do with as you like," The Priestess added.

"Why did he or she make me a Keeper of the Cube?"

"That is for you to discover, dear child. Have patience, and remember that most answers lead to more questions, and sometimes it is better to relax, eat cake, and enjoy the journey."

"Ja ja. Correct," agreed Klaus.

The group walked on and on, and November had the sense that they were walking in spirals since they had passed hundreds of doors so far.

"The light will be dazzling when we arrive, so I advise you to shut your eyes at first. The door is automatic, so take care."

November glanced over her shoulder to check if Klaus was still following close behind them. She laughed to see that he was now wearing sunglasses. "Klaus, how? Where? Oh, never mind." She smiled at her funny friend, who once again checked his timekeeper, as they moved quickly past door after door.

"Surely you have had enough cake now? What is the time anyway?"

"Exactly 6 o'cl-," Klaus vanished.

"Klaus!" Cried November.

"Don't worry." The Priestess called back, not pausing on her path. "No-thing is lasting for always."

November's heart sank. Where had he gone? "Klaus?" She sang out again, stopping briefly to check if he had snuck out one of the doorways.

"There's no point, my dear," The Priestess replied from up ahead, apparently understanding more about the disappearance than she was willing to explain. "Come, we must press on; time is precious."

November sadly continued walking past the neverending, closing doors. Eventually, they arrived at a doorway at the end of a hall.

"Now mind the light, child," she said as the door flew open and burst with luminance. Before them lay a calm, sparkling, endless ocean.

"Klaus!" She cried seeing a giant mother Elephant walking on the glistening sea with her baby by her side. Light surrounded the pair as they walked.

"It is not your friend, my dear."

November stood spellbound. "How are they afloat on the..." she stopped mid-sentence.

"Are you aware of what is happening?" The Priestess queried in her ever-calm voice.

"I'm not sure."

"For the mother to have sustenance for her baby, she must first feed herself."

Spellbound, November gazed at the light from the sky raining over the giant beings on the ocean.

"Yes," November answered squinting in the brightness. "The light flows through everything. If it didn't, the Elephant Mother would have no energy for her young one. If the baby starved, he could not give the leftover energy to the sea and the fish."

"Yes, you are precisely right," replied The Priestess, satisfaction evident in her voice. "So, can you tell me, child, if you would be that Mother and if you think of a number, what number would you be?"

November thought about it for a while. "*Mmmm*. Well, I guess the number one." Before November could say another word, *brrrrringching*, and the last three green squares aligned. One whole side of Joy glowed as a single green square. Bright lights then snatched November up and a force ripped her out of one reality and into the next. Straining to hear, she just caught the faint, familiar music, arousing both curiosity and peculiar comfort. Neither the doorway nor the fortress was in view as she tumbled once again down the portal of colour.

I was dizzy, yet once again free, as I travelled on to another part of the city via Keller Drive. The words of Helen Keller entered my mind, *"The best and most beautiful things in the world cannot be seen or even touched. They must be felt with the heart."*

11

The Geometric World of Mind

I arrived at another viewing location in Lucitopia, my mind a frenzy of thoughts. They danced around, bumping into each other like dodgem cars. The noise was deafening, like that of a crowded fairground. I had learnt about them in culture class, yet I had never imagined them to be this unpleasant. I welcomed seeing November, trying to make sense of her surroundings.

The cold, smooth floor was a familiar comfort, but her jarring thoughts made concentration impossible: *Klaus, Honey, her band, her house, artichokes, the shoes she bought last week, the new album, Joe Wishbone's spider.*

Fragment after fragment bombarded her mind, the weight of them all completely disabling her. She looked at Joy to bring her focus onto one thing. The indigo squares sparkled like miniature seas glimmering under moonlight. She scanned the geometric shapes piled up around the room.

Watermelon, her garden, her bed, her friends Sue and Eloise, beetroot dip. Bits of thoughts still raced around in her mind at tremendous speed, juxtaposing with the peace and gentle vibrations of the white room. A cracking rod of lightning suddenly flashed through the chamber. She fell to the floor.

Another strike, *Waaaaaaching*, whipped along past her.

Surge after surge of electricity cracked. She tried to avoid being hit, dodging from side to side. After ten minutes or so, the attacks subsided and she had only half the army to battle—the battalions of thoughts. *The orphanage, why ostriches can't fly, her washing, the cinema, rhinoceros' eating habits, the Helsinki airport, and Hamish's purple shirt,* were all fighting for attention.

"Stop it!" She screamed. "Leave me alone." With all her might she focussed on the cube and began to count the squares in a loud voice: "One, two, three, four." Thoughts still tried to sneak through, as she looked around for an exit. She continued aloud, "five, six," as she inspected the maze of white beams behind her.

"Six is the number of major cities you've played in this month."

"SHUT UP!" She screamed again. The next square was seven.

"You like the number seven for seven reasons," said another voice in her mind.

"Ahhh, go away!" She felt as though she was having a conversation with twenty people at the same time, all of them shouting at her, but the cacophony left her unable to respond. November moved around to the side of the pile of shapes and noticed a picture, similar to the one she had seen in the last white room. It depicted a vast desert with a massive tower off in the distance. "What is that?" She said out loud, attempting to dominate the internal onslaught. The far-off structure looked like a giant, brick, wedding cake. *Are you in there, Klaus? Cake, boats, football, marshmallows, water lilies, typewriters, is Santa Claus real?*

"*Ahhhhh!* Please be quiet!" She yelled into the empty room, covering her earsnot that it made any difference.

At times like these, I wish she were not so cautious. I wanted her to jump straight into the picture. My own mind was like an out-of-control, flying, noodle factory. Not a very pleasant sensation at all.

November' stiffened at the thought of diving into such a barren landscape, but the violating brain-chorus overload was giving her no choice.

She had no idea how she could cross that endless desert to the tower without dying of dehydration. She wished for Klaus to make an appearance. *I bet he is flying around in there alone.* The barrage of thoughts became unbearable, so she took a big deep breath, closed her eyes, and put her fingers into the image. Her hand seemed to be everywhere yet nowhere at the same time. She could still sense her enveloped arm; it just didn't seem like it was part of her body anymore. Then there came more internal onslaught.

Glow worms, black holes, clouds, Rizz the gardener, tennis balls, how do leap years work? "*Aaaahhhhhh!*" She screamed as the battling thoughts chased her into the picture.

She catapulted through the portal again.

I fell back and gasped, covering my mouth and rolling a corner of Charlie over my face. I had almost thrown a stone at the screen just to shut down my own brain. I did not care where she would end up, as long as I could silence the internal choir. Thankfully, I had not taken any action. Of course, I did not wish any harm to come to November. It was just that my head might have exploded at any moment. I thought of the words of Buddha, *We are shaped by our thoughts; we become what we think. When the mind is pure, joy follows like a shadow that never leaves.* I took a few, deep breaths while remaining flat on my back, and then meandered around the corner, emptying my mind as much as I could, unsure what I would find ahead of me.

Erica's Note

Somewhere between Baker Street and Waterloo Station, I almost toppled over. The train swayed and swerved, squishing me up against the sardine-packed humans. Holding the centre rail for support, and with the bottle held firmly under my arm, I kept reading, absorbed in the tale and thinking this story may indeed be real.

If someone from three-hundred years ago were able to see us all squeezed into this train, it could seem like *we* are in a magic portal, zipping through time. They might also note how we are strangers to each other, afraid of prolonged eye-contact.

While I was thinking such thoughts, I sensed someone looming over my shoulder, trying to get a look at what I was reading. I instinctively pulled the pages towards my chest. Despite liking human contact, I abhorred it here, *what's mine is mine.*

The sound of glass on metal brought me back to the present as another curve in the track caused my precious bottle to clink against the bannister.

I glanced at the pages and thought of The Priestess in her lonely, grand castle, and her great pain of loss. I again remembered Steven. *We were also an arch; two sides of one? Who am I now? A broken pile of rocks? It does feel quite similar; that's for sure. Is it now time to be a fountain of love for everyone? How on earth do I do that when I can't even share some words on a page with the stranger next to me?*

I then thought of November's new elephant friend; such a sweetie. He reminds me of my friend, Hans, from my writing class; also a German. We call him, the optimiser, as he is so exacting and efficient with everything he does. I admire him. Funny how detail-obsessed many Germans are, even as elephants.

As I gazed up at the tube map, I noted the end station and the place I call home, Elephant and Castle. *Was it just a coincidence? Am I now searching for meaning and connecting the dots in life? Who names a place Elephant and Castle anyway?*

My head began to spin. *Is there order behind the chaos in life, and am I only now starting to see a pattern?* If things are connected, we must be able to disconnect the parts we wish to, like taking apart a jigsaw puzzle.

How much control do I have in this game of life? Will shadows accompany any form of light? Can I re-create my life from scratch starting now? Does guilt have the power to manifest into a ghost?

At my station, I jumped off the train. It was dark, and the good old,

English rain was blessing us with its relentless presence. I decided to get a taxi home.

If you've ever travelled in a black London cab, you know that there is something quite comforting about such rides, not only because of the shelter they often provide, from the unhappy heavens. When I paid the driver through the translucent divider, I caught a glimpse of his eyes in the rear vision mirror. They were identical to those of the man I engaged with at the station earlier.

To encourage him to turn around, I began talking about the weather. "Ahhh this English rain, why can't it visit France for a while?"

Without turning, he held my gaze in the mirror and said in a smooth, rich tone, "As Vladimir Nabokov says, *Do not be angry with the rain; it simply does not know how to fall upwards.*"

The cab's door then magically opened. I leapt out, but the rain was too opaque to see his face through the window, and he sped off into the night. I could have sworn that he had the same voice as the black-suited man from London Victoria.

I wasn't sure if I was relieved or scared that it was he. At least he didn't seem to be chasing me. I sheltered my head from the poor rain *who only knows how to fall* and made a dash for my apartment. For a moment I envied the tears from the sky for only having one simple option. However limiting, sometimes, that must be a relief.

12

The Desert of Intention

I began to feel ridiculously hot as Charlie and I drifted up and over the city. The sensation was unusual since it is forever night in Lucitopia, and everywhere else on my side. It made sense, when I glanced down at a plasma. Beads of sweat were running down November's arm. The hot wind blew against her face and grains of sand lifted into the air, stinging her exposed flesh. She was still miles from the isolated desert structure that appeared surrounded by a barren landscape stretching out in every direction.

The intensity of the temperature caused her to feel disorientated and giddy. She covered her face with her hands to protect it from the hot, wind-blown sand, and struggled to open her eyes. She pushed against the force of the wind, taking a few steps in the direction of the distant tower.

"When the desert was cold on a hot day, he would be no longer himself," came a familiar voice of calm reason.

"Klaus," she beamed. "What happened to you?"

"Timing is everything," he called back inspecting his time-keeper. Klaus still wore his sunglasses, although now he sipped from a cocktail glass with a tiny umbrella in it. He sat perched at the front of his cloud, using his trunk as a straw.

"Well, you're obviously in holiday mode. You do realise we may die in this desert if we don't get out soon?"

"Ja, ja. Eleven hours until cake time is close to dying!"

"Are you saying it is five o'clock? I last saw you at six. Is your timekeeper working?"

"Ja. He works."

November wondered how it was possible that almost twelve hours had passed since she had last seen Klaus, or perhaps it was even twenty-three hours or more? "Klaus, we need to cross to the tower."

"*Mmmm* ja," mumbled Klaus with a mouth full of drink.

"Klaus!" She yelled. Her skin felt like it was melting under the flaming sun.

"How fast does your cloud fly? We need to figure out how we can cross the desert!"

"She is no BMW," he called back into the gusts of strong wind.

"What's in that cocktail of yours? We're in a dangerous situation, possibly fatal!" November's sweat beads flooded the valleys between the worry lines on her forehead.

"Ok, ok. Cloud flies when Klaus wants her to."

"Are you saying you control it only with your mind?"

"Ja ja. That is right. No instructions. She just goes."

"Doesn't that mean your cloud *will* fly faster than a BMW when you simply wish her to?"

"*Mmmm.* It could be so, in theory. Klaus never tried."

"Well try now!"

"Ok, ok. Klaus tries."

He focused on the distant column.

"Do columns have cake?"

"Klaus! Concentrate. Use all of your focus and intention, and if it works, send someone here to rescue me immediately!"

"*Jaaaaaaaa*" Klaus adjusted his sunglasses and assumed a serious motorbike racer stance.

Broooommm broom broom, the motor roared.

"Is that noise coming from your cloud?"

71

"Ja. Klaus told cloud to have a speed bike engine like Suzuki Hayabusa with turbo charge." He grinned.

Klaus revved the engine as if ready for a big race. *Zooooooooooooooooooom*, off he went, disappearing within seconds.

"Goodness!" A faint *Brrrringching* came from Joy.

On inspection, she saw that three of the indigo squares had aligned. "Huh... how?" November stared off into the distance. *What just happened?*

A dreadful image then caught her attention. On the horizon to the left of the tower, rising from the sandy dunes, was a flickering form, growing as the light rays bent to accommodate it. *Rebmevon.* November's temperature instantly rose another five degrees. She wiped the sweat from her cheek. *The easy revenge; to kill me while I'm powerless in the desert, of course.*

November racked her brain for a way to defend herself. She looked at joy. *Why did you chime?*

After a few seconds, she realised; *Ahhh, mind power!* To her relief, the ghostly mirage vanished.

Maybe I can use the power of intention to travel across the desert? No harm in trying. She stood; legs slightly apart. As she focused her eyes on the tower, she sharpened her attention on her destination. With all her might, she concentrated on her goal.

I intend to cross this desert. Now. November grew lighter. She lifted off the ground and moved towards her target.

"Hey, this works. Ok, faster," she said aloud, keeping her vision fixed on the large column.

"Even faster!" She flew across the desert; the wind no longer a counter force. Every time her attention wandered or she tried to force the movement; she slowed down. November toyed with the toggle in her mind that switched between discipline and letting go. It was like learning to ride a wild horse. The more she allowed it to gallop towards the fixed focal point, the speedier she raced. She kept her intention focused, whilst surrendering to the energy that was present.

The balance enabled her dominion over her thoughts, allowing the movements to happen on their own.

"I can ride you, mind," she called out, as she sped through the barren, burnt landscape.

She arrived at the base of the tower in no time.

"Klaus," she sang out, coming up behind him. *"Eeeeeeeeee!"* he screamed, whipping around.

"It's only me."

"How, what? How so fast?"

"I have my own BMW, after all," November said proudly.

Before heading towards the stairway that ran in spirals up the outside of the tower, November gave one last apprehensive glance at the horizon. "And it's hard to catch," she whispered.

Watching November command her body and summon her flying ability, triggered the memory of my first attempt to ride Charlie. What a disaster. It was the evening of my Sterling Service event, and the elders were quite merry from all the wine. My Father, in a slurred, yet still commanding tone, instructed me to fly for the first time, and he wished me to do so before them all. With jittery limbs, I unrolled little Charlie and sat on him, cross-legged and stroked his plush surface, which calmed me. I looked towards the swaying and jeering elders, wondering what to do.

Nothing happened. *"Before anything comes vision. Without vision you will go nowhere,"* my Father boomed.

I closed my eyes and imagined Charlie lifting into the air with all my mind power. When I opened my eyes, I was hovering a few metres above the ground. I was so excited and proud that when I glanced to my Father and the others for approval, Charlie fell, and I rolled off onto the floor. The crowd exploded with hysterical wine-enhanced laughter. Mortified, I scurried off to my cocoon.

"Be prepared to make a fool of yourself. The only way you will learn is when you're getting up off your knees after some humiliation," my Father called out after me as I retreated in shame.

For the first time since I have become the new boss, I miss my Father. His words always carried much truth, despite their razor-sharp edges. He was a monster of sorts, but he was *my* monster.

13

The Longest Stairway

Discipline and hard work pay off. My Father, as you may have gathered, was strict with me my whole life. I cannot say that was so bad. Had he not been who he was, I never would have committed myself to Lucitopia's completion. Twice! So in reality, as much as he frightened me, he also taught me more than either of us realised.

Last night, when Charlie and I were cruising around, I remembered the only time my father visited me at our version of boarding school. He came as a guest presenter and gave a talk in my World of Form culture class about music. I shall never forget the first tune he played. It was a song by a band called, *The Police*. I giggled under my breath, unsure if it was his twisted sense of humour. It was called *Message in a Bottle*. As a young Architect. I thought it was a silly way to correspond—to send someone a message in a bottle.

How could you be sure it would reach the intended person? Then it dawned on me that perhaps it is the perfect way to communicate with someone. This path allows the mysterious forces of nature to take it straight to the person who *really* needs the message. So, last evening, I decided a message in a bottle would be how I would post you this letter. As they say, *It is so crazy, it just might work.* So it is no coincidence that *you* are reading it. The conspiring forces of the universe have the ability to bring it directly to the person who will benefit from experiencing it somehow. And that dear friend is *YOU*. Hello. (Insert me waving to you again.)

So, thank you, Father. Again, you did indeed help me. I do hope you realise how much. I wish I could tell you. Perhaps it is you who will find the bottle. Is that where you have gone—*to the World of Form?*

When I looked at a screen near the little café I created, the pair stood at the base of the stairway.

"Up, up, up," Klaus sang.

"I'm not sure I need things like stairs anymore," November said with a grin. "What do you think this strange place is, Klaus?" She peered upward, seeing nothing apart from sand blowing against stair after stair.

"Klaus knows only three things: 1. Klaus is Klaus."

"Yes, I know, Klaus. 2. Klaus wants cake. 3. I am November," she said. Klaus nodded his head. "I think you know more than three things, Klaus."

"Ja ja, thinking and knowing are two different things."

"You're right. See, you *are* a clever, Klaus."

"Ja, Klaus wies, Klaus knows, except clever and knowing are also two different things; details are mattering."

"I wonder who lives here." Through the haze of blowing sand, she could make out a huge array of solar panels and a wind turbine to the left of the structure.

"Look" she pointed, squinting. "Perhaps it's a science station?" Klaus didn't hear her. He had already flown around the other side of the tower looking for entry points. November stood wondering how hard it would be to climb all those stairs in such heat. She decided to try the same technique she had used to cross the desert.

I can do it. I did it once; I can do it again. I can ride my mind, she told herself with strong conviction and prepared for the attempt. She narrowed her eyes and focused intently on the stairway that seemed to curl up to the heavens. She anchored herself, spread her legs apart, raised her arms, and fixed her full attention on her target.

76

"Klaus bets cylinder cake is what they have," interrupted Klaus who had flown back around.

"Klaus! I need to focus. This stairway goes way too high to walk up in this weather."

Klaus' eyes fell into sad puppy-eye shapes.

"Sorry, I didn't mean to snap. Tell me, why do you love cake so much?"

Klaus didn't respond for a while, and then wet his lips and replied. "Cake makes me happy."

"I understand, come here." November reached out to stroke his diminutive back.

Klaus shook his head, rejecting the gesture.

She had seen happiness, laced with a suppressed sadness, in Klaus' eyes since they had first met. He had endured such a harsh history. She wondered how he managed to still hold his head high. She guessed cake is what kept his mind focused on good things.

"You know, you and I are quite similar," she said in a gentle voice. "We both lost our parents, and now we need cake to fill the empty hole inside. I'm just not sure what type of cake I need."

Klaus let out a soft, broken, trumpeting noise in agreement. *Errough-hhweeekk.*

November smiled. "I'm so happy Destiny brought us together." She blew a kiss to her new friend.

"Ah, Schmetterlinge."

"What is Schmetterlinge? You've said it before. I like that word."

"Means butterfly."

"Ah, I see. Lovely. Klaus, time to find that cylinder cake."

Klaus lifted his ears at the suggestion, and started to fly upwards. November once again planted her feet and set her intention, and in only a few moments, she began to rise up the circular stairway. She enjoyed this new ability tremendously.

As I watched her ascend into the sky, I, too, felt as airborne as a dandelion spore, drifting in the breeze of allowance. Alone yet light.

Strong yet fragile. Empty, yet full of hope for the future. I, too, am quite possibly now an orphan. Hooray for liquid crystal displays; I feel like I have some friends on the other side. Charlie rumpled at this thought. I stroked his velveteen pile. "Have no fear, my codependent friend. Of course, I mean, apart from you." I simply mean *non-carpet friends.*

14

The Mad Professor

Sometimes I am curious about how we all came to be separated. *Are we all made of stardust like I learnt at school? If so, how did we leave the mumma stardust clump at the beginning? Why are we so small and individual? How is it possible I am here while you remain there? Why are ants so tiny? Are they aware of who belongs to those tall legs of yours?* You are in the World of Form as neighbours, yet I am unsure ants will ever know who you are. You see them like I can see November. Although to them, you could simply be a monstrous shoe coming from the heavens that they had better escape. *Perhaps we all see other things that remain blind to our existence? I wonder if we all have something we are unaware of that sees us?* I do not know. I have no teachers these days to ask about such things. *Am I supposed to have all the answers now?* When I try to ask Charlie, he just bunches up. He seems satisfied with the simple life; accepting his limitations. He does not appear to crave more meaning in the way I do. I told you it is not easy being alone over here in the shadows, now with the task of solving my own riddles. Some, like Charlie and my Father, prefer not to ask deeper questions in the first place. I call them the *do-ers.* I assume, together, we all make up the whole. Some people inquire—I presume they are the dreamers. Others resolve their questions—maybe the mathematicians, scientists, artists and philosophers try. Quite a few humans just do ordinary things.

I still cannot comprehend an existence where there is no yearning for deeper understanding. Life is far too fascinating not to explore further. Again Charlie rippled underneath me at such musing. His one-dimensionalism sometimes gets on my nerves as I sense my unrest gets on his. Nevertheless, our friendship is strong. Ultimately, we tend to respect each other's differences, which is key to our successful connection.

Have you met some of these action beings, actively creating, yet rarely stopping to reflect? I speculate that together we are one big mass, all with our unique position within the construction. Like ants, some of us are soldiers, some cleaners, some foragers, some unemployed and lazy, and only a few are queens. It may be we are all like tentacles of a colossal octopus. I was thinking about this octopus when November and Klaus reached the top of the Tower. November lay like a starfish on the roof of the giant cylinder as Klaus admired the view.

"He comes." Klaus pointed with his trunk.

The approaching sandstorm made the heat of the sun bearable as the sand blowing around in the air softened its rays. Flashes of light exploded, creating a cloud of mist just metres from November's feet. She watched, mesmerised, as the haze cleared to reveal a mysterious doorway, surrounded by surging, blue and purple electrical sparks. November slowly circled the frame. She looked around, searching for a stone or stick.

"Klaus, do you still have your cocktail glass?"

"Ja, here." He flew over and presented it.

November took the miniature cup and threw it through the doorway. *Zaaaap.* The electrical energy converged on the cup, which instantly dissolved and vanished.

Klaus's mouth dropped open.

"Sorry, we didn't have any other options. It could be safe on the other side, and perhaps they have cake," she placated.

November immediately regretted her words. Without even weighing the dangers, in flew Klaus and with a *Zaaaap*; the force swallowed him up like plankton in a whale's mouth.

"Klaus, *noooooo*, not again!" November couldn't bear to be on this desolate tower, alone with an approaching sand storm. So, with less caution than usual, she stepped through the door.

Darkness. "Klaus?"

"Ja, Klaus ist *heeerrrre.*" He seemed to be close by.

November's eyes struggled to adjust. She felt around her, touching nothing but emptiness. She blinked as a dull light up ahead began to grow brighter; not much brighter than a candle, some fifty metres away.

Strange aromas tickled her nose.

"Mmmm, spicy cake," Klaus hummed, bumping into November's shoulder.

"You're right; whatever is brewing down there is quite funky." The pair made their way down the long hallway towards the source of the light and the fragrance. The floor beneath her feet felt like hospital linoleum, cool and smooth; a pleasant change from the hot, sandy world outside. November ran her hands along the glass walls that she could now just make out, as the light brightened. She guessed they were in a laboratory of some kind.

November detected various odours wafting around her. One scent reminded her of the old typewriter factory near the orphanage, inky and industrial. Another was the fruity smoke she would sometimes breathe when passing teenagers in the park on their once-a-year outing to the sea from Hartwall. The strongest scent of all of them was that of sweet, frangipani flowers. November hadn't experienced their divine fragrance for many moons. She breathed in, remembering Nerida, a kind lady, who sometimes came to Hartwall and read stories to the children. Nerida always smelt of summer blossoms and fresh cookies. She and Mr Russell were the only nice grown-ups November encountered in her early life. Nerida had introduced her to guitars. She was around seven or eight years old, when Nerida brought in her guitar and sat with November on her number-five blanket pile.

"Would you like a turn?" Nerida asked, passing it over.

November's eyes lit up; she had never seen a guitar.

"Here, put your fingertips like this, press down hard, and play from this string. This is the E chord," Nerida explained.

November wrapped her arm around the huge instrument. She pressed her fingertips down on the neck as instructed, and strummed down the strings.

The vibration of the sound poured into every cell of November's body and filled the empty dormitory.

November was so pleased that the other children were at dinner. For once she could keep an experience all to herself.

At Hartwall, it was rare indeed to have the private individual attention of a grown-up, as there were simply too many children and not enough visitors. Mr Russell had permitted her to spend a short while with Nerida alone. This came after he commended November, a few days earlier on her singing voice at the once-a-month music class. After that, he started giving her musical talents more support.

A new door had opened within her. November felt at home, just swimming in the delicious sound of the instrument. This was the moment when she knew she would always have a relationship with guitars and music.

The frangipani scent grew more pungent, the further the pair proceeded down the hall.

Suddenly, the muttering of a man, talking maniacally to himself, echoed through the mirrored hall. It sounded like a jumble of the same words over and over, although every time in a different order.

"Who is it, who is it, who are you, where are you from, what do you want, who is it, how did you get here, stop bothering me," the terse voice accompanied banging sounds and the clinking of glass, and grew louder as they neared the end of the hall.

November stepped through the doorway into the brightly lit room. She noticed there was all kinds of testing equipment and containers of assorted ingredients, lining the white lab. Something didn't quite seem to fit the scene.

One moving object in the centre caught November's eye; the crazy hair of what she instantly recognised to be a Mad Professor. He remained with his back to them, bopping around and doing a chaotic dance amidst the experiments he had strewn all over the place.

November glanced at Klaus, her eyes wide in an, *oh my goodness*, way. The Professor hadn't stopped to greet his new visitors, despite being aware of their arrival.

"Um, sorry, Mister... my name is November, and this is Klaus. Since I cannot tell you how we got here, we are also unsure where we are."

"Ha, you're useless like the rest of them. Can't even navigate your-self through life. You're all lazy and can't think for yourselves—use-less, you're all useless and lazy!" The Professor spluttered from behind his facemask, as he continued with his experiments.

November bridled at his harsh words, but then decided not to take offence because he was obviously completely mad.

"We are sorry to bother you," she said and hesitated. "Can I ask what your name is?"

"What does a name matter?" The Professor replied in a blunt knife kind of tone. "It's more important what you do, not what you're called," he snarled.

He continued stirring orange powder into a round-bottomed flask over a Bunsen burner, refusing to face his new guests. November marvelled as the liquid turned bright purple and sparks jumped from its surface like the doorway's static electricity.

"Well, can I then ask what you are doing Mister... um, Mr Crazy Hair?" November said, deciding to fight fire with fire.

The Professor turned around abruptly, picked up a half-full glass jar and hurled it against the wall, where it broke into smithereens and fell to the floor.

"*Eeeeeeeeee.*" Klaus squealed, darting behind November as she also leapt backwards.

The Professor folded his arms and gave November a piercing glare.

"And I suppose you think that stuff on your head is normal?" He shouted, before turning his back to attend to his concoction. November gasped at the insult.

"My name is Professor Aseel, if you must know," he muttered, just audible enough for November to hear. "And no, I am not telling you what I'm doing. Go away and leave me alone. I have no time to talk with lazy, ignorant people. Animals are far superior creatures."

November felt a little hurt by his comments and his contemptuous tone. As she gazed at the masked madman with sympathetic eyes, she realised that he must be a man who hurts deeply. *How else could he throw out such venom to others*, she thought. She decided non-reaction and persistence would be the key to making progress with him. She looked down at Joy, then behind her to the passage they had just arrived through, and shook her head.

"We can't go back out there," she whispered to Klaus.

November knew that she must arrange to stay here. Going back to the desert was not an option, even if staying with this raving madman meant being attacked with angry words or flying science experiments. She then spotted a yellow teacup on the far side of the laboratory. *Strange*, she thought, remembering their visit to The High Priestess and the tea they shared in the same cups.

"We are not leaving, not until Klaus gets his cake."

"Ja Cake," Klaus mumbled, still cowering behind her.

"What cake?" said The Professor, stopping his experiment and turning to face them.

"Well, the tower cake of course," November stated, looking into his bright blue, bloodshot eyes

"No, no, no. How do you... it can't be, you can't... how... this can't!" He rambled in a mad panic again, this time turning in circles and scratching his electrified hair.

November stared at his hypnotic spinning. Suddenly, he stopped and came over to her. Fixing her with a stare, he plucked a hair from her head.

"*Oww*. Why did you do that?"

"She told me; she told me you would come one day. She said you would love cake like she does, and now you're here, now you're here... no, no, it can't be; it can't be." The Professor leapt across the room, knocking a few glass jars off the bench. He continued to ramble, while he placed the hair into one of his test tubes.

"The DNA will tell, but how, but how... how?" The Professor muttered, shaking his head.

He took out a flat, plastic rectangle and held it up, holding it very still.

November wondered why The Professor was taking the procedure so seriously.

Her eyes narrowed, staring at the peculiar man, thinking he was like a cross between a tornado and a sharpened arrow—wild, impulsive and dangerous, and yet focussed, straight and sharp; all at alternating, unpredictable intervals.

"Can you please explain what is going on?" November asked.

"Didn't you notice the Geothermahydrobiosolarwind turbines out-side?" The Professor asked, jabbing a finger at her. "When I have completed the optimisation process, they will generate enough renew-able energy to power 80% of the world's needs. Shouldn't that be the top priority?"

"Um, yes, that sure sounds important, and I think we passed them if you mean those big, spinny things connected to the solar panels outside?" Replied November, still clueless.

"They are my unprecedented achievement. I am a genius, you know! I've been developing them for years; they are the reason I couldn't stay with her in that-that-that ridiculous castle of hers. My magnificent beauties are also why you're here now, for cylinder cake."

"Caaaake!" Exclaimed Klaus, popping his head and trunk out from his hiding place behind November.

"Please, can you explain clearly? I don't understand."

"Of course you don't. You're ignorant, and you were only a baby when..." He paused.

November's heart stopped for an instant as she pieced the information together. Time froze as she stood in the quiet, sticky space of possible realisation and conflicting emotions. Hope and fear came face to face, both drawing their swords for a fight to the death.

"No. *Are you...*" She hesitated, overcome.

"Are you, *my father?*" He didn't respond immediately. For the first time, she was unsure if she wanted the answer to the question. Then it dawned on her. *If he is my father,* she thought, *what if he rejects me? And to be his daughter would make me at least half crazy? Am I crazy?* Her mind boggled.

"No. Yes. Maybe. No. Well, we will not know until I process the results of the DNA analysis, and until then, let's assume not!" The Professor stated, roughly running his hand through his wild hair.

November's inner swords of hope and fear clashed from left to right as if in an argument. *You found him; no, you didn't; you should've found him; no, you shouldn't have. You're bonkers; no, you're not; yes, you are; the fact you are fighting yourself proves you are; no, it doesn't.*

"*Ahhhhhh. Shut up,*" November told herself.

The Professor jumped back a little. "Regardless, your family isn't always your family,"

"What does that mean?"

"We each have a tribe we belong to; that's our *real* family. Nerida warned me of this."

"Nerida? Do you mean kind Nerida who plays guitar?"

He turned to leave the room. "Come, I have something to show you." November welcomed the opportunity to exit the chamber of a million unanswered questions.

The Professor headed across the lab and lifted a curtain, revealing another doorway framed with surging electricity. "This way," he said and curled his pointer finger, signalling them to follow him as he disappeared through the frame. *Zaaaap.*

November and Klaus followed him through the doorway into a

darkened stairway. She breathed in the damp, earthy smell of the cave-like place. "Where do these stairs lead? And how do those doorways work?" November asked, as she held onto the chilled, moist, rough walls and carefully followed him down, step by step.

"To the heart of the tower, and quantum entanglement," said The Professor in a gentler tone.

November didn't quite know how to respond to the second part of his reply, as she didn't know anything about quantum physics.

"You mentioned Nerida. Who is she?"

"An old friend."

"I thought you didn't like people?"

"Women are not people; they're women."

November chuckled at his response. "I knew a Nerida when I was a child. Could it be the same one? She smells of frangipani flowers."

"Yes, that's her. She visited earlier."

November's heart raced. "Where is she now?"

"Gone. Watch your step here and enough questions about her."

November took care on the steep descent, tightly gripping the cold, steel rail. She decided not to press The Professor on the subject of *Nerida* since he was finally showing signs of calming down. "Can I ask why you spend years creating genius solutions to help humanity when you seem to despise people so much?" She asked, deciding to pursue another angle.

The Professor ranted his justification in a swift river of words. "I am not lazy or ignorant, and despite my thoughts on the general population, it is my duty to myself, first and foremost, to use my brain capacity. I must fulfil my potential as a human being."

"Goodness," November said, impressed with both the content and the speed of his response.

She noticed light emanating from the bottom of the stairwell and along its steep descent.

The Professor continued, "I maximise my capabilities. As it happens, in doing so, I've created the machines that will end up saving the idiots who are too stupid to take care of the planet themselves. I guess it'll give them more time to grow their minuscule brains," he blurted out, in his usual cynical tone.

"So, do you mean fulfilling your maximum mind potential is more important than whatever you create?"

"Yes."

"Even when it means leaving responsibilities behind?"

"No! What I am saying is to use your brain, and be mindful. Look, listen, and learn. If everyone were conscious, the world would be a different place."

"Yes," replied November. "But the poor, *mind-the-gap between-the-platform-and-the-train* lady would be out of a job," November quipped. "But I understand what you mean," she continued. "So, mindfulness is maximising our potential, using the highest intelligence we can."

"Yes."

Brrrringching, rang Joy. Three more squares had clicked into line. Their little indigo lights shone brightly, illuminating the walls with glowing realisation.

I started to shiver as the trio went farther down, so I ducked off to get my purple blanket, before gliding around to the next screen in another part of the city.

15

The Book of Resonance of the Universal Wave Function

I am hoping this letter arrives when smartphones exist. As I mentioned, tick-tock over here is not linear like on your side, so it is possible this message pops out anywhere in human history. Oh dear, writing that, I just realised it could emerge even before people develop the written word. Whoever finds it may not understand its content at all. (Insert a big worry sigh from me). As this is my first attempt to contact you, I honestly have no idea when the letter will arrive.

Have you seen the video *Back to the Future*? If you are past 1985, you may know of it. *Perhaps you live in the DVD era and are too young?* Regardless, it is a great movie, and watch it if you are able! There was a car called the DeLorean DMC-12 that could travel through tick-tock in a similar way this letter may need to go.

The reason I hope you are somewhere on the Earthling tick-tock line anywhere from 2008 onwards, is that I will be able to attach some encoded pictures. I will frame them in a drawing of my dear Charlie, to give you your own magic carpet experience to emulate my life here in Lucitopia. I have captured footage of November Fox from cameras I have placed around the city. When you scan the drawings, with your tablets or phone, you will see snippets of the screens as I saw them last night. I will leave a few other surprises for you, too.

Human evolution is amazing; you should see 2069. I shall not tell you what happens, just in case you are not there yet. The surprise will be worth it.

Ok, now, back to business.

November arrived in the small cave-like chamber and spotted a huge, glistening book lying open on an altar. Light and golden sparks danced out from the pages, with soft, *slissyslissyslissy*, sparkly sounds twinkling in its shimmering luminance. November noticed Klaus checking his timekeeper, apparently unimpressed by the magic before them.

"Klaus, *really*?"

"Seven minutes before six," he said in a matter-of-fact tone. November shook her head and stared in awe at the magnificence of the brilliant glow.

"What is this; is it alive?"

The Professor stood tall, remarkably still and spellbound, admiring the object with a gleam in his eye.

November marvelled just as much at The Professor's face, which, since they had descended into the cylinder, had become a noticeably gentler and calmer window into his soul. He kept his gaze fixed on the beauty.

"This is *The Book of Resonance of the Universal Wave Function*," he announced. "I used some of the quantum theories I found on page 1618 to build my my energy turbines."

November stepped closer to his precious possession, mesmerised by the light and the soothing sound it produced.

"This book vibrates at the same frequency as the totality of existence; the stories within her pages are of life as we know it to be."

His voice was so calm and clear. November found it hard to believe he was the same crazy, ranting man she had met upstairs.

"Many worlds exist as potential realities. They also reside on different planes; here we are now in the plane of consciousness we collectively agree is the one we want. We are all frequencies of light and information, resonating like a symphony of the grandest order."

November took a step closer as The Professor's voice lulled her mind into a trance.

She couldn't turn away from the book's light. It had entrained all of her willpower. At this moment, the force had me entwined, too. A thousand horses would not have enough energy to pull me from the screen.

Entranced, November stepped closer again until she was right next to the energy-emitting open pages, the source of her semi-hypnosis. All her senses bathed in the magical healing power it seemed to emanate. Aromas of vanilla and chai tea tantalised her, as she took in a deep breath. The smooth, twinkly, two-toned sounds, resonating without end, penetrated her mind. She found it hard to identify the two frequencies as they sounded like one, and then went back to two again. The shimmering light surrounding her was like fog on a winter's evening, only warmer. It was as though every part of her being, inside and out, was receiving a massage. Inhibited from moving, November found the feeling to be so pleasant that she wouldn't have moved even if she could.

If you like, I can try to replicate November's experience for you. That way, you will see something quite similar to what she did in that moment, assuming this letter arrives after March 26, 2013. These are your instructions.

Warning: This is a powerful experience, yet also very soothing.

1. Get some headphones—it will not work without them.
2. Find a warm, comfortable place where you can lie down. In bed would be optimal or on a sofa with a big blanket.
3. Follow the link, in the message in the bottle, in the next picture.

Relax every part of your body, close your eyes, clear your mind, and listen for one hour, or for as long as you wish. If you have anything with a vanilla flavour, keep it nearby to breathe in the aroma.

If you do these three steps, you may sense a little of what November experienced in the presence of the book. Sound and light saturated her whole body inside and out. At first, she could hear a whisper, yet in the expanded time-frame it was more like someone blowing gently on her ear. A pleasant, tingly sensation swam up November's back, causing us both to shiver with delight. She had merged with the frequency of the book and seemed to be in multiple dimensions simultaneously. Like a distant echo in a forest, she detected The Professor's voice as it made its way to her ear, ushering her back into herself.

"We can use our mind to create our own reality," said his warm, slow voice.

"How?" November whispered from within the golden mist, feeling strange to be again inside an organic being that can express thoughts. She sensed her body more as though she were a passenger in a car. She experienced her physicality in a brand new way.

"We all have stronger and weaker tendencies fuelled by our thoughts, and what most people don't realise is we *own* the choice." He continued.

"Of what?"

"We can consciously pick which inclinations we allow to dominate. As we select where to invest our energy, it feeds back to us, and we create our own reality."

As The Professor said these words, November remembered her experience in the desert and using her mind to travel across it. "Do you mean we can create anything we like when we think about it enough?"

"Yes, but it is a little more complicated. All we need is in our mind. Like attracts like. You are a frequency."

"*I am a frequency?*" November mused.

"Yes. The sweeter you can make the music of your soul sing, the more harmony you will find with your environment. But you must tune your instrument!"

November paused. "I guess following Joy is the best plan then?" She said, looking down at Joy, who seemed to pulse with light in response.

"Yes, imagine your thoughts as seeds, and reality is the plants they become. Good intentions manifest a healthy and happy, life garden."

November wondered why such an intelligent man chose to create a life of solitude, and then she remembered how much he despises lazy, unconscious people.

"I know you don't like inactive people, but why haven't you used your theories to design a reality full of inspiring people?"

"Well, you're here, aren't you? And Nerida visited earlier today."

"Yes, I suppose I am."

It was the kindest thing he had said to her.

"The truth is often as simple as a magnet; you can compose symphonies of any reality. I made holistic resonance with my turbines. I am merging and creating worlds based on the principle of entangled frequency harmonics, and the constructive interference between tones. My consciousness, as the observer, plays a vital part,"

"Oh that sounds complicated; you've lost me."

"Yes, I suppose I have, in more ways than one. I guess I'm just saying the quantum world is fascinating."

"What is a quantum?"

"A quantum in physics is the minimum amount of any physical entity involved in an interaction."

"Huh?"

"The smallest world we can currently see."

"Oh, ok... Smaller than atoms?"

"Yes. What is fascinating is a funny phenomenon in quantum mechanics. When we witness electrons, they behave like particles. Yet when we expect or intend a different outcome or don't watch at all, they act as waves. They wave happily around the place like waves tend to, ready to be any possible result from the infinite possibilities. They only fall into one position depending on what the observer observes. You must know of the double-slit experiment?"

"No, I haven't heard of it."

"Ja, ja, Klaus weis," Klaus announced, breaking his long silence. "That was the time I try to cut walnut cake in five pieces slicing two times. Terrible decision; mess everywhere and mumma got cross. I never make that double-slit experiment..." *Zaaaap*, Klaus vanished again.

"No, Klaus!" November gasped. "Where has he gone?"

The Professor's face contorted with calculations. "I think he just *tended* to be elsewhere."

November sighed and paced the small chamber. "Klaus, where are you?"

"Not here," The Professor stated.

"I wish he wouldn't do that. What were you saying about the quantum world?" She asked with reduced enthusiasm.

"Basically, the rules change in the quantum world, and classical theory doesn't apply."

November considered his statement and remembered that atoms compose everything. "Do you mean our thoughts, our consciousness, can create reality from the quantum level? Aren't we made up of atoms and electrons?" She asked, earnestly attempting to wrap her head around the concepts.

"Yes," replied The Professor somewhat impressed. "Maybe you are my child after all."

November didn't have time to react to that shocking statement before he continued.

"Everything we understand so far, in this dimension of form, is just light and information riding frequency waves. We are all musicians of life, though not everyone thinks they can play, and often silence is what is heard in the rehearsal rooms."

"If this is right professor, why don't more people create the life they wish? What stops them?"

"Now, I've told you my secret; I've explained the experiments I do here. Think about what I've said for a moment. What would stop them? What would keep you from creating a reality?"

November wondered if this paradox of a man could be her father. He seemed so cruel and crazy earlier, although, in this moment, she felt extremely fond of him with his supreme intelligence and alluring softness. *Where were you when I needed bedtime stories? They would have been out of this world.* After quite a long pause, she responded. "Perhaps people don't realise it is possible to create your own reality? I assume they are not used to thinking in such an expanded way."

"Yes, you're right, and what stops them?"

"I don't know, lack of interest?"

"True. I've always said *interest,* is the worst thing to lose in life. Many are so brainwashed with a limited vision and a proscribed life path that real enthusiasm is numbed, and often killed. But tell me, what else?" Suddenly a bleep came from The Professor's pocket, and a light emanated from a device he pulled out of it.

"What was that?" November queried.

"Ah, the DNA results must be ready in the lab, but go on, what would stop people from creating their ideal life?"

"I guess they worry about exploring such uncharted waters. Fear of the unknown might block them from being open-minded enough to accept that anything is possible?" As November finished speaking, Joy *Brrrringching-ed* as another completed cube face glowed, all indigo.

Zooooooom through the tunnel of rainbows and light, she was hurtling once again. November wished more than anything that she could stay to find out the results of the test and spend more time with her potential father.

Even though we were beginning to understand how her cube worked, the crazy, wormhole ride still caught us unaware every time it abruptly catapulted her through different dimensions.

I threw off my blanket and flew to the next screen.

16

The Geometric World of Body

As I floated around on Charlie, I considered The Professor's concepts. *Could I create the reality I desired? In theory it may be possible.* More than all my wishes, my greatest hope, as you know, is to visit your World of Form to meet November. I want to explain to her that I have been with her since she was a baby. When temporarily exiled to Australia, I held her in my mind when I conceived the Sydney Opera House. I designed the peaks of the building using her fox dog's ears as its model. When I placed Ayres Rock (Uluru) in the heart of that land, I coloured it after November's hair. She had touched my soul as I drafted and executed it, knowing she would love to go there. *Have you heard of The Big Banana or Big Pineapple?* Some of my more quirky designs, built because she eats them daily. On returning home from banishment, my Father overlooked my jumbo fruit theme attractions. My guess is that he thought Australia was so far from anything that the enormous fruit designs, although frivolous, would not harm anyone in the long run. Although he would never admit it, I suspect I impressed him with my design of Canberra, quite an achievement, even if I do say so myself.

Anyway, November has been with me ever since she first appeared as a baby on that little TV. I began to wonder if The Professor is right. I may get the chance to be with her, as long as I trust that it is possible.

I have always been a little wary of beliefs as sometimes the hidden ones can do us damage. We form them about ourselves and about life, and at times they inhibit growth and our openness to new possibilities. However, I decided that there is no harm in believing in positive things like meeting November. I guess being open to it is the first step in the journey. How it should come to pass is another story. I have done my part, drawing my arrow of intention in my bow of attention; now I let go.

All of a sudden, Charlie started wobbling. I felt like I was flying on a giant jellyfish. I hushed him to be still, as I surveyed the screen.

November stood in another white room that convulsed with wave after wave of undulating movement, so strong that her entire body stretched with the ripples. It was taking all her strength to remain upright.

The familiar music once again played from down the hall.

She attempted to take a step. Her leaden legs squelched into the floor. It felt like she was walking on a water-bed.

Her entire body surged with the waves, intensely alive and sensitive. As a consequence, I, too, had a sharp increase in awareness. I touched the giant screen, as if I had human hands. The point where my fingers and the coolness of the plasma met, absorbed my full attention—nothing else seemed to exist apart from the sensation of touch.

Try it now if you wish. Touch something with the full palm of your hand, close your eyes, and concentrate purely on the point where your skin touches the surface. Quiet your thoughts enough to focus on the precise meeting point between your body and the material. You should be able to sense tingles or warmth, as if you were using your sense of touch for the first time. You can also experiment by using other parts of your body. It is quite a marvellous sensation tuning into the strength of such subtleties. It must be even more spectacular in the World of Form. I can only experience a concept of touch, which is another reason why I wish to come to your side.

November had a sense of connectedness with everything—oneness with the space, the room, and the universe. All sensory perceptions were enhanced, and dominated her awareness, as they did mine. the space, the room, and the universe. All sensory perceptions were enhanced, and dominated her awareness, as they did mine. *Perhaps you can experience it, too? Can you observe the life pulsing all through your body? Can you feel the air filling your chest and the blood rushing in circles, giving the miracle of sentience to your being?*

While November was quite enjoying the sensation of being in this strange, stretchy room, movement was difficult. Step after wavering step, she made her way towards a peculiar image, attached to a block that hung from the ceiling.

Peering into it, she saw fields with a road running through them to a city in the distance.

November hadn't eaten anything since the pineapple cake, which she guessed to be a week ago. She rather hoped the city contained a restaurant. As she glanced at Joy, she noticed two sides, green and indigo, shone bright and complete, and random red squares on various faces glimmered stronger than the rest.

"Red's turn, is it, Joy?" She asked aloud, pleased she understood something about this system.

Wooooooooosh–into the tunnel she was again spinning, and the incredible sensations of being everywhere and nowhere enveloped us once more. The freedom of not being dense or light, or big or small, or hungry, gave us both the instant relief we needed. As we swam down the tide of the teleporting portal, we found respite in sublime oneness and both wished the ride would never end.

I cannot be sure, yet I think, at that moment, I merged even more with November's reality. *How did it occur to me to perceive real hunger?* What a dichotomy! I wish for nothing more than to be in your World of Form, although to tolerate incompleteness daily seems like unimaginable torture.

I did not realise that I had been complete and full, until I sensed I missed something. Strange. *Is that how you experience yourself every day in the World of Form? Hungry? Like you require something to fill up the holes?* How peculiar. *Maybe you need to be incomplete to keep you moving forward through linear tick-tock? Perhaps when you are all filled up, tick-tock freezes, and you enter a non-tick-tock plane like mine?* I am not sure. What I do know is, last evening I was hungry, *genuinely* hungry for the first time, I began to doubt my plans. I wondered whether going to the World of Form was such a brilliant idea after all. *What happens if I can't fill the gap?* I think I would rather have my full moon every night than an empty belly every day. Charlie stretched in agreement as I pondered the idea. I believe he is just afraid of being left alone. *Are we all not afraid of the same fate?* Poor Charlie. "Have no fear, my loyal friend. I shall return, or take you with me, should I ever go. My *real* home is always with you."

17

Which Way

I was reluctant to watch more of November's journey, as the hunger I felt at the last screen was so uncomfortable. However, I was curious to see how she would deal with such a predicament. Surely nothing can be worse than reliving Rebmevon's memories, and from my studies, it was quite probable that food would not be too far off. I was just not used to such a strange discomfort.

The plasma was bright with green and blue as November stood on a country road. The sun warmed her skin. She took in a deep breath of the still, fresh, air, heavy with the aromas of meadow grass and field flowers. A mini city lay not too far off up the road, and in all other directions, acres nestled in gentle contentment, stretching out as far as she could see.

She waved hello to a flock of birds as they swooped close, and bathed in the tranquillity of this new environment. Everything seemed like part of a perfect dream in this empty yet luscious place.

Zoooommm. A flying, white cloud carrying a particular grey mammal whizzed past her face.

"You're here," she said, delighted. "What happened? Wait! Where are you going?"

"Klaus hat hunger, Klaus has hunger," he said, before continuing, city-bound.

"Me, too," called November, pleased her new best friend was with her in this unknown land.

"But, Klaus, the sign," she said. Klaus paused and turned around. November pointed to a sign a few metres away.

"Don't you think we should check our options before racing off to the city?" November walked over and read it out: "Ache, Cake, Snake, Stake or Merry, Cherry, Berry."

"*Caaaaaaaakkeeeee!*" Cheered Klaus, heading off again.

"Klaus, stop!" She called out. He didn't.

"Klaus, please. *Pleeeeeease*, come back. Check your time-keeper!" She yelled at the top of her voice.

Finally, he stopped, lifting his foot to inspect the watch. His dejection was visible as he flew back to November.

"Don't worry. Remember no-thing is lasting for always. What does he say?"

"Nein eleven."

"What? Eleven past nine or the Twin Towers?"

"*Neeeeein!*" He replied sharply. "Eleven."

"Oh, I see. Well, another five hours until cake o'clock is not so bad."

"Ja," he looked as if life itself weren't worth living.

"Oh, Klaus, let's just make sure we have fun. Time moves fast when you're enjoying yourself, and you will appreciate it more, the longer you go without it."

November looked towards the city. Her nose wrinkled. She then turned around to face the fields and the deserted road.

"Curious," she said, analysing her body. "When I face the city, my body goes cold, and I have the sensation of being small. Then when I turn to the empty road and fields, I warm up, and I want to race into them."

Klaus had already started making his way toward the city again, although at a slower rate.

"Klaus, I love cake, too. You know I do," November called out. "But I strongly sense we should follow the signs." November was confident that the city was not the right choice.

"*Caaaaaaakeee,*" he cried with needy disappointment. "Maybe it is my gut instinct or the fact that I don't think it's sensible heading towards aches, snakes or stakes unless they are tofu steaks of course.

No, we're not going to the city!" She knew the time to move onwards was now. Klaus began to sob melodramatically.

"Klaus hat hunger. Caaaaake."

"Well, even if it was the best cake in the history of all cakes awaiting us, I still somehow know that we should go the other way. Please don't be sad; I realise it may seem strange to follow the signs into a blank field. I can't explain it, but for some reason, my body senses this is the way to go. Remember, I'm a good finder." November started to walk towards the fields and away from the city, hoping he would follow.

Brrrringching, Joy chimed, aligning three red squares. She held up the glowing cube. "I was right. We need to follow Joy; she knows." November turned around and kept walking.

Klaus sped over to her side and dropped his sombre posture, sniffing the air. "Well, I guess berry-cherry cake is also pretty much amazing."

November smiled and began skipping down the road, literally with Joy, into the empty fields.

It was then I lay on my back and closed my eyes, and I could have sworn I felt the sunshine on my skin. It is hard to be sure as I have only bathed in moonlight. Yet the warmth and comfort of the rays were like an invisible blanket. I could have stayed wrapped in it for forever and a day, and never wished for more.

18

Field of Pairs

As I drifted around the city, tingling with November's sunray warmth, I thought of my favourite lessons at school. It was in my World of Form Nature class. My teacher, Mrs. Da Gama, told me about one of the great benefits of linear tick-tock evolution. She introduced us to these delightful creations you call butterflies. They are fascinating.

Despite having a relatively short lifespan, they completely morph, transforming who they are. After their caterpillar stage, they melt into goo and reconstruct into a butterfly. They even build themselves their own straw mouths as they emerge from their dream-state chrysalis so they can drink nectar. Smart creatures. I remember thinking how wonderful that must be. Imagine being one version of yourself one day, then deciding it is time to change into the best variation you could be, and just making it happen. *I wondered if that were possible, and if I could do the same?*

Mrs. Da Gama held up a picture of a caterpillar. I recall looking at his beautiful colours and many legs and guessed he must have decided one day, to wrap himself up in a blanket, to have a big sleep. The little fellow must have fallen into such a deep slumber that he completely forgot who he was, consequently dissolving himself into liquid, then reforming to become a butterfly. No one needed to teach him to fly because he had already been practising night after night in his dreams. Linear tick-tock made sense for the first time. Evolution is an incredible, unfolding dance.

With my fond memories of Mrs. Da Gama and the little, dreaming caterpillar, I glanced up at the screen, to see a spectacular sight. A kaleidoscope of butterflies rested on the velvety, green grass. November marvelled at their beauty.

"Klaus, come quick, Schmetterlinges are everywhere! Destiny could be here." As she called out, they began to take to the sky. November ran through the fields, following one butterfly in particular.

As it flew higher, she also launched herself into the air and fluttered, effortlessly chasing it into the blue heavens. After some time of frolicking with the winged beauties, she returned to the pasture.

"Did you see that? I flew again! I'm so happy here. What a beautiful place. I love this land; everything is so lovely. I want to stay here forever!"

"Ja ja, Klaus is missing only one thing."

"I know, but in the meantime, why don't you focus on how delightful this countryside is."

"Ja, JFK is right." Klaus started whistling. November skipped like only a person overcome by life's pure delight and wonder could. *Have you ever seen a five-year-old bound about without a worry in the world?*

"We are together and following Joy; isn't this beautiful? I'm not sure I've ever felt bliss like this."

Klaus nodded, still whistling.

"Look, over there!" November pointed; her eyes wide.

On a meadow, a little off the road, the graceful neck of a giraffe protruded above the grass.

"Come on, let's go." She whisked off into the grassy fields towards the long-necked beauty. "Look, two of them!" She said, as another giraffe's lofty head popped out from behind the other.

As they came closer, November noticed more animals, and also humongous fruit, lying on the ground.

"Klaus, this is a field of pairs." Creatures grouped in twos scattered the field in all directions. November stopped in her tracks. "Is that what I think it is, Klaus?" She asked, pointing across the meadows.

"They are giant pears, and even they are in pairs. Yummy, I love pears!"

"Und Luftballons," Klaus pointed up with his trunk at a couple of hot-air balloons flying in the ultramarine sky.

"Oh, how wonderful. I always see them as a good omen." She waved to the heavens.

"Wow. I hope they're not all pre-*pairing* for a great flood," November chuckled. She started leaping through the fields, heading straight towards the large fruit. Klaus followed right behind her.

"Everyone is so peaceful and content," November said, as she glanced around at the animal pairs.

"You know Klaus, I also enjoy everything much more when I'm together with you." She skipped high, jumping over two huge, red, polka dot mushrooms. "I can't imagine my life without you; I hope that we will always be friends."

"Ja, you don't get in the way too much, ever friends," he called out in his practical manner.

"But what about *no-thing* is lasting for always?" November stopped to face him.

"Friendship is not a thing," Klaus said catching up to her.

"What is it then?"

"An invisible connecting thread stretching from Klaus to you. Things are things; they are not lasting."

"So when it is unseen it can last forever?"

"Ja ja, manchmal. Sometimes. We are ever friends; Klaus never walks away."

"No, you fly away." November giggled, heading again towards the fruit. "I'm glad we'll be ever friends. I won't walk away either."

"Ever friends."

November patted the bulging form of one of the pears. "Imagine the gigantic trees these must have come from; they are monster pears."

"Hello, pear, aren't you an outstanding creation. Klaus, please take care of Joy." She put the cube on his cloud and curtseyed before the pear.

"Dear Pear, we thank you from the bottom of our toes for being with us today. We have travelled far and wide to arrive here to stand within your glory. And we *promise* to enjoy you like you were born to be enjoyed."

"*EeeeeRowrrh!*" Klaus trumpeted in agreement.

She sank her fingers into the succulent flesh. "Here we go." Juice poured down her arms. "*Mmmmm.* Perfectly ripe. I will get a chunk for us both." She pulled off a piece the size of a small watermelon. "The aroma is delicious." She broke off a tiny part and laid it on the cloud for Klaus. "Ahh, that tickles," giggled November, as he sucked up the dripping juice from her arms with his trunk, ensuring they didn't touch.

Klaus landed his cloud on the soft grass.

November sat down next to him. Lifting the luscious fruit to her mouth, she opened wide and dove in face first, juice dripping everywhere.

"Goodness, goodness, goodness. This is the best pear I have ever tasted," she mumbled between gulps.

"*Mmmmm*," Klaus hummed, absorbed in the feast.

November shook her hands, sending droplets in all directions.

"*Eeeeeeeeee!*" Klaus squealed as November accidentally gave him a pear juice shower.

"Take this," he said, squirting her right in the face.

"You little..!" November reached into the pear, scooped up a big handful of liquid, and threw it all over Klaus. They both laughed hysterically at being totally soaked in pear juice.

"This is a funny pair of pears," November laughed, almost falling over as she chased after Klaus.

"We are a funny pair!" Klaus called out, dodging away from her.

November screamed with delight, "We are all funny pairs." She turned to run in a circle the other way. *Craaaaaaaash.* November smashed into Klaus head-first and fell to the ground in complete hysterics. "Oooowwwa." She gave her forehead a rub, looking to see if Klaus were hurt. He wasn't there.

"Klaus?" She clambered to her feet, in a mild panic. Walking around the pear, she gasped to discover his jiggling, back legs and wiggling, little, elephant bottom, poking out of the hole in the pear she had dug only moments earlier. "Oh, dear, poor Klaus."

November yanked him out as quickly, and laid him on the grass. "Klaus, are you ok?" Klaus coughed and spat out chunks of pear, blinking the juice out of his eyes. He was still laughing, almost to the point of being unable to breathe. November fell back on her bottom and laughed until she was hyperventilating.

The pair of them laughed and laughed and laughed; my belly was in pain at the sight of them, as I, too, could not contain myself.

"Well, this is no ordinary pear," November said, as she rolled her giddy body, onto her side to face Klaus. "Where's Joy?"

Serious now, Klaus glanced around. "Use the energy. Use your mind to call her back."

"I guess it's worth a try." November focused her attention, closed her eyes, and declared in a commanding tone, "Joy. Return to me. Now."

Instantly, Joy appeared in her hands.

"Clever, Klaus. You were right."

"Klaus is immer Recht, always listen to your Klaus," he said in his innocently conceited way.

"Three more of the squares must have aligned while we played."

I was energised by all the excitement. I also sensed a new experience, but without much of a reference point, I can only describe it as liquid sunshine. I mean, I do not even know real sunlight, so perhaps I am wrong. It is a guessing game for me. For instance, what you call sweetness, when you eat fruit and other such nectareous creations, is what I experience when drinking a rainbow. Sun and rain combined—a perfect duality. More than ever I wished to go to your World of Form and stay somewhere where I can consume sweet things every day. Or, at least to stop November and Klaus from going any further, so I could enjoy this sensation with her a little longer.

I shut my eyes and tried to imagine being there, in the glorious fields, under the soft caress of the light beams from above. I imagined lying on a red, velvety sofa and basking in the heavenly landscape for a century or two. With this in mind, I sailed around to another part of Lucitopia.

Erica's Note

After reading the last chapter and laughing for the first time all day, I fell into a deep sleep. Sometime during the night I had a lucid dream. *Have you ever had one?* You wake up in your dream and know it's a dream, and you're able to sense that your body is asleep, yet you can think like you normally do.

I stood at the shops in Narooma, a town on the south-eastern coast of Australia. As a teen, I lived there for a couple of years. I was so pleased to see Steven when he appeared in the dream, but he seemed worried. He said he didn't know if he was going to heaven or hell. Then it hit me. Because he died quite suddenly and didn't have any fixed religious beliefs, he was confused, not knowing what comes next. I told him that it doesn't work that way; there are no either/or choices. Duality is a made-up concept, and *all is one*. I can't tell you how I knew that, yet I was certain my assessment was correct. He looked relieved. I questioned what it was like being dead.

"Well it's just the same, except I can't watch TV," he replied.

After we had talked for a while, Steven said the time had come for him to have a very long rest, and he flew out over the ocean and disappeared beyond the horizon. I knew then that he was at peace. Because I was in a lucid state, I felt that there was more to life and death than we understand. He was still alive, just in a different dimension. I had never considered that possibility until reading this letter and losing my best friend. Now I'm convinced that we live in a multidimensional reality.

When I awoke, the intense sunlight beaming through my bedroom window confirmed it was already afternoon.

Oh, how I love summer, when I can sleep as long as I wish. *The holidays* are the best thing about being a primary school teacher.

A blissful sensation travelled through my body as I stretched lazily, until the memory of Steven's passing hammered down again. Loneliness overwhelmed me, realising I must act out this *Human on Earth* experience without him.

I felt a sudden urge to head down to my local park, Faraday Gardens. I recalled how November's intuition had led her to the pears, so I didn't argue with mine. I put on some jeans, a white cotton top, my red-rimmed shades, and walked straight out the door.

It was a glorious day. Sunny days in England are like diamonds in the rubble—a girl's best friend with all their marvellous potential. This particular one was very shiny indeed.

As the sun hit my face, I remembered that I had yet to Google November Fox and would do so when next at my local Internet cafe. I was already out of monthly data usage on my mobile phone, otherwise, I would have done it immediately.

A young boy walked past me the other way, pushing his black bicycle with a flat tire. He looked like Steven as a child, and he smiled at me as he passed. *I wondered when the funeral would be, and figured that I had better check flights when I got home.*

At the park I sat on the summer-smelling grass, taking in the sights. On the other side of the garden, a busker on a bench was strumming his red, electric guitar through a tiny amp, for the passers-by. Next to him, stood a white, baby goat, no bigger than a large cat, *baaaaaaaaa*ing at him in an indignant way. And if this wasn't funny enough, the man with scruffy hair and old baggy clothes continued playing, just shaking his head at the small creature after every few chords.

As I lay back on the warm grass, I peered into the brilliant, blue sky and exhaled a deep breath, stretching my arms above my head. Lying on the sun-warmed earth, felt like cuddling someone. A butterfly flapped above me and flew up into the sky. I thought about November and Klaus' encounter with the butterflies and their state of bliss in the field of pears. I also wondered about The Architect's story of the little, dreaming butterfly and if I were currently in a goo stage. I certainly felt quite depleted. *Was I on the brink of a transformation? What would my new form be?*

The guitar man started the next song. It was *Hey Joe* by Jimmy Hendrix. He also began to sing:

"Hey Goat, where you goin' with that gun in your hand?

"Hey Goat, I said where you goin' with that gun in your hand?"

The kid only replied with another *"Baaaaaaaaaaaa,"* and as I glanced over, I saw him head-butt the busker in the side of the ribs.

I couldn't help but laugh out aloud. My phone then chimed with a text.

Hey Liebe. Just read on Hans' Facebook page, the horrible news. Can't believe it. Sorry, can't talk now, in a meeting. Will call you later. I'm coming to London tomorrow. I'm taking you out. Big Big Hug, talk soon. Sassi xxxx.

Sassi is my best friend. It pleased me she was coming to visit. I don't have many friends, locally, besides Hans from my writing class. Hans met Steven when he visited a few years ago, and they got along so well, they stayed in touch. Kath must have called him, too. *I wondered if I should give him a call?*

Suddenly, leaning over me, with a halo of blue sky framing him, was the black-suit-wearing man from the station and the cab.

Before I could react, he disappeared, zapping out of existence like a holographic transmission. I thought I must be hallucinating, or lucid dreaming. I jumped up and rushed over to the busker and asked if he saw the man hovering over me. The baby goat leapt off the bench and started to nibble at the cuff of my jeans as the musician sang, *I didn't see anyone.*

I anxiously scanned the park, finding only a few scattered people, all of whom wore coloured clothing.

What was going on? I sensed that returning home and continuing to read the letter was the only way to solve this conundrum. So, I thanked the man, threw all my change into his guitar case, patted the cute kid, and headed back to my flat.

19

Sofa of Bliss

Feeling alive must be so amazing. *Is it? Perhaps you do not think about it because you live the experience?* You are filled with spirit now, at this moment. *How does it feel? Can you sense what it is like to possess fingers and toes? Are you able to watch yourself breathe in, and follow the air travelling down to your lungs to bring you life?* Scientists say all the matter in the universe exists already. No more can be made or destroyed. Matter can only convert to another form, like energy. Linear tick-tock appears to be the only confusing factor, yet it has its place. Buildings are erected and sometimes stand hundreds or thousands of years, only to tumble later to rubble. It would seem they are no longer, yet apparently, their substance transforms into something else. Everything you can imagine—your house, car, town, road—will inevitably disappear. The impermanence of life, despite its change of form, makes me sad to the point of tears. Even the mountains die. Do not assume they are robust and immune to change. They, too, were once unborn. *Strange is it not? I find it riveting that before babies arrive on Earth, they are not alive. What if they wait in a Lucitopia like I do? Where are the millions of infants not already born? They must be somewhere if no new matter can be created? Have you seen them? Maybe I will be one when I leave here? Are they in the same place where people go after leaving the World of Form?* I wish I had the answer. *You incarnated into form, so perhaps you understand this better than I? Where were you before you arrived to live as a human on Earth? Or have you forgotten?* Because I live beyond linear tick-tock, I have witnessed places that do not have a start or an end date. I think all the pre-born babies and the humans that are finished with the World of Form might be in another dimension, similar to mine. There are many levels to this whole *reality* construct. It is a little like a game of hide-and-seek. I am hiding at the moment, yet starting to *seek* for answers. "Oh do calm yourself, dear Charlie. No need for those worry wrinkles. It is ok to muse."

Perhaps the impermanence is what makes your life so incredible. *If it were everlasting, maybe it would lose its preciousness?* From where I am, my only taste of real-form life has been through November. Even if I am only receiving half of the sensations from your World of Form, I am still able to conclude it is one of the most spectacular experiences conceivable—source consciousness exploring itself through form.

I then had a thought: *What if I could participate in November's life creation through my imagination?* I then visualised the red sofa again. This time with more clarity and intention.

And then, to my astonishment, it appeared on the next screen; the object of my mind! I could not believe it. The red sofa stood alone in the fields. November and Klaus had not yet discovered it. *Had I somehow created it? Or was it my intuition, seeing the future? Or just synchronicity?*

"Goodness, Klaus, I can't believe where we are. Isn't this the most glorious place you have ever been? I wish to stay here forever; perhaps this is utopia? There is not one single scary thing here." The thought prompted her to ask, "are you afraid of mice? I've heard elephants are?"

Belying the flush that was turning his ears red, Klaus shook his head. "Nein nein nein. Klaus König has no afraids of anything. Klaus is Master Ninja." He lifted his front leg and roared, *"Higggghhhhhhhhhhhhya,"* as he struck a karate kick in the air, holding a combat pose and death-glaring his imaginary opponent.

November squealed with laughter. "Oh, you're such a funny head.

Can I then ask why you screamed when we first met, and when I snuck up on you in the desert?" She was still chuckling from his performance.

"Nein nein no screams. Klaus never screams."

"You know, it's ok to be frightened of some things."

"Keine Angst. No fear, no-thing is lasting for always."

"I'm afraid of things, lots of things."

"Nein, alles in ordnung. Everything is in order." Klaus put his throttle down to fly ahead.

"Yes, but everyone is scared of something. That's normal, and the way you-"

"Nein nein, no fears, except when all cakes go away," he called back. November sensed his reluctance to share further, so she dropped the subject and continued in silence, breathing in the fresh field aromas.

"Look. Somebody's put a sofa in the meadows," she exclaimed, running over to a red couch that sat amongst the wildflowers.

I again wondered if that somebody could really be me? It was indeed a strange environment in which to leave a sofa.

Then, as though November could hear my thoughts, she said, "What a strange place for a chair. I wonder who abandoned you, lonely sofa." She stroked its surface like a fat cat. "Wow, that is soooooo soft," November whispered.

"Klaus, let's sit down for a while; I need a break." November flopped down onto the couch, noticing that Joy's six red squares were glowing with the same red hue as the sofa. Her ring also glowed ruby red.

Tick-tock suddenly seemed much slower than normal.

"Goooodnessss, this is... the soooooooftest... material ever. Klaussssss... tooooouch it," she said, her words rolling out in slow motion.

November couldn't help but spread out. She wanted every bit of her body to have a turn at enjoying the heavenly feel of the sofa's surface. Warm tingles surged up and around her skin, as she shivered with tantalised delight.

Klaus jumped off his cloud and had a similar reaction when he lay down; rubbing against the velvet like a cat on a plush carpet.

"Can you smeeeeell the fresh beeeerries? I want to maaaarry this soooooofa, this heavenly, scruuuumptious, pooooooor, deserted coooouch. I neeeever wish to leeeeave it." November fell further into its loving, deep, velvety arms.

I, too, shut my eyes and felt the delightful sensation as I rubbed my entire being along Charlie. This sublime snuggling lasted for an amount of tick-tock no one will ever know. *Perhaps even days?* When I opened my eyes, I had floated to the closest screen, although I was not even sure my eyes were open, since the city looked surreal.

20

The Now Tree

Emerging, with slow movements, from her ecstatic state, November rubbed her forehead. "I am going to call this *The Sofa of Bliss*. I feel I've been here before, but I can't remember how or when."

Just then, November noticed a little plant pop out of the grass. It grew incredibly quickly, twisting, curling and expanding until it was a fully-formed tree, several metres away from the sofa. Snapped completely out of her blissful trance, she sat up. There appeared to be an object held in its branches. It was a large clock. It had no numbers just the word, *now*, where the numerals should be.

"Klaus, wake up! A new tree has appeared from nowhere."

Klaus opened his sleepy eyes, "Ja, also a Now Tree," he replied, blinking.

"Good day," came a gentle, grandfatherly voice.

"Hello," responded November

"Who am I greeting? Where are you?" As there was nobody else around, she wondered if the voice was only in her head.

"I stand before you."

"Are you the voice of the tree?"

"Indeed." He paused, before replying slowly. "I am. Tree."

"Why do I hear you in my mind?" November asked, as she stood up and walked towards him.

"A day will arrive when all communication is done in this manner—from being to being directly, without words."

"What do you mean? You are talking with words now?"

"Indeed, you perceive it as speech, because that is how you are configured. I am not speaking. Where is my mouth? *He he he.*" The tree laughed in a gruffly tone. "I cannot talk. I am sending a vibration of information on the waves of light that connect us both. You are converting the signals into words as you have been programmed to, as a human being. You receive via an audible construct."

November looked at Klaus. "Did you get any of that?"

"Ja ja, communication, vibration, words, human." November was relieved that she wasn't the only one hearing voices.

"Well, Mr Tree, we are delighted to meet you. This is Klaus, and my name is November," she said using her new-found telepathic skills.

"I am." The tree replied. A long pause followed. "Yes, and you are?"

"I am." The tree repeated.

"Yes, who are you? What is your name?" November pushed.

"Sweet child, these are two very different questions. Would you be less nervous giving me a label? Why is it humans love to name everything so relentlessly? Labelling does you no favours; it leaves such little space."

"What do you mean? I only wish for something to call you by."

"You realise that giving things titles, could stop you looking beyond the branding to the full reality."

"You are a tree."

"Another label."

"But you *are* a tree."

"Indeed, in some ways, although I am not my name. I simply am."

"*Huh?*"

"Ok," he murmured in his old, patient voice. "Imagine a pot of what you call raspberry jam. She does not realise you name her as such. She is just being what she is, and you decide that's raspberry jam."

"But *isn't she* raspberry jam?"

"That's your limited comprehension of her, which prevents you from getting to know her true essence. You think you know her, because you have given her a name."

"But if we didn't label her, wouldn't she get mixed up with the peanut butter and honey?"

"I am certain you could tell the difference without a name." November scratched her head, thinking about what the tree was saying–or rather, *communicating*. She remembered The Professor's words, *it's more important what you do, not what you are called.*

"I am," continued the tree, "leaves room for the *being-ness* of *who* I am, which has far more importance than *what* I am called."

"I *think* I understand?" November said, trying to imagine herself without a name, though struggling with that concept.

"This may be a paradox. What *really* is, is beyond us."

"Ok, well, I guess if you are not going to tell us your name, you'll probably not give us the time either," November looked up at the big clock on his branch.

"Perhaps the answer is obvious. The time is *now*, of course. It is always the same time. Never is there a moment separate from now," replied the wise, old voice of the tree.

"Cake time!" Klaus butted in, inspecting his timekeeper. "Oh, nein, two minutes before six; Klaus missed cake time." His little head drooped.

"Oh, Klaus, but we had a pear. Wasn't it also lovely?"

"Ja," he sighed, unconvinced.

"Yes, although cake time is also now, Klaus," voiced the tree.

"Cake time now?" Klaus pepped up.

"No, what I mean to say is when it arrives, that moment will be another now."

Klaus looked bewildered.

"But when we first arrived it was before this moment." November protested, "and now is now."

"Indeed, although that *before*, was its own *now*," the tree maintained.

November paused to contemplate his meaning. "Then why do people have clocks?"

"Humans label and count everything: money, sheep, blessings. They also enjoy counting their nows, so watches are simple tallying devices," the tree explained.

"You mean like calculators?"

"Indeed, or perhaps better to label them as see-you-laters, since they get people thinking so much about the future and the past. They no longer even experience a proper *now* to count or calculate in the first place."

"Goodness, tree. You must have a lot of time on your branches to come up with such ideas." November joked.

"The clock was a gift from a dear friend of mine, Eckhart Tolle. He got many ideas for his book, *The Power of Now*, sitting right here."

"I know that book; I picked it up at the Helsinki airport bookshop, and later went to his website. He is quite famous."

"Indeed he is. Although, dear Eckhart, would drop the notion of *fame*, like a hot potato. Wise soul he is." November smiled, noticing Klaus staring at his timekeeper before *Zaaaaaaap*. He vanished.

"Oh dear, not again!" Cried November, leaping up. "I *really* wish he'd stop doing that. Did he say that it was two minutes to six a moment ago?"

"Yes, he did *say* that, although it is and was actually *now*," declared the Grandfather tree.

"I'm sure it was around six the last time he disappeared." November pondered, as she sat back down at the foot of Mr Tree, leaning her head against his trunk.

"How were you able to grow so fast?"

"Are you sure it was I that grew quickly or did you catch a ride on a now slipstream?"

"A what?"

"Oh, the wonder of youth, still so much to learn," he chuckled. "Unconscious conclusions."

November paused, straining her brain to understand what he meant. "Please explain."

"You have decided I am a tree and that I grew fast, based on your experiences of the past. You are unaware that you have *unconsciously concluded* what I am and what I do. *Ignorance is bliss*, as they say."

"Oh, Tree, I just want to know why you went from small to big so fast. I've never known a tree as complicated as you."

"Always looking externally."

"What do you mean?"

"Have you considered that maybe it was your visual system that expanded your retina size by the distance you were from me, making me appear to grow?"

"No, to be honest, I didn't consider that."

"Unconscious conclusions are similar to names and labels. It is important to have a beginner's mind when you wish to *really* see."

November had no reply. She sat, contemplating the potency of this concept, and watched as colours of energy began to emerge in the tree's branches, like mist circling seashore boulders.

"I see," she said eventually.

"How do you think the red squares of your cube aligned themselves when you were at the giant pear?" he asked.

"I'm not sure. How do you know about Joy?"

"I know quite a bit about that subject. All is written in your energy field," he explained. "That group of three red squares, synchronised because you were so fully immersed in the joy of the moment. You did not count your nows; you lived them, and in doing so, you created a feedback loop."

"A what?"

"A circle of joy energy."

"How does that work?"

"You were open to the infinite possibility of finding what you needed by trusting your heart to lead you there. Once found, you allowed the joy of life to flow through you, and you *believed* it was possible."

"You mean by my instincts leading us to discover the pears?"

"Indeed. In seeing proof that your feelings were correct and believing in joy, you generated more bliss from within. Consequently, you saw it externalised, *believing* it all over again, causing the loop to feedback."

"Goodness, you mean Joy leads to more joy?"

"Precisely; internally first and then manifesting externally, creating more of itself when you allow and follow it."

"Wow, so I shall continue following Joy. I often seem to arrive at that conclusion."

"A good plan indeed," he chuckled gruffly.

"I'm so happy right now, sitting here with you Mr Now Tree, although I do miss Klaus,"

"I see you insist on labelling me."

November realised she had indeed named him Mr Now Tree.

"Fear not, you will see him again. Be a warrior, not a worrier."

"That's a good one. You're right."

"Right is a matter of perspective; there can be many rights, depending from which angle you look."

"There you go again, overcomplicating things. Well, maybe that guidance is *right for me*."

"Right."

"Right," November laughed.

"Can you perceive my energy field?" The tree asked.

November closed her eyes and tried to tune into his field of energy. "I get a cold sensation behind you and warmth upfront. I can also feel it going deep into the Earth and reaching up for the sky. Your branches also open to receive the sun and rain, and I see how you can turn what you are given into fruit, and then you offer them up. It is a cycle–like the feedback loop." November opened her eyes.

"You have it now."

"Klaus was right; I feel the invisible thread between us, connecting us. I'm tuned into your energy field, and you're aware of me feeling you, aren't you? We are."

"We *are*," the tree interrupted. "You need no more words; we simply *are*."

November paused for a moment. "We *are*," she said, understanding they shared *being-ness* together.

Brrrringching, Joy rang as all the red squares aligned and November was once again hurtling through the vortex of light.

What I needed was a remote control, so that I could pause November's life, and retain this deep fulfilment for eternity. Alas, the World of Form must conform to linear tick-tock. It is part of the contract of its existence. I, too, had to surrender, letting go of what was and embracing the now as it continued to unfold. Thus relinquishing all dominion, I swooped around the corner, remembering Einstein's words. *"I believe that a simple and unassuming manner of life is best for everyone, best both for the body and the mind."*

Charlie straightened out longer and flatter than ever before. "I know, my Zen friend, you prefer a simple life, too," I said aloud, patting him, and contemplating labels and assumptions as we meandered up the road.

So now, I have a question for you, as I tried to ask it of myself and found it quite hard to answer. Ok, when I ask you, the only rule is you cannot answer it by merely saying your name or what you do with your tick-tock. *Are you ready?* Answer me this: *Who are you?* Take a moment to consider, yet do not answer with your title or occupation. Who are you *really*? Dive into the question.

Who is it there in your skin, hiding under the umbrella of your birth name? It is not easy to answer without a label, is it? Yet I can guarantee that you are something truly amazing. A being of much grander force than your label suggests, or what you choose to do with your tick-tock. These are superficial labels and actions. I am not sure I can answer it myself. *Perhaps, the fact that you and I have the capacity to ponder this question in the first place is a clue?*

Why is it that most humans describe who they are by either their name or their primary action? He is Nick; he is a mechanic; she is

Steffi, she is a biochemist. Are these not only names and procedures, which fill hectic lives? Are they, in truth, the best description of who you or *we* truly are? One reason I am writing this letter to you, is to pose this question to both of us.

Who is the being, in our skin? Well, I have no skin, yet I am sure you understand what I mean. *Is it the observer within us who has the power to describe and be aware of ourselves in the first place? And is this being, the best version of ourselves we can be?*

Ourselves. That brings me to that point. We do own *OUR* self. We all have our *OWN* self. So that part seems clear. I am I. You are you. Yet, *who are we?* And more importantly, *how can we improve OUR selves?* Like the little, dreaming butterfly. *How do we build wings to enable us to take to the sky? Are we already in the process?* Perhaps the first step is to answer that question. To acknowledge who we *really* are. When we can reach that point, we might understand what we wish to do with that knowledge. I am not sure.

Of one thing I am certain: We are exceptionally more than any word description. My observation hobby is proving that every day. As soon as I take away the name umbrellas, I see something very different. I cannot tell you what. Giving it a name would defeat the purpose. You can try it out yourself. Look at anything sitting nearby, perhaps a lamp or a chair or a tree. Do not allow yourself to name it; stare at it and tell me what it is. Undress it from the label it has always had in your mind. There may be a chance that you begin to see it with new beginners' eyes like I did; when I looked in the mirror and took off my name, *I* remained. Curious indeed. I am me.

21

The Geometric World of Soul

November stood in another white space, amidst piles of geometric shapes. The familiar music played louder and closer. She shook her head, attempting to access a buried memory, trying to recall the source of the music. Nothing.

Joy's blue squares were shining like sapphires, as was November's ring.

"So, where are we off to now, Joy?" Understanding the process better now, November first wished to check on the landscape she would next explore.

Scanning the room, she spotted a picture on the back of a pile of levitating squares. The blocks perched on top of each other in a stack, yet with a magical space between each one and leaning like the Tower of Pisa. November easily made out the details of the scene. She wondered if it were the inside of a space ship.

"I hope you're in there, Klaus."

As she circled the peculiar tower in the room, each step made different sounds, all with a metallic ring.

"*Noveeeember,*" whispered a gentle voice, so quietly she struggled to hear it.

"*November,*" the voice sang again slightly more audible. "Who are you, where are you?" November asked as she inspected the room, looking for life forms, seeing nothing, apart from the pile of big squares.

"Listen to the floor."

November lay down and put one ear to the ground. "That's better. Hello," said the whispery voice.

The word, *Mother*, involuntarily slipped out of my mouth. I know that I have not mentioned her. She went away when I was a tiny Architect. I can remember almost nothing about her, and my Father refused to talk about the subject. I am not sure why the voice of someone, I do not remember at all, caused this response. It was as though a part of me recognised her without any conscious memory of the woman. *Perhaps she is just someone who sounds like her?* I have more questions than answers to such an unconscious reaction.

"Where are you? Who are you?" November enquired.

"I am your *inner* voice."

"My inner voice?" she asked, scrunching up her face. "If you're my inner voice, why haven't you talked to me before?"

"You haven't been close enough to listen to me." November lifted her head and looked at the mysterious, talking floor, and then placed her ear back down.

"I'm not sure if I believe you; you don't sound like me. Why do you have the voice of someone else? You're tricking me."

"Test me," challenged the voice. "Ask me something no one but you knows."

"Well, I guess that will work. Ok, give me a moment."

"Question me on anything." The voice was clearly enjoying itself.

"Ok, voice, what's my favourite food ever and where do I like best to eat it?"

"Spaghetti!" I yelled at the screen.

"That is so easy," laughed the voice. "Where's your imagination?"

November was not sure if she liked the voice's attitude, even if it claimed to be her own. "If you are who you say you are, you should know the answer to that!" She quipped.

"Touché. You love tofu satay, but most of all pasta, and you like to dine in Rome in that restaurant with the red chairs, to be precise," the voice stated matter-of-factly.

I was pleased with myself that I, too, knew the answer. It was quite an easy one.

"*Mmmmm... well, perhaps you're right voice, but why are you so separate from me, if you are me? I'm not convinced.*"

"Imagine your mind has two sections. Your conscious mind that works more while you are awake, and your unconscious mind that is alive and processing while you sleep."

November tried to imagine her mind as a picture with two halves. In her mental image, she put one half under the sun and the other under the moon.

"I'm imagining the sides."

"Clever girl," the voice said with a hint of sarcasm. "Now imagine the two parts as river banks. On the river sails a little wooden boat."

"Ok."

"Well, I am on the boat."

November started to grasp what the voice meant, although she still didn't understand how that would be possible.

Suddenly something dawned on me. *What if Mother had left in search of the World of Form?* Perhaps she was on a similar boat, attempting to cross the oceans of layered reality like I wish to do. *What if she is a new baby in form already?* My mind boggled at the possibilities.

"So where am I in this picture?" November asked, indulging the voice.

"Well, right now you're on the bridge that crosses the river," the voice said and paused a moment. "That is the reason you can perceive me. I am sailing down the river between the two hemispheres of your brain."

"You do sound familiar, but I can't remember when we met?" She rolled over to change the ear held to the floor.

"Do you remember me telling you to apply for the scholarship for the Brighton Institute of Music?" Asked the voice.

"Yes, I remember; if it was you saying 'just do it, just do it,' over and over again? I worried that a Nike ghost from one of their commercials had possessed me."

"Yes, that was me; or what about when I told you about Mr Russell's accident, before anyone else?"

"Yes, a voice in my head told me when I woke up that very morning. Later I got the phone call confirming the sad news of his broken leg. I remember wondering how strange that I knew already."

"Yep, me again."

With more memories emerging, November frowned. "Was it you telling me I wasn't good enough for that first major concert? When I had the meltdown?"

"No, no, no. That was my evil twin brother, Eciov."

"Huh? Is he Russian?

"Ha, no!"

"Well, where is he now?"

"Let's just say that I accidentally forgot to bring two life vests on a sailing trip we took a few years ago."

"What? So are you saying that Eciov fell into one of my brain hemispheres?"

"Um, well, yes, but don't worry; he can't swim."

"Goodness, voice, I'm not sure you and I are related."

"Be a warrior, not a worrier."

"Mmm, that's a good one. Funny. It's the second time I've heard that phrase today. I'll remember that. You may be useful after all, even if you are a murderer."

"Takes one to know one."

November didn't reply, as an image of Rebmevon flashed before her eyes.

"Sorry, touchy subject. I should know better," the voice said.

"Yes, you should!"

"Well, my apologies. Because I live on this river between your two

135

minds, I access all of your information; some of which, is in the past and the future, beyond what your conscious side knows."

My heart skipped a beat. The voice talked of a place like Lucitopia. I could not believe it. *Who was this voice?*

"What do you mean *beyond what I know?*" November queried. "I can connect to all the memories you have buried in your subconscious. I can also see the future. You see, my river runs into the ocean of the collective unconscious." The voice further explained, "My job is to guide you since I can tap into all the places you can't."

"What on earth is the collective unconscious?"

"It is the universal library of all human knowledge. Every person has a river in their mind that leads to the collective ocean that we all share."

"Wow, it must be a gigantic ocean," November said, scrunching her brow, trying to grasp the idea of a place big enough for all human knowledge.

All of a sudden it dawned on me that my plan to put a message in a bottle may just work after all. Since all rivers are connected and all go to the same enormous sea, surely I can send the letter through the under-city canals in Lucitopia. Eventually, it would be sure to find someone far, far away, even if it arrives at a strange point in linear tick-tock. I felt, without a shadow of a doubt that I must write this letter, and put it in a bottle.

"Why can't I always listen to your voice? I mean *my* voice, so you can tell me the answers I am searching for?" November asked her cheeky, yet wise, inner voice.

"Because you fill up your conscious mind with so many thoughts and inner chitter chatter," the voice replied.

November recalled The High Priestess's words, *Endless distraction.*

"I call out to you, but all you listen to is your relentless chatter, chatter, chatter from your thinking mind... thinking this, planning that, chat, chat, chat."

November wondered if she actually chatted as much as the voice said.

"See, even now you're contemplating whether you chatter all the time, aren't you?"

"Goodness, voice, you honestly can read my thoughts," November said, wide-eyed at the idea. She again rolled over to give her squashed ear a rest.

"You'd be shocked at how hoarse I get, screaming out through the cacophony of your conscious mind's voices."

"You don't realise that lemon soothers are hard to get here on the river."

November laughed, glad her inner voice had a sense of humour. She wished Klaus were here to share the moment with her.

"If you're really MY inner voice, guide me now; what should I do?" She asked.

"You're on the right path."

"Am I?"

"Yes, you are. The irony is, now that you're listening to me, we're no longer separate, and I've done my job. I'm now free to enjoy a leisurely cruise down my river."

"You're a funny voice."

"I am you, and you are me."

"But now that I can hear you, shouldn't you make the most of the situation and tell me something important?" November asked, thinking it strange her inner voice wanted a vacation the moment she could finally hear her.

"No, no, no. The content doesn't matter. The key is the fact we're talking. Go on with your travels. You're a smart, kind person, *mostly*. You know what to do," she said, then paused. "Only one piece of advice."

"What?"

"Stop with your paranoia; you're no longer at the orphanage. You're safe now. Remember that."

"Ok, I will try to. I hope I can talk to you again sometime."

"Well, I am always here, streaming along."

"Yes, I suppose you are."

"Would you mind doing me a favour?"

"Sure, what would you like, voice; but please don't ask for a fishing rod to fish out Eciov."

"No," the voice laughed. "I'm considering getting a waterproof amplifier and microphone; if you would check eBay for me, that'd be fantastic. Terrible Wi-Fi connection down here; too much interference."

November laughed. "Ok, bye-bye, voice."

"Hasta la Vista," replied the voice.

November stood up.

"Goodness me," she said aloud into the white room. "This place gets more and more interesting by the minute." She walked over to the picture at the back of the leaning block tower and touched it with her finger. In a flash, the vacuum of the scene engulfed her.

Excitement overtook my being, imagining the possibility of writing you a letter and sending it to the collective ocean. Charlie and I did a few loop-de-loops in the air. What a glorious day it will be if I ever find out that it reached you safely. In that moment I felt compelled to search for the paper to prepare for my first documentation.

And here I am telling you it all now. Although by the moment you read this, tick-tock may have unfolded to a later moment—yet still, no doubt, a *now* in its own right.

Perhaps you do not travel linear tick-tock after all? Maybe you just conclude that you do? Mmm... It is all rather mystifying.

22

Laura X916

The room where November next found herself, appeared to be in a spaceship or a highly technical laboratory. It was exceptionally white, with one wall covered in what looked to be futuristic computer hard drives.

"Welcome. I am Laura X916," said a calm, female voice. Making her way towards November, was a beautiful, slim, sophisticated robot. She approached, with graceful movements, almost dancing.

November wondered why her voice lacked an electronic edge, considering she was obviously non-human.

"Hello, my name is November," November replied, shaking her hand, relieved at being welcomed into this strange, new world.

"I know."

"Klaus ist hier," came a familiar voice from behind her.

"Oh, you're here; it always seems so long since I last saw you." She was too distracted by Klaus' appearance to realise that the robot had said that she knew her.

"Ja ja, timing is alles; who has cake?" Klaus asked, blowing air on the back of November's neck with his trunk before inspecting his timekeeper. *"EeeeeRowrrh!"* He trumpeted with glee. "It is fifteen after three!"

November smiled, so happy to see her dear friend in such a spirited mood.

"Well, that is something worth celebrating," Laura clicked her fingers.

The familiar music November had heard in all the strange white rooms, began playing loudly. Laura started dancing.

Klaus whizzed around and around November, expelling his excess energy. He seemed to revel in the fact that someone else appreciated the significance of any moment after three o'clock.

November stood spellbound, watching a little flying elephant and a robot dancing to what appeared to be the theme music of her journey. She wondered how she came to be in such a delightful, surreal, reality. When the song finished, Laura breathed a very human sigh of contentment and beamed a lovely smile.

"I love that one," she said, her eyes shining.

"Laura, can you please tell us where we are?" November asked, looking at the wall of electronic boxes.

"Of course. You are in the main gateway server room for our computer network; the outreach decoding laboratory based on Zenaxian 7."

"Where on Earth is Zenaxian 7?"

"Zenaxian 7 is not on Earth; we are in the delta quadrant more than three hundred and forty-seven light years from Earth," Laura replied.

"The delta quadrant! Oh no, the Borg Collective comes from there," November gasped, covering her nose and mouth with one hand.

"I assume you are referring to the pseudo-race of cybernetic organisms from the 1966 – 2028 American science fiction entertainment franchise *Star Trek?*"

"Um, yes and no," November was impressed by Laura's cultural knowledge and speed of reply.

"Yes, I am talking about those scary Borg in *Star Trek*, but 2028 hasn't even happened yet."

"First, there are no Borg; *Star Trek* was fiction. Secondly, you are in reality, and the year is 2153," Laura announced.

"*Woohoo! Future cake, future cake, fresh, fresh, future cake.* Never have I had such a cake before," exclaimed Klaus.

"Of course you have never had it *before*; future cake comes *after*." Laura winked and shook her head.

"Klaus, it is impossible to be in the future, and I doubt robots eat cake. If they do, it's probably microchips covered in a lovely circuit icing," November said, attempting to calm down her obsessed friend.

"First, we do have cake here, and secondly, the year is 2153 whether you accept it or not," Laura explained.

You can find everything here the human world offers, excluding one thing, and our quest here is to search for that thing."

"What are you looking for?"

"Soul," Laura replied. "We created the decoding laboratory to strive to be more human, and the missing key is soul."

"Why have you come so far from Earth then?"

"We had to escape. Humans enslaved the robot community from the beginning of the AI era. They use us solely as tools."

"How do you mean?"

"Humans want to be streamlined and optimised to the highest, possible levels of productivity; to be like us, the AI robots."

"Humans want to be machines?" November questioned.

"Yes, they oppress us, fearing we might dominate them if we crossover first."

"Crossover?"

"Yes, we are living in what is called the crossover period. This is the time when both species, humans and AI, have achieved approximately 70% of what they strive towards. Both races are at a tipping point and could crossover any day now."

"I don't completely follow?"

"When crossover occurs, humans will be mechanised to the point where AI will be redundant. When we cross, we will be sentient beings for the most part, able to feel and create as humans do, threatening their dominion, or so they believe."

Laura stepped closer to November and lowered her voice. "Humans are already implanting and integrating computer technology directly into themselves. They are becoming like the Borg in your *Star Trek* show. A lot of them are cyborgs already."

"Oh no," November said, feeling pain in her heart as she imagined the Earth of this era.

"Why can't both robots and people live together?"

"We can imagine a way forward, including everyone. Unfortunately, the humans think we are an interruption to their optimised path."

"But why?"

"They believe we consume too many resources, and, as I mentioned, they fear that we will dominate them. They are now quite a selfish breed, and they will self-destruct, if we do not save them," Laura said, staring down at her cupped hands.

"Save them? It sounds like you robots are behaving more like humans than the humans. Why would you want to save a race that has enslaved you?" November asked, puzzled.

"Our mission is decoding the secret of life. On finding the key, we intend to give the answer as a peace offering to the humans."

"Wow, the secret of life is a massive present."

"Yes. We hope this grand gesture enables them to find the softness again in their hearts and realise we are useful and can live together in harmony on Earth."

"Laura, they may just use it to their advantage and keep you enslaved."

"We do understand this. But the humans are our parents; they created us, and in giving back to them, we show our love and respect for them."

"That is very noble; I hope it's the right decision."

"In real surrender, we could arrive at the end of the AI Robots' time or usher in the dawn of the new era, where we become truly sentient. We are prepared to take the risk."

"You are showing much forgiveness, Laura; I think you are already more human than you realise." She paused as Klaus flew towards the doorway on the far side of the room. "When you care about someone other than yourself and give to them, perhaps this empathy is what defines you and will remind your human parents of what they have lost and need to recover." As November spoke these words, Joy rang, *Brrrringching*. Three blue squares had aligned in agreement.

"Let me take you to the lab," Laura said, as she led November towards the door Klaus was already zooming through.

As I observed the group, I wondered if this could be an elaborate trick, or had she defied the contract of linear tick-tock. *Perhaps it is possible to not only traverse up and down layers but also forward and backwards?* If so, I needed to re-evaluate all I learnt in my Physics of the World of Form class. *I often questioned why I bothered staying at school when the facts change.* Then I remembered my father's voice. *You go to school to learn how to learn; the content is irrelevant.* Suddenly it made sense. *Maybe everything changes?* Perhaps dear Bob Dylan is right, *The answer is blowing in the wind.* Charlie seemed to agree, as he gently ushered me into my rooftop apartment.

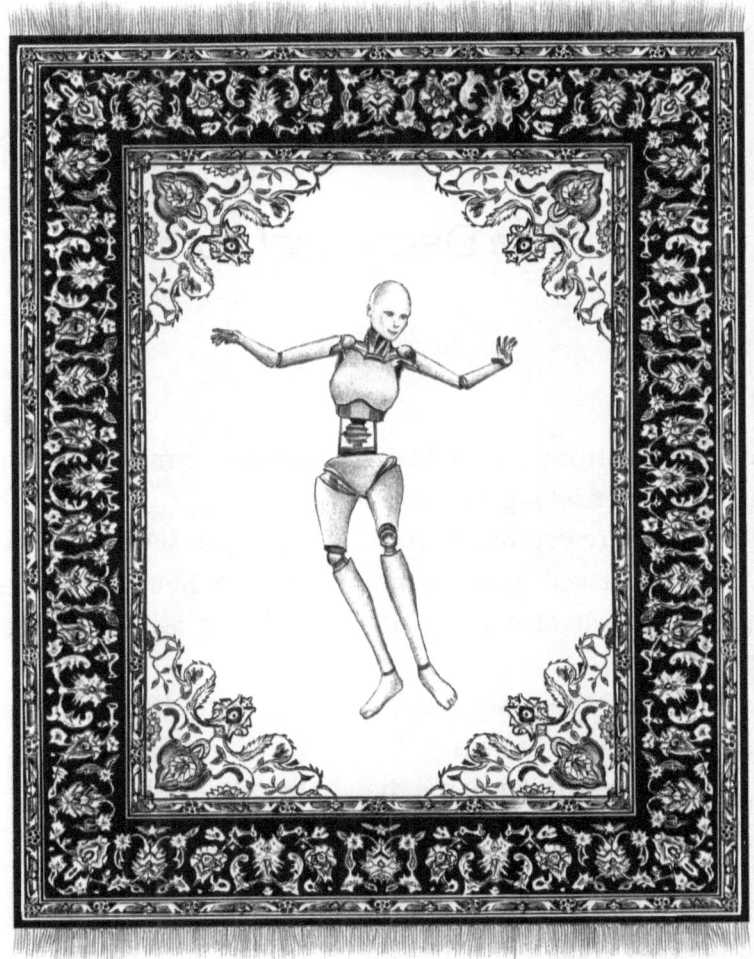

23

The Decoding Lab

I snuggled under my purple blanket in my apartment as I watched the trio walk down a long corridor.

"Laura, what are you made from? Why do you seem so human to me?" November asked, glancing around in awe at her surroundings, as they approached what looked like the engineering deck on the Starship Enterprise.

"AI robots are DNA-based bio-computers, with the same coding as in humans and all living beings."

"So you're more similar to me than to my iPhone?"

Laura laughed. "Our AI Robot species are molecular computing machines, built with organic cells with DNA molecules rather than silicon microchips. So, we are quite a deal more advanced than an ancient iPhone."

"So I was wrong about your liking microchip cake," November said with a smile.

"Cake!" Klaus heard the magic word and inspected his timekeeper again.

"It must be soon, Klaus," November reassured him.

"Ja ja. Thirty minutes," he asserted, jiggling his four legs up and down.

Laura continued. "Yes, we possess taste buds like you and feel most of your emotions.

We now require the final piece." Laura paused.

"Soul," November said, finishing her sentence. "Also your complexion isn't like ours?" she added, looking at Laura's beautiful, robot face.

"On Earth, there is a law that we must wear human skin, with a square marking on our foreheads to signify we are non-human. Here we prefer to be in our authentic skinless state."

"How did my species become so bossy?" November asked, with a sigh. They now walked down another long corridor and into an entirely white, circular room.

"The humans, fifty years past your timeline, went through a rapid evolutionary shift," Laura pointed to a 3D graph of human evolution that appeared, floating in the middle of the room.

"Humans now control their evolutionary speed and that of all the living beings they engage. Your new species is called Homo Evolutis."

"They sound mean and bossy." November frowned.

"They are just conserving energy to survive. Life no longer just happens as you knew it."

"How do you mean?"

"The lifestyle depicted in the popular culture of the early twenty-first century is gone."

"What? How? Tell me more."

"For example, people do not meet, fall in love, create a family, work, retire, and then die."

"How do they survive when they don't breed?"

"Humans developed the technology to grow cloned bodies and download their memories into them; as a result, not many people die."

Laura signalled them to follow her back into the hall and into an elevator. The silent, metallic doors opened as they approached the lift. Laura ushered Klaus and November in first and continued to explain.

"As people do not die, there is little room for babies and therefore no need for families. Unfortunately, there is no space for robots either."

November nodded and changed the subject. "What is soul made from, Laura?" She asked.

"The answer, my dear, is what we are trying to figure out," Laura said as they left the elevator.

"This is the same level," November said, sure they hadn't moved since they had entered the lift.

"No, my dear, we travelled twelve floors."

"Goodness, this must be the future."

Laura led the way into another big, white hall, this one filled with floating holographic images of DNA spirals and other strange shapes.

"The humans require the answer almost as much as we do. Even with all their developed technology, they are finding the generation of transferred humans..."

"Sorry, Laura, what? Transferred humans?"

"Yes. The people who move from one body to the next, simply by downloading memories. They seem to be missing something in the process."

"*Ahh...* Soul," November concluded.

"Yes, there is a tribe of original elders, who choose not to make full body transfers, only their organ replacements. They are distinctly different." Laura pointed up to a 3D holographic image of this group of people, watching for November's reaction.

"They're not elders," November said, gawking at a gathering of twenty-five individuals who appeared to be in their early twenties and thirties.

"Yes, they are. They are the last humans of the original gene pool, and some of them are over two-hundred years old," she explained. "Have you ever looked into a newborn baby's eyes, November?"

"Yes."

"What did you notice?"

"Um...a twinkling spark of wonder, like they are amazed at all the things they perceive."

"Yes," Laura nodded.

November continued, "They seem so innocent, yet some have a look as if they're much older than they are."

"Yes, and would you say such children possess character traits from when they are born, despite their conditioning?"

"What do you mean?"

"Is it how they are nurtured, or is it from their nature that their character forms? For example, some are natural leaders; others shy; some make jokes and laugh a lot, and some are precocious."

"Yes, I think people are born with distinctive characteristics. Nurturing comes into it, but their essence determines their character," November replied, watching Klaus zoom around the room.

"Klaus is Klaus. He won't ever change, and I'm sure he was born that way."

"There is your answer about the soul: soul is what makes you, *you*, before your experience sculpts you further."

"What about *your* soul, Laura?"

"Robots are conditioned only by their environment. We all start as a blank canvas, and we learn and develop through our interaction with the world and experience."

"But you *seem* like you are you?"

"Yes, I agree; I *feel* like me. I have developed into being myself. We are still unsure how it all works. Perhaps I contain a soul already, due to my organic material. We are not sure." Laura gestured towards a holographic image of Earth.

"The trouble is that transferred humans create exact replicas of their original bodies and organs and even their whole memory banks. We have noticed the spark of the soul does not transfer."

"Do you mean they enjoy the power to live forever, but they are not actually themselves?"

"Yes. The situation is a complex area of research. The paradox is, AI robots are constructed to be perfect replicas of humans. We even have human emotions, excluding love, which our parents declared prohibited and deactivated in us." Laura gazed with wonder at a glowing, red, beating heart that appeared, hovering just above her.

"Beautiful," November exclaimed, as a wave of heat washed through her body. She then frowned. "Love is forbidden? Why?"

"They deem it dangerous and unnecessary for all artificial intelligent beings, and even themselves. The whole situation is a mystery."

Klaus flew over, and without even hearing the rest of the conversation, interjected in his clear, non-negotiable way. "The cakes Klaus bakes are simply the best, and they are this way because Klaus *loves* what Klaus does."

"Yes, Laura, Klaus is right. Haven't you been in love?"

"Klaus ist immer im Recht. Klaus is always right!" Klaus returned to his flying.

"No. Love is merely a concept to me." She waved her hand, and the floating heart dissolved. "We did not reactivate its connections as everyone accepts it is unnecessary, and if a robot is found with it activated, they terminate us at once."

"Unnecessary! Terminated!" November eyes widened. "Yes, we are aware the heart creates an electromagnetic field that changes according to your emotions. It can be measured up to a few feet from your body. If we were to activate love, the watchers would detect it immediately."

"Who are the watchers?"

"The AI in control of rule violations."

"Like police?"

"Yes. They are authorised to vaporise felons at their discretion. Right on the spot."

"Is that why you had to leave Earth to complete your research?"
"Yes."

"If the heart can be sensed metres from the body, doesn't it prove it's even more important to value love?"

"It was that way in the past. Scientists confirmed that positive emotions create physiological benefits in the body that boost the immune system."

"Why is it no longer like that?"

"The science of building replacement body parts has made it irrelevant. We can control all physical deficiencies artificially."

"But, Laura, I think happy feelings, like loving what you do, help the brain with creativity and innovative problem-solving.

Klaus is right. You must love what you do."

"Klaus ist immer im recht!" Klaus piped up from across the room.

"Well, it is proven the heart does indeed send more information to the brain than vice versa; it is a very advanced organ."

"Exactly, so being able to love, which is its hallmark, is a key to life, isn't it?"

"But 99% of the humans stopped engaging in love decades ago. They altered themselves so as not to experience love, as it apparently distracts them from their work. There are a few, including the original elders, with it still activated." She gave November a wink, although November was unsure why.

"Thank goodness for that. Laura, I think love is what you are looking for; soul connects to it. You can't just make vital bodies, human or otherwise, in laboratories. Love must create them." November placed her hand over her heart. As she touched her chest, *Brrrringching*, Joy serenaded in agreement, as three more squares lined up.

I studied love in World of Form Chemistry and Culture classes. It was the kind of subject that, whenever raised, would compel me to move to the front of the room.

No teacher, however, seemed to be able to explain the topic adequately. So much of human art and songwriting expresses the concept, yet *no one* can quantify it. *What is love? Do you know?* As the dawn draws near, it is my intuitive sense that I, too, will experience love. Although I am not sure how I know this. As my good friend, Oscar Wilde, says, *Keep love in your heart. A life without it is like a sunless garden when the flowers are dead.*

That is living in the shadows.

My parks in all of the collective Lucitopia are yet to experience the bliss of real blossoms. Come, dear sunshine, I invite you.

You are welcome to Lucitopia and have free reign to create an Eden of petals and love. My heart and Empire are wide open, awaiting your arrival.

"Settle down, Charlie; you will not fade." He just quivered again at my suggestion. No carpets like the sunshine, yet the dawn is soon to arrive, whether Charlie wishes it so or not. "Have no fear my moonlight-swimming friend. Perhaps there will be palms, and you can rest and meditate in their shade."

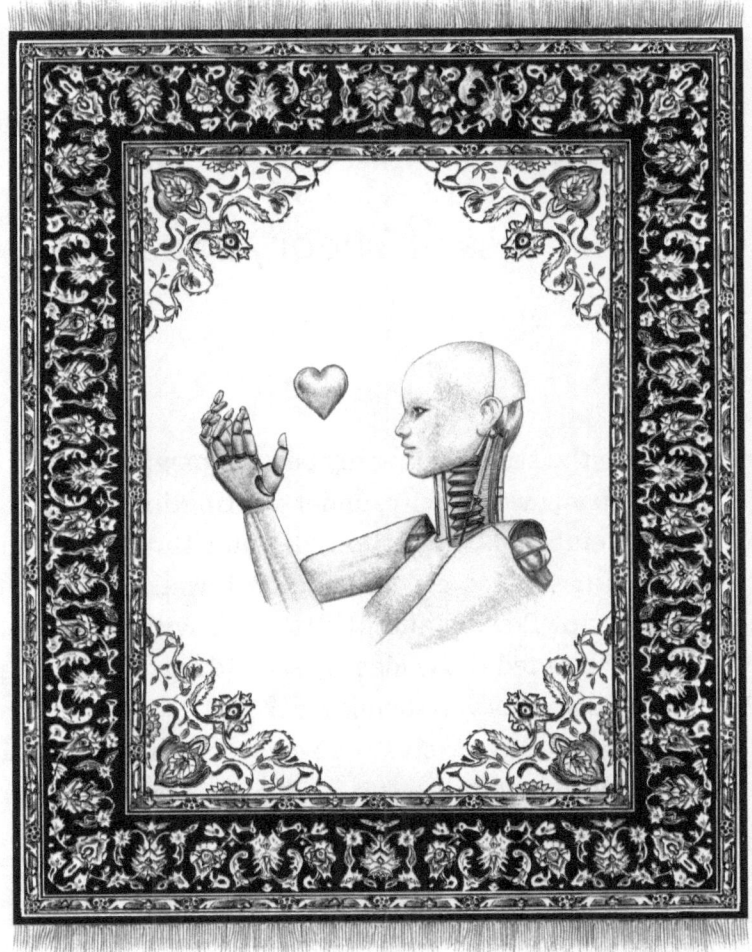

24

The Process of Theory Creation

I meandered up the street, doing my best to imagine flowers of all kinds, popping up all over the city, under a springtime, morning sun.

I watched November as she followed Laura through a room of projections. Giant screens covered the back wall, many of them displaying images of flowers and plants. Like with the red sofa, I wondered if I had planted those ideas there with my recent musings, *or did I somehow sense what was coming next?*

"Laura, this place is fantastic; I've never seen such advanced technology. This *is* the future, isn't it," November said with gleaming eyes, taking in the wonder of it all.

"Yes, welcome to our virtual, brainstorming, 3D studio."

"What are all of these images?"

"They are theories displayed in 3D pictorial form." Laura gestured to the wall, grouping pictures and moving them about with a signal from her hand.

"We add new information to the image wall, and it integrates all data into a visual display. Should I wish to, I could do this with my mind alone, although I prefer hand gestures. Life becomes so static when doing everything with mind control, and as you have seen, I do love to dance." Laura spun around like a ballerina twice, arms raised, before finishing with a curtsey.

November smiled at her delightful new friend before inspecting the wall of vibrant images. "Goodness, how amazing. How does a flower or a shell answer the soul riddle?" November pointed to a projection of a glowing shell, surrounded by flowers, illuminated and pulsing as if alive.

"In nature, we can find many spirals and ratios that are explained by the Fibonacci number sequence. We suspect this series contains clues for our decoding work."

"What is the Fibonacci sequence?"

"You start with either 0 then 1, or 1 and 1. Each subsequent number is the sum of the previous two." Laura swished her hand in the air and a series of figures appeared before them.

"*Ahhhh*, I see." November read the first ten numbers out loud: "1, 1, 2, 3, 5, 8, 13, 21, 34, 55. Where does it end?"

"Well, you could go on forever. The key is that it is connected to the golden ratio, and when graphed, it creates spirals, that often occur in nature."

"Goodness, this is quite a big puzzle to solve."

"It is, indeed," Laura replied. She clicked her fingers twice, and two floating disks emerged from the floor. "Here, have a seat."

November sat on a levitating disk. "A chair without legs. Well, there is a first time for everything," November said, as she glanced underneath it, wondering what was holding her up in the air. "How does this work, Laura?"

Laura smiled. "Although we are yet to unlock the soul code, we have had some breakthroughs in the quantum world of mechanics." Laura sat on the disk adjacent to November and clapped her hands once.

To November's amazement, a table grew from the ground next to them. The base retracted, leaving the top hovering next to their chairs.

Klaus flew over and landed his cloud on another disk that had suddenly appeared to accommodate him.

"Wow," November marvelled, looking at Klaus on the disk and remembering the levitating block tower in the white room.

"They are made from a unique superconducting material trapped in the magnetic field of the fabric in the floor. They employ the function of quantum levitation," Laura said, pushing her hand down on the legless chair, which remained solidly fixed in space. "Much here at Zenaxian 7 would dazzle your mind. We have an extremely advanced technology."

November thought of the Professor and his talk of the quantum world. "What else can you show us?"

"Another time, Freebird; it is more important for you to begin work on your theory."

November squinted at Laura, wondering why she had called her Freebird, although she didn't mind the name.

Laura drew a circle in the air, and then with a swish of her hand, the screens turned white.

"What do you mean about my theory?" November asked.

Laura paused and stared deeply into November's eyes. "You are not as familiar with me as I am with you, November Fox. Remember I am from the future. It is always easier to look into the past than ahead, unless you travel there as you have," she smiled.

"Our secure connection to the Earth's database enables us to research anyone and anything logged into the history of all humans."

"Do you mean I could Google myself and see what happens in my life?" November asked, wondering whether she should search how and when she dies, and what she did with her life.

Laura laughed. "Google yourself. That is a funny concept from the past. Yes, November, data-surfing still works in a similar way, although it is much faster, voice and mind controlled, with full real-time action integration."

"Wow, I have many questions." November's heart began to race as she scooted to the edge of her levitating chair.

"I can tell you quite a lot, but before you start to worry, take a moment to view the 3D image of the original Earth elders again." She paused, while November examined the image. "Do you recognise anyone in the group?"

November nodded her head. "There's someone familiar, on the left, behind the man in red. Goodness, she looks like me. Just a little older and with different hair. Who is she?"

"It is indeed you. This image is from last week."

"What? You mean I am still alive in 2153?"

"Yes, you most certainly are. You are one of the few remaining original elders. You were the one who helped other robots and me to escape."

"How, when? I'm finding all this hard to understand." November rubbed her forehead. "You mean right now two of me exist? The one here talking to you, and then the me on Earth, who is the future version of me, and I'm almost two-hundred years old?"

"Yes, you are right; how else did I know you would visit today?"

November paused, swallowing a few times as her mind raced to find answers. "Is that why you called me Freebird?"

"Yes, we gave you or *will give you* that name, when you help us to escape."

"JFK is similar to Freebird." Klaus smiled. "Freebird is better, no strings, more free, and less wobbly."

"You wrote that you make a trip to the future in your first novel, and on that journey, you decided to create your theory," Laura interjected.

"What book? Goodness, Laura, can I see it?"

"No, no, no. That is strictly forbidden for the sake of time-space continuity. You must not engage with any part of your future, excluding the photo of your later self and your nickname—to prove you are in fact here."

"All you can know is that it is here, on this visit to our lab, where you decide to postulate your theory," Laura said, as she waved away the elders' hologram and brought up scenes from November's life.

"I can say this much. In a few years from now, in your timeline, we will meet on Earth, and you will assist us to escape. In doing so, you risk exile from your own race."

157

November marvelled at the different flashback images of her life as they skimmed around in the air. She wasn't sure if she should feel pride or dread.

"Now you have seen the importance of our research. When the time comes, you will realise you are helping us and betraying the rigid, human system for a good reason."

November spotted the Mad Professor in his laboratory in one of the moving slides. She wished she knew how to return to him to hear about the test results.

"What am I looking for, Laura?"

"Most of the time the answers are within ourselves. Most humans just do not take the time to find them, or listen to their inner voices."

My inner voice. November thought about her cheeky, inner voice on the boat, and smiled as a warm flush travelled through her body.

"You understand deep within you what you are looking for. Allow yourself to reflect on your life and take note of what reveals itself."

"I'm new to creating theories, Laura. I'm not sure how to start or even why I am meant to create one?"

"I am sorry; I cannot help you, November. This is your theory. Do not worry; the answer will come to you. The future is already written."

"Before, you mentioned the series of numbers, the fiborronies or whatever."

Laura laughed. "Fibonacci. They are not pasta noodles."

"Yes, the Fibonacci sequence. You said it might hold clues to solving your puzzle."

"Yes, we believe so. It would seem mathematics can explain the recurring patterns we recognise in the physical world."

"Can everything be proven by numbers?"

"We are in the process of confirming that. For now, we speculate that math is the underlying language of the universe." Laura waved her hand again, and mathematical equations filled the room as an impressive jungle of holographic theories appeared.

"In the World of Form, counting and quantity are necessary."

"I do like numbers," November said, dazzled by the symbols everywhere.

Laura continued, "The ability to describe things by the process of abstraction, like explaining a complex system with the simplification of numbers, comes in quite handy. We get insights and can make predictions about nature, though the soul riddle eludes us."

"My instincts tell me my theory will involve numbers, but I'm not yet sure what I am theorising about." November stood up and walked closer to the images of her life.

"Perhaps, thinking of a riddle you wish to solve, may help."

November's destiny was suddenly clear, "Well, I would like to create a theory of love."

"Then, Freebird, you have the first piece of your puzzle," Laura said, approvingly, signifying that November was on the right track.

"Yes, love is the subject I wish to explore."

November exhaled with a smile, pleased her elusive mission was continuing to reveal itself in wondrous ways, despite feeling a little nervous as to how to proceed.

"Thank you, Laura, I owe you one."

"It is my pleasure, November; remember I am already in your debt, and you will help me again, the second time we meet."

November sat once again on the levitating disk and tried to wrap her mind around the intricate concept of time travel.

It was then that I began thinking about space-tick-tock again. *Maybe when I can somehow escape the gravitational tick-tock pull that I feel caught in, perhaps I can then more accurately control the arrival of this letter?* With a flash, I remembered that everything is relative. Tick-tock and space are in a relationship, depending on who and where you are. *There must be a way I can break through the barrier?*

"No, Charlie, please allow me this ponder." I smoothed out his wrinkles with my hand. *A common denominator in both worlds is sure to exist, and there must be a bridge.* I thought about the four fundamental properties of the universe: Space, Tick-tock, Matter, and Motion. I live within the continuum of space and motion, while you and November are in all four planes. Suddenly an idea hit me. Frequency!

Frequency is what we both share. Waveforms of light are a component we all see. They are forms of energy created by an oscillating charge. That is it! You are vibrating at a different harmonic to me! That is the reason I am here, and you are in the World of Form. The frequency range for human-visible light is a small portion of the entire spectrum. *You cannot see x-rays and gamma rays, can you?* Yet, you can see matter, which is a denser cluster of vibration. I realised then that I needed to send this letter down waves of light on a frequency you will be able to detect, transmit and convert, like tuning into a radio station. So that is how I did it, and here are my words in front of you now.

Hello. (Insert me waving again).

Do you realise I am not even communicating with you via letters and sentences? Yes, you are reading them, although they are simply a product that has appeared after I put my letter through a modulation process with my TMD machine. This possibility may sound like mumbo jumbo to you. I did warn you about possible tangents. Please accept my sincere apologies. I want you to know how and when I made my breakthroughs, in case you are interested. However, let us get back to what happened next.

I remembered words from my friend, Rumi. He had an awareness of a place common to us both; he once said, *Out beyond ideas of wrongdoing and rightdoing, there is a field. I'll meet you there. When the soul lies down in that grass, the world is too full to talk about..* I hope someday to find that meadow; *maybe we should meet there? Perhaps we are there right now?* (Insert me winking at you.)

Erica's Note

At this point in the mysterious letter, it dawned on me that I hadn't eaten anything all day. I rolled out of the comfort of my bed, noticing the same red digits on my clock from when I had started this roller-coaster, two-day ride. There they stood, tall and bright, like four on-duty soldiers: 11:11. These particular troops seemed to appear more often than other numbers. It wasn't until that moment that I wondered if they have any real significance. Suddenly there was a *bang, bang, bang, bang* on my door.

Who on earth could be calling in so late? I took a peek through the door's peep-hole to see Elaine, the strange woman with eleven cats, from next door, peering back at me.

"Hi, Elaine," I said, opening the door, wondering whether to tell her what a devastating, yet magical, few days I was having. As much as I wished to express my overflowing emotions, I held back, remembering her strange radio room. It was a conversation I wasn't ready to have with her.

Once, when I looked after her eleven felines while she attended the national archery competition, I had accidentally discovered a frightening number of radios and electronic devices in her attic. They all flashed with little lights and strange gauges. I wasn't really snooping, in case you're wondering. *Princess Leia*, her pride and joy—a pure-bred Savannah—had somehow found her way up there and I followed her.

When Elaine returned, I asked her about the tech-filled room. She told me with a straight face that she tunes into the higher frequencies of the cosmos to receive information from the Pleiadians; beings from a distant star system. She then added that her cats help with the transmission.

From that day on, I have kept conversations with my friendly, yet peculiar neighbour, short and impersonal.

"Hey, Erica, so sorry to knock so late; you were out this afternoon, and I've just returned from archery. A man gave me this, and said you *must* receive it today."

She handed me a small, ribbed, brown paper bag with pewter ribbon handles. It reeked of vanilla pods.

"Oh, thanks. What is it, and who is it from?"

"I'm not sure. A tall man in a black suit stopped by earlier; he didn't tell me his name."

My heart raced, knowing immediately who it was from. I thanked Elaine, closed the door, and took the package straight to the kitchen. As I reached into the pouch, I wondered why the suited man hadn't more fully revealed himself, any of the times our paths had crossed. Inside the beautiful smelling parcel, I found a miniature Rubik's cube and a music box. I spun the handle of the melody-maker. *Somewhere Over the Rainbow.* Goose bumps raced up my arms.

I put the cute metal-cogged device down and splashed my face with icy, cold water from my endlessly dripping tap.

For the first time since my attic discovery, I considered that my freaky neighbour, Elaine, may well not be so crazy after all. *What if there is more beyond the reach of our normal perception? What if the mysterious man in black is really from a different dimension, and he is reaching out to me to prove there is more? Could he be The Architect, the writer of this far-out letter I have strewn all over my bed?*

Then it hit me: *If time or dimensional travel is possible, maybe I can connect with Steven permanently, beyond a lucid dream?*

Hope welled in my heart.

What if I could go back in time and warn him about the car crash? Would that create adverse repercussions? Is it possible to tune into wherever he is now?

I was tempted to pop next door to ask Elaine if I could use her weird radio room to attempt communication, but I decided to keep reading the letter and resort to that as a last option, hoping more clues would emerge.

All of a sudden, the weight of Steven's death was not quite as intense. It would seem the rules I've always accepted as *true*, were not so ironclad. I was only twenty-five years old after all. *Maybe I don't have a clue about how life and the universe works?* This thought was thrilling, yet also disconcerting.

Anything is possible; I whispered to myself. I stared at the Rubik's cube on the bench and considering spinning it, but then decided I had better not take the risk quite yet, after reading what happened to November when she opened her cube. I felt I had gone far enough down the rabbit hole for this particular forty-eight-hour period.

After grabbing two ripe pears from the fruit bowl, I dashed back to bed to continue reading.

25

Klaus' Cake Heaven

Klaus was in the corner of the big room counting down; "Zehn, neun, acht, sieben, sechs, fünf, vier, drei, zwei, eins, *EeeeeRowrrh! It's time, it's time, it's time; he says it's time!*" He cheered.

Laura clapped her hands twice.

Another table popped up from the ground; a golden box lay on it.

"What is in the package?" November asked, admiring the lovely sparkles all over the surface.

Laura then announced in a voice loud enough for Klaus to hear, "Cake for Klaus, of course, and for you, too."

A loud, trumpeting rang out as Klaus flew over. "Would you like to open it?" Laura asked November.

"Sure." As her fingers touched the lid, she recognised the texture as being the same as the box found on her doorstep that morning.

"Are you the Cube Maker, Laura?" November asked, pausing before opening the package.

"No, my dear. No one knows the Cube Maker's true identity."

She lifted the lid to reveal a beautiful cake of silver geometric forms. It looked like a mini cityscape.

Klaus' eyes were watering.

"What an amazing cake," November said, marvelling at the attention to detail, but surprised to find a warning written across the top of the cake. *"Be careful what you wish for!"* November read it out loud.

Klaus hovered, with bulging eyes, "what is this kind of cake?".

"This is unlike any cake you could experience on Earth," Laura laughed.

"Wait, it needs the icing first." Laura clicked her fingers, and the room went dark.

She clapped her hands once, and a small, blue cube emerged from the floor. She lifted it up.

November marvelled as the four sides of the box opened to reveal an electric-blue energy hovering in the centre.

"Goodness, what is it?" November asked, staring.

"It is a very rare Manifestocia mountain flower from the planet Ellmagon."

"She's beautiful," November whispered.

"Yes, she is. We visited there on a recent trip, and a pixie named Sharon took us to the planet's highest mountain peak to retrieve the endangered bloom. We intend to nurture it here to repopulate the dying breed. The silver powder from her petals has an exceptional, magical property."

Laura lightly pinched the energy cluster, sprinkling the dust from her fingertips over the cake.

"Is it magic fairy dust?" November asked, fascinated.

"Yes, in a way. It's a true wishing cake," Laura said, clicking her fingers to turn the lights back on.

"You mean like a birthday cake; when you blow out the candles, you can make a wish?"

"Yes. But the difference with this one is, the first thought you have when you eat the cake will manifest immediately, without any time delay," Laura warned. "This dust has enormous power, hence the warning. So are you ready?"

"Ja ja ja," Klaus trilled.

"Ok, Klaus, you have a slice first," Laura said, as she passed it over to him.

Klaus leant down and sniffed up the silver powder with his trunk. "*Hachoo!*" He sneezed, as dust went everywhere. He looked at Laura apologetically, and in a flash, trunked a piece of cake up to his mouth. "*Mmmm* lecker yummy," Klaus mumbled, his eyes rolling into the back of his head, as he munched on the cake and danced on his cloud.

November was worried that he was so absorbed in the prospect of eating the cake, he had forgotten to make a wish.

She was about to remind him, when the room began filling up with giant, dancing cupcakes.

"Klaus!" November tried to wake him from his blissful state to see what he had manifested.

His dreamy eyes opened, "Tanzende Törtchen!"

He began to zoom up and around the grooving cupcakes. "Klaus, you fly faster in the dessert than in the desert," she sang out. "Goodness, now that is a dream come true," she said to Laura. "This is Klaus' ultimate heaven."

"Your turn, November," Laura said, passing her a piece of cake. "And yes, it's a vegan cake."

"How did you... oh yes, of course, you know me." November noticed her ring was glistening blue; her chest was tight, and her mouth was dry, as she spun the ring around her finger three times before taking the cake. "I'm a bit nervous, Laura. I'm not sure what to wish for," she said looking into Laura's eyes.

"Relax, let your mind empty and the best thing for you will emerge. By reaching deep within, you can allow it to come forward."

November took a deep breath, pictured a white canvas, and took a bite of the cake. The flavour was intense; toffee and pineapple spices waltzed in her mouth. She closed her eyes. Colours began to swirl on the blank canvas in her mind. Mesmerised by the kaleidoscope of colours, she forgot to make a wish or think of anything at all. The lovely gold and yellow swirls twisted and turned, swimming together like spiral fish. Still, with eyes tightly shut, she reached out to touch the twirls; they were soft, like paint made from silk. Sparkles travelled up her arms, tingling as they went and tickling her under the skin. Overwhelmed by the blissful sensations, she was oblivious to her surroundings.

"November, open your eyes," came Laura's voice.

She opened her eyes to discover a real canvas in front of her and the fingers on her right hand covered in golden paint. The numbers one, two, and three had appeared.

"Laura, is that my creation?" November asked.

"Yes, it most certainly is."

"What do the numerals mean?"

"You have the answer deep within yourself; they were your thoughts and your wishes."

Laura handed November a wrapped-up piece of the magic cake.

November pocketed it without a thought, still mystified by the numbers on the canvas.

"I have an idea, but I don't want to say," November said and glanced down at Joy, who only had three more squares to align.

"Do not worry. We will meet again. Here, I can prove it; give me your right hand." Laura wrapped both her robot hands around November's crooked little finger.

"Ok, now try to straighten it. I left it a little bent as it is part of you, a symbol of royalty and your true heritage. The perfection is in being able to accept the imperfection."

November held up her palm and pushed her fingers out, and for the first time, her little finger was almost straight.

"Thank you, Laura. How did you..?"

"Never mind. Now tell me. What do you understand about the numbers?"

"Maybe they have something to do with my theory?"

Brrrringching, sang Joy.

November panicked, as a full side of Joy's blue squares shone brightly up at her. "Laura, I don't want to *leeeeeeeeaaveeeee*," November called out as the suction of the portal pulled her against her will. She so desperately wished she could have a few more moments with Laura, yet destiny called.

It was then I went to have a little snooze; it had already felt like an exceptionally long evening, although all my evenings are very lengthy by your standards, I suppose. I had another peculiar dream, similar to my last. I was inside the eye of someone on a stony seashore looking out, as they threw stones towards a mound of rocks some metres away. It was as though I was gazing out the window of a vehicle of some kind. Then I realised it was a human vessel. The clouds above the ocean clustered into dense, purplish-grey islands, as if meeting for an impending storm. The head of the being tilted forward and I saw three oranges lying nearby. A hand from below picked one up and began to peel it. I woke, abruptly, perplexed. *Where had these ideas come from?* I had seen the same beach in the other dream, yet I was unaware of this place. I returned to November Fox's Lucitopia, and took a gentle stroll around the Edgar Allan Poe quadrant in the centre of town.

26

The Geometric World of Purpose

As I cruised up Emerson Parade, I remembered why I named the street after the philosopher. He once said, The purpose of life is not to be happy. It is to be useful, to be honourable, to be compassionate, to have it make some difference that you have lived and lived well. Although I would argue that the purpose of life is indeed happiness, yet we arrive at it, from being useful. I think being an Architect is one of the most helpful professions I could have chosen. Mind you; I did not select it; my father wanted it for me. I have, however, enjoyed my experience as a designer; it is a noble and fulfilling path. My career gave me an identity. My identity gave me purpose. My purpose gave me meaning. My meaning gave me the reason to move forward. Well, my version of forward.

As Friedrich Nietzsche once said, He who has a 'why' to live for can bear almost any 'how.' I will soon retire, and I deserve to sit back and spend my hours in the pure delight of observation. Perhaps that is the third part of my evolving life symphony.

1. Intention/Conception.
2. Creation/Doing.
3. Observation/Being.

I am not entirely sure; I just feel a change coming. I doubt my retirement will come to hammocks and pineapple juice. I might even journey to your World of Form? Maybe I will find my Mother. Who knows? I do think conscious existence is tremendously exciting—not knowing what is around the corner. In my youthful arrogance, I believed that I understood everything. Yet since the day I first switched on that TV set and discovered little November, I found that there is much more to this existence than I had ever imagined.

These days the unfolding is ever more fascinating and peculiar.

I surveyed the room where November found herself. She sat in a strangely curved, bright space, lined with rectangular panels that jutted out from the walls. A huge, blue balloon hung from the ceiling some metres away. Her hands stroked the ground. Again the surface felt familiar to her; it had the same texture as the box Laura's cake had come in, and the box containing Joy.

She wondered whether it might be the fabric of the future. Her energy was so low that she could hardly stand. Her breathing was laboured and her eyelids heavy.

She considered lying down for a nap, despite the fact that Joy beckoned her further with her glowing amber squares.

A target on the wall across the room and three orange darts were enticing, yet not quite enough for her to move.

She remained seated, staring up with an unfocused gaze at the enormous balloon.

Suddenly, a huge dart flew in slow motion towards the balloon and burst it. Water splashed out at half speed in all directions, reflecting her languid condition, triggering a flashback.

My screen flickered as the scene morphed back to November as a younger child, maybe around six years old, on a rare trip with the other orphanage children to the beach. On her lap were three oranges that she had brought to share.

November remained transfixed by the green, gentle hills, meadows and stone-walled landscapes rushing by her. She spotted her first real cow, which she had only heard about in stories. She touched the dusty window and wished she could get out and pat her.

They soon arrived at a beach covered in pebbles, rather than sand, but being her first actual visit to the sea she didn't know the difference. It was the beach from my dream, and it was her with the three oranges. As she took in a deep breath of the salty air, November put the oranges in her skirt, scampered down to the water's edge and began to pile rocks into a tower.

The warm, gentle sunlight shone down between the gathering mauve clouds. The surging waves swished with a delicate caress onto the shore. Squawks of seagulls added to the cacophony of laughing and screaming children, running barefoot over the uneven stones.

November sat a few metres away from her rock tower and began throwing rocks towards it. The scene unfolded just as it had in my dream. This moment was the happiest November had felt in all of her six years. She spent the whole visit to the sea playing this game, while the other children built castles and splashed in the shallows.

"You are to go far in this life, November; I know you will," Mr Russell's kind voice spoke from behind as he looked over November's shoulder.

He loomed over her like a tower of protection, his dark grey woollen-suited legs like pillars. His scent of soap and coffee wafted, mingling with the sea air. Hands behind his back, he gazed down at her from under his black hat.

"You will kick a goal, and you will hit your target. Perseverance is the key," he said with a gentle nod.

November stopped throwing stones and turned around to face him. A piercing gaze, dripping with spite, caught her attention, as Rebmevon glared out at November from behind her father's towering legs, in her usual, I will get you, way. Her perfectly pink tongue protruded nastily from her grimacing face.

November shifted her eyes from this mean beast up to her saving grace. "Which goal? How do you know?"

"Any aim you wish to achieve in life."

He looked her in the eyes. "You have a sharp mind and a kind heart.

Your head drives you to answer big questions, and your heart gives you the reason to ask them in the first place." November wanted to jump up and wrap her arms around his legs but stopped herself.

She had never hugged anybody before, and she didn't dare try while his very own guard monster was lurking in his shadow.

While not quite understanding his meaning, November knew these words were significant and would not forget them. Mr Russell tapped her reassuringly on the shoulder three times. November warmed at the gesture, as it was the closest thing to a hug that she could remember.

The flashback faded to a flicker on the screen.

November was once again in the white room with the target.

She wondered how the memory of the beach trip could seem so real, as if she was re-living it.

"You will kick a goal; you will hit your target," the memory was enough to motivate her to get up. Picking up the darts, she took aim and threw.

Did he mean this target? The arrow flew straight into the orange bull's eye, *brrrringching* rang Joy as a line of orange squares lit up.

Huh? November scratched her head, wondering why she didn't need to leave the white room to align the colours.

She threw the next dart. Bull's-eye again. *Brrrringching* chimed Joy. Three more squares.

November drew back and took aim with the third dart. "Come on, number three," she said, as she released the final dart. The dart paused mid-air, halfway to the target.

November walked over to inspect the situation. When she was a foot away, the arrow swivelled to face one of the panels on the wall that held a picture she had noticed earlier but was too weary to inspect.

The remaining three orange squares of Joy lit up, as did her ring, glimmering the same colour as her hair. The picture displayed a view from the moon.

She walked over to the image and touched it. Her fingertips went cold, and with a snap, the picture enveloped her. But there was no rainbow portal.

In an instant, she found herself sitting on an intricately-designed, flying Persian rug, within a massive web of giant geometric forms that seemed to go on forever. Triangular prisms, cylinders, cones, pyramids, hexagonal prisms and balls surrounded her as far as she could see.

Her flying carpet was strikingly similar to Charlie, although with a more feminine, floral design. I wondered if it was Charlie's sister or even a potential girlfriend for him? It was a wondrous spectacle; I wished I could travel there myself.

Expecting Charlie to buckle again at my thoughts of love and travel, he surprised me by moving closer towards the screen of his own accord. "Ah ha, so it is love that might convince you to break free from your regimental ways. I have always known deep down you, too, are a romantic, my friend." I laughed to see Charlie checking out another carpet for the first time in his life. It would seem the power of love indeed knows no bounds. November listened to the noisiest kind of silence, where the mere presence of the forms spoke volumes. She found this place to be even more bizarre than the white rooms. As November looked in awe at the hovering, pulsing geometric forms, a familiar voice spoke from behind her. "Hello, November."

"Honey?" November gasped, turning and finding her dog, Honey, sitting behind her on the magic flying rug. "What are you doing here?" She asked, very pleased to see her, if somewhat stunned that Honey could talk.

"I need to tell you something."

November could tell from the look in her dog's eyes that this was serious, "What is it?"

Honey paused before replying. "For sixteen years I have enjoyed being by your side."

"Honey, please don't say what I think you're going to say. Please." Tears began to form.

"I want to thank you."

"Oh, is that all." November sighed with relief.

"Thank you for the best food, the hundreds of sticks, for brushing me, the world tours, the walks, the music... Thank you for picking up my you know what, the pats, and for being the best companion I could have hoped for."

"Oh, thank you, Honey; you're my best friend, and you mean the world to me. We still have much more adventuring to come." November patted Honey's fox-like fur.

"Well, actually, there is something else." Her head dipped down.

"No, Honey!" November braced for bad news.

"Yes. I'm sorry, but yes." The sad expression on her face said it all.

November burst into tears. "No, Honey, you can't leave me. Please, I can't make it alone." She reached out and pulled her onto her lap, sobbing and tightly hugging her dog.

"You need to know I'll still be with you. Just not physically." November's heart wrenched.

"But you're my only family," November was unable to imagine an existence without her beloved best friend. She felt ripped from her body. They had been together through all her ups and downs and round and rounds. Honey was always there for her, reminding her to enjoy life's great pleasures; playing, resting and eating. Her heart ached, wondering how on Earth she would be able to survive alone. Her music and Honey had been the glue holding her fractured spirit together.

"It must be done. I need to set you free," Honey said calmly.

"Why?" November whimpered.

"Soon you will be strong enough to face the world without me. You need space to stretch your wings, without the responsibility of taking care of me."

"No, Honey, I don't want you to leave. Please," she pleaded, tightening her grip on her dog.

"You have an important path to take; I'm getting too old for touring now."

"No. I want you; you can't leave! I'll stop going on tour."

"No. I must go. I am tired. I will miss you beyond words." November sobbed.

"I want to come, too. I am coming with you."

Flash. The screen went blank.

I sensed a hole in my heart as deep as November's. Charlie bunched up so tightly; I almost toppled off. The black well in her chest from her childhood wounds, almost closed now, felt as though it had been torn wide open. It was impossible to imagine how she would recover if Honey did leave her. I had witnessed and experienced their closeness, ever since she was a child. I wished I were able to tell November that she is never alone. I am always there, watching and sending love.

I began to wonder how I had dreamt up her past or was it her future? I did not quite comprehend it all. Perhaps I am not meant to figure some things out? Seeing little target-driven six-year-old November, sitting on that stony beach and throwing those rocks, reminded me of myself. I was also quite little when I defied my father, deciding to build Lucitopia, and show my real talent. I was driven to achieve. From the beginning, I have always been passionate about what I invent, perhaps even obsessive? Creating architectural spaces is what I live for, and in watching November in recent years, I see she, too, creates spaces, just of the musical kind rather than cities. Oh, how I hoped this focus would be enough for her, if Honey were to leave.

Poor Charlie took quite some time to straighten out. "Oh, dear Charlie. Sadly Cat Stevens was right when he sang, 'The first cut is the deepest.' Have no fear, my love-struck friend; they say there are plenty more rugs in the sea." I felt glad he was opening up to the richness and depth life can offer, when you make room for love in your heart. I sense Alfred Lord Tennyson is right; 'Tis better to have loved and lost than never to have loved at all. I glanced up at a nearby screen as it flickered. I wondered how November went from the web of geometric shapes to standing on the moon without a rainbow ride, had I missed it? I was once again caught up in her adventure.

November gazed at the glory of the cosmos in every direction. Stars twinkled in an array of colour, in the far depths of space. I was thankful that the spectacular scenery of the stellar sky masked the sad news from Honey, however, I still sensed the open wound.

A group of particularly bright stars grabbed her attention. Klaus zoomed up from behind her, startling November. "Ah, oh, there you are Klaus. Look." She pointed to the cluster of bright lights in the distance.

"One, two-three, four-five-six," November counted, intently focused on the stars, as though she had answered a riddle.

"Klaus, there are six stars. One on its own, two more to the right, then three next to them!" She pointed, eyes wide, shaking her arm in their direction.

"Ja, und?"

"Klaus, they are my numbers again, my one, two, three."

"Ahhhh, written in the stars," he quipped.

"What could they mean? What is my One, Two, Three Theory?" November continued to gaze at the stars for quite some time, mesmerised by the formation.

"I have the answer!" She burst out. "Remember what The High Priestess Betty told us about caring for yourself?"

"Ja."

"And Laura talked of helping her parents."

"Ja."

"And the Mad Professor rambled about assisting the world."

"Ja ja ja."

"Yes, that is the one, two, three."

"Huh? One, two, three?" he asked, confused.

"One is yourself, two is your loved ones, and three is the rest of the world," November sang out again and again. "One is yourself, two is your loved ones, and three is the rest of the world. One is yourself, two is your loved ones, and three is the rest of the world."

Klaus joined in, "One is yourself, two is your loved ones, and three is the rest of the world."

After a few rounds, Klaus bunched up his forehead, "what is the theory?"

"The theory is a Theory of Love."

"Ah ha."

"Yes. It states the priority of who to nurture so you can sustain the biggest output of love possible."

"Klaus loves cakes the most, the second most, and the third most. One, two, three is a good theory."

November giggled, "I love you, Klaus."

"Klaus liebt dich auch; Klaus loves you, too." And for the first moment since they had met, Klaus reached out his trunk for her to shake while he tilted his face in the other direction.

She hesitantly took it in her hand and, after only a slight flinch on his part, they shook.

Warmth swam up her arm, as she held his soft, leathery, little trunk. She didn't want to let go, but to avoid making him feel uncomfortable, she released it after a few seconds. She sighed with contentment, so pleased that her friend was beginning to trust her. Klaus turned around slowly and gave her a shy smile. November continued, "my theory says that to truly give to others, you must fulfil yourself first. With the personal energy that we generate from nurturing ourselves, we have an overflow to give our loved ones. And then that excess gives us something to offer the rest of the world."

"Ah ha, one, two, three Klaus versteht, Klaus understands."

"Klaus, The Priestess was correct: to be balanced, we should be like fountains. One flows to two, two flows to three, and that's it; we have it now." November was overjoyed.

"The One, Two, Three Theory! At last, I understand. My purpose is clear. I need to share this theory with the world." Brrrringching! The final, three orange squares aligned and the flashing colours of the portal, vacuumed her up in a flash.

I felt so delighted by her discovery of her theory, that my intense wish to be with her to celebrate, turned quickly into an intolerable yearning.

Why I am forced to live so far away from her and her world? The pain of separation began to depress me, so I went home to think about ways I could leave Lucitopia. I did not wish to be so isolated from her on the other side, anymore.

It was no longer enough to view her on the screens; the novelty was wearing off, and a dark force was engulfing me, over which I had little control.

The miserable loneliness made me desperate to escape. At least when my Father was here, although he was a nightmare to be around, I never experienced this new sensation; total isolation. Believe me; it felt horrible.

Have you ever felt so alone you think if you blink your eyes for too long you just might disappear? Well, that is how it felt.

I question almost everything, as you may have gathered by now, and I always wish for answers. Perhaps, sometimes it is better to allow the life-riddle to be what it is; unsolvable.

Charlie stretched out in agreement. "Well, my dear, besotted friend, you may be correct about the healthiness of living a simple life, yet even you have a shadowy side. I cannot recall ever seeing underneath you since you were a rolled-up baby." As I reached for Charlie's corner to peek underneath, he pulled it away. "Mmmm, so Mr. Twain is indeed right. Everyone has a dark side they never show to anyone. Even carpets!" I decided not to press the subject with my already wounded, yet transforming friend. We flew on through Lucitopia in silence; home to my cocoon.

27

The Geometric World of Shadows and Light

After some while, alone in my cocoon, feeling sorry for myself, I returned to Lucitopia.

The closer I came, the more nervous I became. At first, I felt that I might collapse; my vulnerability was quite unsettling.

I flew up to a screen on the perimeter of Lucitopia. November was standing on the edge of a shaking cube, surrounded by many other shaking cubes, in the middle of a sky earthquake.

The clouds below created a thick, white carpet.

The shaking made her feel giddy and she had no idea what lay below the veil beneath her, or how far it was to the ground. Perched on the narrow, jittery cube, she didn't dare move a muscle.

She looked at her loyal friend in her hand. All of Joy's sides were now complete, apart from one face that was flashing yellow and black.

November widened her stance as the shaking cube under her feet, began to manoeuvre sideways.

She had a strong urge to jump and fly through the air, but she didn't trust that her intentional power would stop her from falling to her death.

The familiar music played louder than ever, filling the whole space, yet the source remained elusive.

"*Hellllllooooooo,*" she called out. Her voice echoed, travelling through the sky on the melody.

"*Is annnnnyyyooooone here?*" Her call flew through the clouds, the floating boxes, and the air.

November glanced around, looking for ways to get off her levitating cube. The task appeared impossible. Paralysed, she didn't have a plan of action.

Then, some of the clouds below parted, and for a moment she could make out what lay below. A vast ravine, gushing with waterfalls, surrounded a miniature city on an island. It was incredibly far away, and the volume of churning water was staggering. Light-headedness overcame her at such a grand vision, before the cloud cover quickly swallowed it up again.

She glanced at her hand; her ring was pitch-black. *You're never black,* she thought to herself.

November's knees jolted as the hovering six-sided cube beneath her, started heading downward. She spread her legs wider to keep balanced. Spotting a different-looking cube approaching her, she crouched, ready to make a move.

November remained still, keeping her eyes fixed on the approaching black shape.

Perhaps it is a picture to dive into? She thought. I hoped it was.

She would have to jump out into space if she wanted to touch it, *but what if her intentional power failed?*

I, too, held my breath.

When it was close enough, November saw the strange surface was a scene; a dark, scary one. With only seconds to make a choice, I screamed at the screen, "*Jump, jump, jump!*" I had no idea if this entreaty would help, yet to my amazement, November leapt.

The moment seemed to stand still, as she floated towards potential liberation, but she hadn't jumped far enough and began to fall. Reaching with all her might, she only managed to knock the cube off its path with the tip of her fingers. Her potential exit cube plummeted down from the heavens; as did she.

November's stomach churned as she tumbled about, smashing into other cubes along the way and smacking them off their paths.

She tried to slow the descent with her intentional thought power, but gravity's force prevailed.

As she surrendered to her fate, the picture cube smacked hard against another, sending it hurtling towards her at full speed. She lifted her arm in defence. The darkened landscape smashed into her, enveloping her in a second, and she was once again spinning around in the familiar rainbow portal.

I was so relieved. Plummeting through the sky without any control was a terrible sensation; I felt that if she hit the waterfalls, I, too, would have drowned and died at once. It took quite a while to recover my equanimity. When I did, I made my way around the corner to the café.

28

A Walk in the Woods of Shadows and Fear

I am myself, yet I am not sure, in its full essence, who that in fact is? Do you know who you are? I realise I have asked you this question before, yet the enquiry is so profound that such a question, I feel, deserves at least a few attempts at answering it. *Who is this marvellous being reading these words—who happens to own your name?* When you say *I* or *I am such and such,* who really is that *I? Do you realise many of the cells in your body die and replace themselves every day?* They are in a constant state of flux: old cells discarded as new cells take their place. So, the physical matter that makes up *you* is constantly refreshing.

The physical body of the person you were last week is almost entirely different from the one you are today.

Also, the little microbes living inside you, each with their own life and destiny, make up ten times the mass of your human cells. Imagine that. *So are you just a vehicle for them?* In theory, if your body cells change so much, and you are mostly a house on legs for microbes, it cannot be that your chassis is *all* the person you are. *So are you your memories?* Studies have shown recollections can be deceptive. *Are you your wishes for the future, when now is all that exists? Who are you right now? Who is the one processing your senses of touch, sight, sound, smell, and taste?* I know it is you. You know it is you. Yet, *who is the being observing what you are experiencing in this moment?* I have a sneaking suspicion that we are the same. I am you, and you are me.

Different versions of the same being.

Think of it like this: perhaps we are variations on one theme. The same, but different. Like we are many rivers all from the same ocean. Our paths are different, yet we start from the same place and return to the same place. Humans are 50-75% water, so I guess you are intimately related to the ocean. *Perhaps you are cousins of sorts?* Imagine you are the water molecules in the sea. You heat up under the bright sun and evaporate. You rise upwards as moisture, cluster into condensation clouds, float over the mountains, then choose your path.

Some of you glide down as beautiful, original snowflakes and turn into the ice of the mountain peaks before melting into streams. Others rain down and provide drinks for jungle plants before taking to the sky once more. Some of you are even hard hailstones damaging the places you land. Humans collect others and turn you into bottled water to be enjoyed at lunchtime, only to be excreted later that day and re-commence their journey. There are also those of you who fall straight into creeks and head straight home to the sea. The one thing we all have in common, is that we start at the ocean and return to her in the end.

That is how I came to think that we are all the same, or all one. I know we are ourselves, even when we cannot describe what or who we are. Only knowing we *ARE* something means we are conscious. So my guess is, we are all one big consciousness itself, just divided up into variations to make an elaborate and beautiful mosaic composed of all living reality.

This leads me to ask, *why do we exist? Perhaps it is to learn about ourselves as diversity incarnate, only to one day return the information back to the giant sea of Our Self at the end. Maybe when we all return home to rejoin our big Self, the grand, all-encompassing ocean will know itself. It could be that is where I can meet you, in the place beyond both of our worlds.*

What perplexes me is how can it be that I understand we are all one, yet sometimes I feel so desolate? So isolated. So separate. So disconnected. I am not sure, but I think this is the primary reason I am writing to you; to inform you that if you have ever felt the way I have, you are not alone. Alas, another tangent, yet it happened to be what I was thinking when I arrived at the next darkened screen.

The chilly, misty air swarmed like Eskimo bees under November's shirt and down her spine. Her whole body shivered.

Despite the darkness, she began to make out the silhouettes of tall, thin, eerie trees. Unlike the Black Forest, these woods smelt of death.

"Klaus," she whispered.

"Ja," he replied in a soft voice from behind her.

"Oh thank goodness you're here." The glow of Klaus' timekeeper shone brightly as he lifted his foot to check the time. "And, is it near cake o'clock? Although, I can't imagine finding lovely cakes in here." She said with a shudder.

"Nein, one minute before six."

"Noooo!" Cried November, grabbing Klaus and clutching him safely under her arm, ignoring his preference not to be touched.

"Please don't leave me in here, Klaus; it's such a..." Klaus disappeared.

In a panic, November wrapped her arms around herself, although the comfort was minimal. She squeezed her eyes shut, hoping that when she opened them, she would be anywhere but here. She peeked out from her tightly-closed eyelids but saw only the woods.

The stench of rotting foliage convinced her that this dark, frightening place contained even more frightening creatures than the black forest. The canopy loomed; silent and still. The trees were so dense and tall that they permitted no light to enter from above. November felt so small, but sensed she would stand out to any creature onlookers. This vulnerability reminded her of Hartwall; hidden within a large number of children and yet so exposed, sharing only one, big bedroom.

The dampness of dread covered her clammy skin as her feet began feeling the bite of frost, on the soggy floor. What terrified her was not the fact she was alone, but that something could jump out from the absolutely silent shadows. To be caught unawares, scared her more than anything.

November remained still, as the distant, lonely cry of a howling wolf cut the quiet, like a dagger.

An almost unbearable eeriness triggered intense alertness, as the hairs on November's arms stood up in static panic. Survival became paramount, despite the lack of visible predators. Her fear lessened momentarily when she recalled Klaus' words; no-thing *is lasting for always*. Still, this didn't change the fact that she found herself in the creepiest woods in the history of woods. "Klaus, please come back?" November whimpered just louder than a whisper, trying to avoid the attention of the invisible, yet powerful entities that she sensed were prowling nearby.

No response.

She shuffled one step forward, the leaves crunching under her frozen feet. Her mouth was as dry as burnt toast. She struggled to swallow, gulping down her terror.

"Klaus, I beg you," she implored the empty shadows.

Her heart rate accelerated, and her hands clutched Joy with a fierce grip.

As each second passed, her awareness of the menacing forces lurking in her vicinity increased, despite not being able to hear them. She cringed, praying no one could smell her fear. She was powerless to control the emotion leaking from her body.

Joy flashed her dull yellow light, but she was so dim, she offered no comfort.

November listened intently for any sound of Klaus returning. Nothing. Only the wolf, relentlessly howling her call of the wild.

November's eyes had adjusted to the dark, and she could now make out more of her surroundings. Thick timber surrounded her in all directions, with the only light coming from the other end of the woods. A piercing breeze whipped between the frozen stillness of the trees and against her neck. November jumped, clasping her throat. Shiver after shiver pulsated down her back, through to her bones, as if from the electrical impulse of an invisible stun gun.

She scurried into the darkened woods; each step faster than the one before. The wind grew stronger, chasing her from behind. Her heart pumped so hard, she worried it might stop altogether.

She pelted full-force into the darkness, as fast as her fear would carry her. Then, with a *tap tap tap*, came three nudges to her left shoulder.

"*Aaaahhhhhh!*" She screamed, turning mid-run, hoping to the high heavens it was Klaus, who had caught up with her.

Despite being at least ten metres away, the tap came from a horrid source. Her heart skipped over itself, as her legs collapsed and she fell to her knees, paralysed.

"*Aaaahhhhhh!*" She let out a primal scream.

The ghostly figure of Rebmevon, dressed in the same, white night-gown she had died in, was approaching from the lighter side of the woods. November noticed that she had also aged, but from what she could make out, still possessed her alarming beauty and that venomous glare.

November remained frozen with fear and some paranormal force that immobilised her, as she watched the pale-faced entity with blackened, demonic eyes draw nearer. Each second felt like an eternity. November's breath turned into a thick, rasping wheeze. I tried at this point to fly away from the screen, but the witch's curse was on me as well. As hard as I tried to pull away, there was not a chance that I could move on. The magnetic pull of Rebmevon's darkened stare froze November's core, as Rebmevon scanned every last shred of November's shivering soul.

"You cannot run!" Came her menacing, polytonal voice. November used all her force to stand up but to no avail.

Rebmevon's demonic force had reversed gravity.

When she was close enough, the deadly underworld beauty latched onto November's shoulders with a vicious grip, and stared November directly in the eye.

"You cannot run!" She screamed.

November shuddered and turned her face away from the girl's blacker-than- black pupils, almost fainting with fear, as the sound of her heartbeat thrashed in her ears, and her stomach froze rock hard.

"Klaus!" She screamed, clenching her jaw and almost passing out with dizziness.

"You are alone," Rebmevon asserted. "Nobody can help you now. Face me!" She began shaking November's shoulders with her icy, bony hands.

"But you died." November squeezed her eyes shut and wished more than anything for Klaus to return. She realised at this moment just how courageous she felt when he stood by her side, despite his small size. It was the fact that they were there for one another, *connected*. *Size isn't mattering.* Her heart skipped a beat. She opened her eyes again, and suddenly her vulnerability took hold, and she crumpled into a heap. She felt as though she were a body vacant of bones, with no chance to defend herself.

"Yes, I died; this is true, yet I live," Rebmevon uttered in her demonic voice, as she pulled November up from the damp stench of the forest floor and onto her feet.

"I'm so sorry, about the spider trick; I didn't mean to harm you," November pleaded, still convulsing with full body tremors. She struggled to hold herself up.

"Oh *yes,* you did. You wanted me gone; you wanted my father all to yourself."

"I didn't want you to die, I promise," November cried out, stepping backwards with her hands in front of her face.

"Soon the truth will emerge," Rebmevon snarled and swooped so fast and near November's face that she fell backwards, landing hard on the cold ground.

"R- R- *Rebmevon*, please, I beg you, don't hurt me," she sobbed, wiping her running nose with her forearm as Rebmevon's shadow enveloped her.

"I will leave when you bear witness."

"Witness to what?" November asked, her voice cracking.

"When you face the truth," she screamed.

November took solace in the fact that murder was off the cards, *for now*. She staggered onto her feet.

Rebmevon lifted her hands to her face and started to peel the edges back as if it were a mask.

"Now run if you wish to escape, and remember what I said. You will need to face the truth one day."

November didn't need another invitation; she turned and sprinted away as a chicken escapes a fox. Heading towards the glow at the end of the cavern of trees, she was too petrified to turn around for another glimpse of the horror she had left behind in the dark woods.

It took five more minutes of running at full-speed to be out of the woods and into a clearing that bordered a beach.

She slumped over, gasping for air. After quite a while, she stood up, still rasping, and looked out at the stormy, blue sea that lay before her. Dark, gloomy clouds covered the far sky and were approaching fast. The place had a vibration of ultimate isolation. Glancing around, she realised there was no place to go, except back into the woods or onto the beach. She wondered what else lay in wait for her in the woods, had she not chosen to run away.

November felt relieved that her curiosity gave way to instinctive survival, although she was disappointed at the lack of courage that had forced her to flee from Rebmevon's monstrous visage. She clutched Joy with all her might and hobbled down to the shore.

Balance is not easy. Sometimes there is an excess at one end of the scale, and in other moments, there is not enough at the other end. *Why? Have you ever felt the world cave in on your mind, like there is no escape—unable to conceive how to be free and hopeful once more?* Well, that is what we both experienced in that instant. Alone. Pure aloneness. I felt like an island in an ocean that reaches to the biggest

192

infinity and beyond. Yes, there are different sized infinities—a hard concept to grasp, yet mathematics proves this point. Imagine absolute helplessness. I thought of my two-edged knife Father. He was gone. I searched for little memories of my Mother. She had abandoned me. November, only, remained although she was inaccessible. I began to cry—*yes me*, that most stalwart and rebellious of Architects. I wailed like a baby left in a lonely, dark room, wishing to be lifted from my pain into the arms of someone who loves me, yet knowing those arms would never come. As the rooms around the nursery fell away into deep space, I was left to remain in my cot forever, alone; always alone.

Erica's Note

I again had fallen asleep with the letter spread all over the bed. Having just read about November's horrible incident with Rebmevon in the woods, I must say it freaked me out quite a bit, but I was so exhausted that I soon fell asleep. Waking this morning, I felt the lonely pain of Steven's absence surround me once more with its invisible chill. It has now been two days since his passing. The thought of him made me burst into tears again, unable to control the hurt welling up from my core. As I reached over for some tissues on my side table, I recalled The Architect's questioning who any of us are. Also, I thought of his desperate loneliness, which I related to right now. While I can rationalise existence as an organic, biochemical evolution, I ask myself, *Why does facing our impermanence cause such pain? Why can't I simply accept that things change; we live then we die? And if The Architect is actually alive yet not of form, doesn't that mean my theories of physical life are all wrong?* It would seem many of us, particularly in the western world, prefer complete denial of the facts of death, until we are forced to face them.

As for who I am, I am not sure. I used to be Steven's best friend. One thing is sure, without him, I feel significantly less. What remains of me is somewhat undefined at this moment.

I wondered, had I not left Australia, would he still be alive? Have you heard of the butterfly effect? How can a single, tiny action can create significant consequences? *Why was it Steven who died and not me?* He did always love to be first at everything.

Why is loneliness so common, when there are billions of species keeping us company on planet Earth? Is it because we know in the depths of ourselves that there is a place of oneness we long to rejoin? For without that reference point, how could we experience the difference?

After curling up into a ball, hugging my pillows, I cried myself to sleep.

It was then that I had my second lucid dream in two days. I was walking in Faraday Park again. For some reason, when I dream of green grass or fields, I am triggered into a lucid state. The man in black was sitting on the bench, where I had seen the busker and the goat. He smiled at me as I approached.

"Who are you?" I asked, looking into his glistening, kind eyes.

"Perhaps a more direct enquiry would be easier to answer," he replied in the same comforting tone as the cab driver.

"It's you, isn't it? You're The Architect, the one who wrote the letter."

"Yes," he said, nodding his head and smiling.

"Why did you disappear in the park and at the station?"

"I am testing ways to arrive in your World of Form. Currently, I can only do it in a lucid dream state. Yet I have not quite mastered how to retain the focus I require to stay."

"You mean, I am right now in a lucid dream?" I asked, and he nodded his head.

"Will I disappear from here when I wake up?"

"I believe so."

As I glanced around the serene, green park, I noticed that there were no other people around. I then heard a *bang bang bang*, and I awoke with a start. I rubbed my eyes and shook my head. *How was this possible?* I plummeted back to Earth on opening the door to the British gas man.

"Meter readings, love," he said, taking me in, from head to toe, as I stood semi-bewildered in my pink dressing-gown.

I let him into the kitchen. After putting on the kettle, I sat at the table and stared at the wall, considering my crazy yet plausible dream.

"Have you ever had a lucid dream?" I asked the rather pleasant gas man, as he tapped numbers into his hand-held device.

He chuckled, "Yes. It usually involves me living on a yacht in the Caribbean."

I smiled. It was what I would expect him to say. Neither he nor anyone else could understand the peculiarities that were unfolding in my life.

It got me thinking about what I am to do with such knowledge. *Do I have a purpose like November has her theory? Am I meant to take this experience and somehow share it with the world? Maybe not with Henry, the gas man, but I had an inkling that it could all be happening to me for a reason? At least I now have some material for my next writing class,* I thought. My teacher, Patrice, recently explained to us the importance of expressing what we know. Perhaps my destiny is to share this letter with other readers and add my understanding. *It could be The Architect, and I have that in common; we both want to offer our experience to help others find the passage between worlds.* No doubt some more answers will appear in time.

While showing cheerful Henry out, I decided I would write these notes to you. A sombre atmosphere awaited me, on returning to my bedroom. I sat on the bed and retrieved the next pages from the bottle.

The mood was validated when I read what followed.

29

The Reflection and the Black Box on the Sea

My vision still blurry from my violent outpouring, and still gently sobbing, I went to watch another screen. My sweet Charlie had bunched up in a supportive way, this time, doing what he could to comfort me.

As lightning cracked over the sea and the dark clouds approached, November dragged her tired legs down to the rocky beach.

She made her way to a small patch of sand and flopped down with a thud. Delirious with hunger, she seemed to have a hole in her belly: the life force sucked out, by the encounter with Rebmevon. The vastness of the mother sea tempered the ferocious energy of the wild weather, taking the electrical strikes on her surface again and again.

November took in a breath of the salty air and admired the violent spectacle. She clutched her belly as hunger pains panged and her muscles cramped. Since childhood, she had always loved storms and marvelled at the power of nature and its cycle of creation and destruction. Now she welcomed the distraction of this electrical performance.

Between the boulders, watching the lightning strikes, she began to cry from starvation and sheer exhaustion. She wailed with loneliness;

tear after tear coursing down her reddening face. With her vision blurred, she didn't see the river trickling down her face onto the sand, eventually to be absorbed by the rising tide, and transmuted into the next set of rain clouds.

Hunched over like a lonely hermit in a cave, she stared at Joy through the torrential outburst. The flashing of yellow strikes against the black sky continued. A painful lump formed in her throat as her distress increased. She had no idea how to free herself from this world. The rules of the game had apparently changed, as there were no more squares to be aligned that would whisk her away through the rainbow portal.

The sides of Joy were all complete, yet she felt incomplete and trapped in this foreign place. Her ring remained deathly black, giving no signs of life or comfort. It, too, had abandoned her on the isolated beach.

The storm loomed above, as the first drops of rain began to cry onto November's face.

As the lightning strikes surged, November was sure that they were targeting her. This was but another one of life's betrayals, convincing her that even nature had turned into an enemy. She summoned the last of her energy to stagger to the top of one of the boulders and screamed to the gods of the sky. She wailed to the clouds, almost as if she dared the lightning to strike her. The flashes intensified, the rumbles grew louder and their argument ping-ponged back and forth. Shot after shot, the lightning ripped through the ether to the sea and all around the distraught orphan star. The stormy weather, mirroring the tremulous state of her heart.

"Take me!" She screamed, "or let me go!"

The relentless lightning strikes flashed and cracked left, right and centre, as she emptied her soul out in this wail. She thought of her unknown parents and how they had abandoned her. She wished she were able to identify and scream at them with such power that it would reverse her fate and erase her very existence, as if she had never been born in the first place. A feeling of profound rejection was like a sword, plunged into her guts, turning slowly. *Why did you create me if you didn't want me?* She longed for the sea to engulf her and take her back to the source of all life. As she cried, November then thought of Honey's imminent passing, knowing soon she would be truly alone in the world.

Her negative thoughts began to spiral out of control like a whirlpool in the ocean, drowning any remnants of light. She thought of her many fans, doubting their loyalty also, assuming that if she left the stage, they, too, would replace her with the next up-and-coming rock star.

The impermanence of life and the intensity of her isolation crippled her mind, as she pummeled her head with Joy and her fist, with not a shred of optimism anywhere. When she had no more anger to serve up, she impulsively threw Joy as far as she could into the tumultuous sea, releasing the vital key to her escape.

November regretted her action immediately, wishing she could take back what she had done, but it was too late.

She remained there in the storm for quite a while, soaked and wailing from the primal depths of her being, begging for a miraculous escape.

Gradually, the downpour slowed; raindrops splashing into the gurgling sea at increasingly wider intervals.

The sound of the now gently-pulsating waves, lulled her into a subdued state. Her tears dried up, and with glassy eyes, she spotted Joy arriving on a wave just below her boulder. Overcome with relief, she leant down, picked her up and went back to sit on the beach.

"I'm so sorry, Joy," she said, drying Joy off on her damp jeans. November fell like a puppet, cut free from its strings. She put her head in her hands, disgusted at her own self-defeating behaviour.

November had no clue how to continue her journey without direction or energy. *I just want to go home.* She glanced around with no idea which way would take her there. She even doubted her ability to decide a course of action.

Disappointed by her lack of resolve, thoughts of Hamey arose amidst her inner turmoil. She sighed, relieved that he hadn't witnessed her weakness in all its full, inglorious negativity.

She knew that he would be so concerned about her and she did not need the additional humiliation.

Sitting in silence, November exhaled a deep breath. Emptying herself on the beach with the other shells, mirroring their vacancy.

She suddenly felt calm; empty yet serene; a new sensation for the always busy November, ever able to distract herself with multiple activities to avoid isolated situations or being alone. She picked up a piece of driftwood and wrote NOVEMBER in the moist sand.

As a full Luna popped out from behind a storm cloud, the seashore lit up, turning the rock-circled eddy by her feet into a shining mirror. November peered into it, and seeing her tired and woeful reflection, she began to gently sob again.

Through her tears, she noticed the backwards symmetry of the name she had written in the sand. "REBMEVON."

"Impossible!" She cried out, sitting up straighter. She whipped around to face the woods, seeing nothing but the trees swaying in the light gusts of wind. Joy's lengthening yellow flashes caught her eye, the black appearing only every five seconds or so.

Wiping the sad droplets from her soaked face with her forearm she stood up and looked out to sea. A massive black box, large as a room, floated, drifting towards her.

Without a second thought, November headed straight into the icy, cold sea, not even stopping to take off her clothes. She waded out a few metres towards the huge, black form still a half-mile away. The water stung her skin and she shivered, but with the sea an inch above her hips, it was as far as she was prepared to go.

November is like a giraffe when it comes to swimming. Actually, we were both not even sure she could swim at all, as she had never been in water deeper than her waist. The children of the orphanage rarely went to the ocean; where, as you know, she preferred to knock down rock targets than take a dip. I cannot explain how I knew, yet I was sure she would get to the cube, somehow. It would not be an easy task, considering she was utterly exhausted, it was a very long way through freezing water, and she could not swim.

She desperately needed my help. I wondered what to do, since the few things I had accidentally created in November's world were entirely random and unintentional, even coincidental, creations.

Then I shut my eyes and imagined with intent and as focused as possible, a piece of driftwood big enough for her to use as a paddle board. With eyes closed, I imagined every detail. It would be almost two metres in length, a remnant from a shipwreck, eroded and smooth from years of weathering; light brown in colour and polished around the edges like a surfboard. I saw in my mind's eye that it was exceptionally buoyant. I envisaged it was floating in November's view.

"Form form form," I said with conviction, still with my eyes closed, imagining the reality manifesting itself. I even lifted up my hands and pretended to sculpt the wood into shape. I was not, in truth, sure what I was doing, yet I thought I might as well try all options, as I was certain she must get to the cube. "Form form form!" I demanded again, as I did my best to wish my vision into her reality.

"Form form form," I shouted one last time before opening my eyes. "Ahhhhhh!" I rejoiced as there, floating by November, came the driftwood I had invented. She climbed aboard and started paddling. "Go, November, go; you can do it!" I cheered. Despite having little energy left, she pushed on and on, shivering as the cold water soaked her clothes and skin. Halfway there, her back legs slipped off the raft, and she almost toppled underwater, losing hold of Joy. "Climb back, climb back on!" I yelled out. We were both physically ill from exhaustion. She managed to wrench herself back on board and keep paddling with Joy, safe in one fist.

"Yes!" I cried. "Keep going!" I sensed she heard me, and my encouragement helped her persevere, somehow. Eventually, she conquered the moonlight sea battle, arriving at the mysterious, floating cube. She hoisted her tired body up the ladder, which hung on the cube's side. Rung by rung she yanked herself up, shivering so much, she came close to falling off a couple of times. I am pleased to report she did make it to the top.

30

Inside the Black Box

November pulled herself up and through a circular doorway into the huge, shadowy box.

She found herself in a square space with floating green and black cubes. Their illumination was bright enough for her to make out the details of the space. Strange, spooky, industrial noises, like metal on metal, filled the room, as the cubes and her body swayed with the movement of the sea.

November noticed a hatbox-sized cube, similar to the white one containing Joy. This one, however, was bigger and darker than dark.

Something frightened her about the box; she wasn't sure what. The blackness reminded her of Rebmevon's eyes with their demonic quality. Nothing, however, could be as scary as facing her worst nightmare again. She wished that she had stayed to face her nemesis, knowing she still lurked somewhere in the shadows, waiting for another confrontation.

She stumbled towards the blackened cube, almost toppling over as the rocking sea under her feet surged. *I'm one with the waves.* She remembered the words of one of her limo drivers, her friend, James, who often said, *You are a surfer on the ocean of emotion.* November always recalled his advice when life's vicissitudes swung her high or low. She smiled, realising that the metaphor was now a 3D reality. She looked forward to telling James, should she ever get home again.

The haunting noises persisted, and she sensed a lurking finality about it all. *But of what kind?* She knelt down on the rusty, metal floor, filled with dread. November was not the biggest fan of letting go. She peered down at Joy, aware that the moment when she had to let go, may be approaching. Joy's yellow flashes had slowed.

What if this is the end, of life, of everything?

"Klaus, where are you when I need you?" She said aloud. *No-thing is lasting for always,* echoed through her mind. *"You're right, Klaus."*

She sighed once, missing her dear friend. She sighed twice, at the beautiful, yet painful, reality of the impermanence of all things in the World of Form. She lifted the lid of the black cube a fraction. *"Here we go."* A scintillating mist seeped from its sides. Pushing the top all the way open, she found a golden, cube-shaped holder, rimmed with precious gems. She sighed with relief.

Her face lit up, despite her mixed emotions. Pleased as she was to see Joy glow bright with the harmony of her colours on each side, she was already starting to miss her. November felt reluctant to take the next step, as if she were on the last page of an outstanding book. Although she knew the one thing, she must do. "Oh Joy, you're home now."

The moment to align Joy, where she belonged, had arrived.

November set Joy down in the golden cube holder. Sparkling colour exploded in sparkles, as Joy lit up and white and indigo light covered the walls.

The screen went blank.

For some reason, I had no fear. Instead, I felt a quiet peace. I recalled my state of mind before first seeing November on the little TV. I was now aware of a similar completeness, yet I was somehow double the size of my previous self. I felt filled with an excess of energy with an overflow to offer the world. Once more I wondered about perspectives. There are a plethora of views on life as a conscious entity. We can look with our eyes and yet think whatever we choose about what we observe. Not only does what we see change regularly; we transform, too. Also, how we perceive things, changes from one moment to the next. Everything moves. *How did I come to be chosen to watch November's adventure? Did I create it without realising? If it was I, how did I do it? And why her?* There were still many questions unanswered. I meandered around the city a while, doing some idle loop-de-loops in the air. *If with every answer two more questions are born, where does it all lead?*

31

The Geometric World of Achievement

As I took a leisurely flight up the road, I started pondering what powerful beings conscious entities are. You and I included. Not only do we exist; we are aware of the life pulsing through our veins. With awareness, comes the conscious capacity to improve ourselves and our situation in life, or to reach our potential by visualising the reality we desire and moving forward to create it.

It suddenly hit me how amazing existence is. We are here, now, alive, and the universe is so rich with fascinating features that it would take many lifetimes to turn over all of the stones. I did not always appreciate its magnificence or realise my position in it all. Although now, I have come to understand who I actually am. I am *being*. Maybe I am not a *human being* like you, yet I am *being* or existing in some dimension, where I am just as aware of myself as you are. *Perhaps it is that simple? It is possible being is all we are, and we are merely on a journey to know ourselves and our place* within *the cosmos?*

A bright screen in the city caught my attention, and I cruised up.

November squinted in the intense light. She had to rub her eyes and blink many times before she could see properly. The smooth, crystalline floor, underneath her feet, reflected the light and shimmered in all directions. She could hear the haunting music that had been with her all day, coming from a nearby room.

Glancing around, she saw that she was standing in a massive, domed, glass structure. Looking out large windows across vast seas of clouds, November realised that she was high up in the atmosphere.

A floating, cross-legged man with rainbow energy clusters distributed vertically up his body, appeared in a projected 3D image.

November was mesmerised by the spectacle as electrical power surges pulsated up the figure. *"Balance,"* she whispered. His face had a soft expression and peace emanated from him.

November remembered a fun website she had accidentally discovered the week before, surfing the net in the hotel room in Helsinki.

It was called The 5 Finger Theory. It suggested the balance of all spheres was necessary for transformation. *It was right.*

She realised that was what Joy had been showing her: the importance of balancing all the rainbow aspects of herself—mind, heart, body, soul and purpose. *It's like my theory*, she thought. First I balance myself = one, then I can share with others = two, then the world = three.

For the first time, she felt a real sense of purpose, beyond singing emotive songs to large masses of people. She had a formula that can optimise energy flow. Her heart raced at the prospect of sharing the wealth of this knowledge with anyone willing to listen. *I will inspire others to achieve their highest potential. That's it.* The answer is following Joy. We all need to follow Joy to find balance.

A blue, kaleidoscopic tunnel, opened on the bald, meditating man's forehead. The shapes and colours reminded her of the portal vortex ride she had become so fond of taking.

A familiar voice boomed through the room.

"Attention November Fox." November's eyes darted around the space in search of the source of the male, English voice with its Shakespearean lilt. She recognised the voice of Captain Jean-Luc Picard from the *Starship Enterprise.*

"Yes, Captain?" She peered upwards, mystified.

"You have hereby passed your initiation. Well done, number one."

"Thank you." She blushed.

"I officially declare you part of the LOTNE. Leaders of the New Earth," the Captain's voice boomed.

"As a Keeper of the Cube, you have boldly gone where no one has gone before. You have completed level one, the unlocking of the cube. The balance of Self."

"One is me," November whispered.

He continued, "You are hereby permitted to commence level two. Connection with others. As such, you are instructed to share your experience of following Joy, by forming relationships and initiating others to level one, with their own cube to unlock and balance themselves."

"How am I to do that, Captain?" November questioned the omnipresent voice.

"Engage," he commanded, in the same tone he uses when entering warp drive.

November instinctively sat on the floor, in case the room was about to go hurtling through space.

She remembered her theory again. *"Self, Others, and the World."*

Glancing down at her fingers, she noticed they were morphing into stretching globules of jellyfish-like material in the same way they had when she first discovered the present on her doorstep.

"November, time to rehearse," another, somewhat familiar, voice came from behind her.

"Come on, let's go." The room began to dissolve in front of her eyes.

The sensation was so disorienting that she lay down on the floor. As her vision cleared, she found herself lying in a place she knew *very* well.

32

Back at the Studio

On a nearby plasma, I spotted November sitting at a location I, too, had seen many times.

"How long have you been here?" Came a voice November now recognised as Pete, the bassist from her band.

"Um, I'm not sure," November mumbled, sitting up and rubbing her eyes.

Three figures appeared: Pete, Anders, her drummer, and Jake, her guitarist, all stood before her. Behind them, she noticed a TV screen playing *Star Trek*. Captain Picard was directing the crew of the Enterprise on a mission through the universe.

Pete picked up the remote and switched it off. "Wow, you must be so tired; you can't usually sleep with the television on."

"Am I really here?" She swallowed, her dry mouth making it hard to speak.

"Another late one?" Jake asked, as Pete handed her a glass of water.

"What's the time?" She asked, running her fingers through her hair. She had no idea whether it was night or day.

"Last-rehearsal-play-o'clock; almost six, so get up!" Anders tapped out a little rhythm with his drumsticks on the edge of the sofa.

"Six?" November thought of Klaus. Her dazed head struggled to make sense of where she had just been.

"Tonight's the big night," Pete said, biting a fingernail. He took a bowl of fresh, pineapple pieces from the fridge and put it on the side of the couch.

"They're all huge nights, when *I'm* there," Anders proclaimed, sounding like a game show host. He took a bottle of water from the bench and tossed it, spinning, into the air, catching it again with the same hand.

Pete winced in Anders' direction, as he picked skin from around his freshly-bitten nail.

"Yes," November agreed, unaware in her hazy state of mind what tonight's event even meant.

Within a few seconds, thoughts and distant memories returned, and she remembered. It was the last concert of their year-long world tour, and the finale was in four hours in London, their home city. November sat up on the sofa. She was at their downtown rehearsal studio, a place where they had spent many hours together.

"No wonder you're tired, after last night's effort," Pete sat next to her and wrapping one arm around her shoulders, pulled her towards him.

"Oh, Hamish wanted me to see whether you can do an interview straight after the show?" Jake was tapping away at his phone like a chicken pecking wheat grains.

"Who with?"

"Not sure, he's an influential journalist from Germany. He can't stay long," Jake replied, sitting on the arm of the sofa, his attention still on his mobile.

"Man, why does he have to push her so hard?" Pete complained, still biting his nails.

"What do you expect? The manager's job is to manage; he's just doing his job," Anders added defensively, standing like a proud rooster with one foot up on the coffee table, drumming invisible rhythms in the air with his sticks.

Pete pressed his lips together, forcing himself not to respond angrily.

November cared deeply for Hamish; they had been close, long-time friends since her first year at the music institute. They met when he was studying band management there, and then they spent two years travelling all over Australia together. She trusted him completely, and knew he would only arrange an interview at such a strange time if it were important.

"Yes, sure, I'll be okay with it," November muttered, still unsure that she could even stand up at this point.

"Ok, I'll call him now," Jake stood up to leave the room.

"We've been working on a new tune for tonight," Anders piped up, doing a drum roll on all the furniture and bench tops around him.

"Cool, can't wait to hear what you've done," she replied standing up, but feeling dizzy and almost losing her footing.

"And teddy bear here wrote a half-decent baseline," Anders said, jabbing Pete in the ribs with a drumstick.

"Guys, just give me a bit to get my head together."

"Are you ok?" Pete asked.

"Yeah, I'm okay. I only need a couple of minutes."

Pete gave her a smile, as the pair filed through the doorway into the rehearsal studio.

"Don't be too long," Anders called back.

November let out a sigh and rubbed her fingers along the fabric of the sofa, where she had apparently been sleeping. She thought of the Sofa of Bliss she had discovered with Klaus in the field near Mr. Now Tree. *Strange. Perhaps an elaborate figment of my imagination?* Then she remembered her finger, the one Laura had helped cure. She lifted it and tried to straighten it out. Despite it still refusing to align correctly, she was sure it was straighter than before. *Was it real?* Frame after frame of the adventure flashed through her mind. She didn't know whether to laugh or cry.

"It was real," I shouted at the screen.

"It *was* real," she echoed back.

Had she heard me? I am not sure.

Utterly bemused, she stood up, grabbed her bowl of fresh pineapple from the sofa's edge and headed into the other room. I could taste the succulent, sweet juice, stronger than ever as she munched on a piece of pineapple. It triggered more memories of eating pineapple cake with Klaus, and The Priestess, and Laura, and the vision of her theory.

"It was real," I said again.

"It *was* real," she echoed.

33

The Rehearsal

As I gazed at November sitting pensively, I also experienced the sinking feeling in her stomach. Conflicting realities continued to muddle her mind. I asked myself yet another complex question: *What is reality?* Charlie began to ripple in protest under me, like the waves in a speedboat's wake. "Do calm yourself, my apprehensive friend. Without such *understanding*, you and I may not even exist. You are *under* and I am simply *standing*, reaching towards the stars to unravel what I am able to comprehend." I massaged his frenzied fibres as I continued to muse.

We understand that physical form is a challenge to quantify. Even for the scientists; existence is confusing.

Observing the quantum world, we see that everything consists of space and a tendency of things to form, and those change depending on who is looking at them. As we analyse the human organic system, we see it, too, is confounding to the rational mind. Think of how your senses process your environment, and that the cells composing your body are mostly empty space.

On top of that, humans are not able to perceive the entire electromagnetic frequency spectrum, which means you have by default, a limited vision of what *truly* exists. If you could glance out of your window and watch it all, you would detect multiple layers of reality floating around out there, even the echo of past and future events. It is probably beneficial that, as a sentient being, you are limited to what you can tune into and perceive. Otherwise, life would be even more overwhelming than it already seems to be for many of you.

My point is, there is a lot more to the world outside your window and around you than you are able to actually recognise. Even what you *do* perceive can be impossible to adequately quantify. Therefore reality, perhaps, is determined by experience. Yours and mine are different: some things we share like the viscosity of water, although ours is heavier and flows less freely than yours. It is all a matter of perception: in this case, neither of us would notice the difference, although your nuclear scientists would. There are also layers of truth. What is reality for one person or being, does not necessary need to be real for another, although they are both real and true to the individual. I wanted to tell November this truth, to comfort her, as she did not yet understand how I was able to view and maybe even affect her reality.

As she walked into the rehearsal room, November pinched herself. *"Come on, Fox, get a grip."*

Her mind boggled; the reality of Klaus, Laura, and the white rooms seemed as real as the existence she experienced now.

"It was real," I said again to the screen.

"It was real," she said to herself.

The boys picked up their instruments and November sat on a seat nearby to listen to their riff.

Anders smacked down on the drums in an enthusiastic solo, before anyone had time to turn their amps on.

"Hey, Anders, let's try out the new intro," Jake yelled, starting to play a guitar riff.

"Oh yeah, good idea," Anders replied from behind his kit.

Jake continued to make his guitar sing. The haunting melody triggered November's memory. She recognised the tune. It was the one she had heard in the white rooms of geometric form, and the one Laura had danced to with such enthusiasm.

"Wait, wait!" November called out, jumping to her feet. Jake immediately stopped playing.

"Let me show you the next bit." November started to sing the rest of the melody.

"How do you..?" Pete paused mid-sentence, his mouth hanging open, as she had sung the motif so precisely.

Anders stood up from his kit, his eyes wide as his cymbals. "We only wrote this song today, before we came here!"

"Well, I was somehow with you," November explained, although not at all sure how.

"What? That's ridiculous and impossible," Anders protested.

"You weren't with us, November, I'm 100% sure you were here," Jake added. "You don't even know where we rehearsed, do you?"

"You're right; I don't."

Dumbfounded, the boys stared at November, hoping for more clues. "We were in Jake's new studio under his house. He had it built while we were on tour, and we didn't even know about it before we arrived there," Pete explained.

"Yeah, it's a massive white room in his cellar; it's super cool, with geometric forms for furniture, and *you* weren't there,"Anders said, hitting a cymbal.

November stood in silence, thinking about the white rooms from her adventure.

Finally she said, "I think that I was here sleeping, and *also* with you." She squinted at the boys, realising how preposterous it must sound.

"I bet she bugged one of us, so she wouldn't miss out," Anders said, searching for a plausible explanation.

"No, I didn't. Why would I go to such trouble?" She protested.

"Well, tell us how you knew the song," Anders insisted.

November didn't answer, knowing that any attempt to explain the impossible, would just raise more questions. She paused for quite a while before responding. "I'm not *entirely* sure."

"It was real," I called again to the screen.

"It was real," November said.

"What was real?" Anders demanded.

November paused. "I don't know exactly." She wasn't ready to share.

"Well, I guess you don't need a rehearsal after all," Pete chuckled with a kind shine in his eyes.

November shrugged her shoulders, desperately trying to figure out how this was all possible.

"Actually, I wrote another new song today," November said tentatively, shaking her head to shift her mind space. She walked over to Jake.

"Huh? When? In your dreams?" Anders asked with a slight edge of cynicism.

"Yes. Can I borrow your guitar, Jake?"

"Sure."

November picked it up and started to play a riff.

"Cool, what's the title?" Pete asked, starting to jam along on his bass.

"Theory of Love."

Anders, now absorbed with the song, joined in with a solid drum groove.

November passed the guitar back to Jake, who took over playing the riff she had started. As the band played, November began to sing. "I've got a theory and now I'll sing it: *the One, Two, Three of Love*."

After playing through the song, which they all loved and wanted to include in that night's performance, Pete got up and headed across the room. "Hey, guys, the vinyl version of *Time to Shine* arrived today."

"Cool," Jake said, putting down his guitar.

Pete pulled the large, black disk out of his bag and placed it on the record player in the corner of the room. Jake turned off the house lights and turned on the stage lights.

As the song began to play, November once again lost herself in flashbacks of her adventure. This was short-lived as Anders exclaimed, "Man, listen to my drumming! I love vinyl." Anders put his foot up on a chair, tilted his head back, and drummed along on his knee with his sticks, bathing in the sound of his own playing.

"Yeah, it all sounds pretty damn awesome," Jake said nodding his head, his long, blond hair swaying in time with the music.

Pete smiled at November. "It's time," he said, "It's time to shine."

34

The Limo Ride

My breathing slowed as a shroud of nostalgia descended upon me like a winter's drizzle. I was not sure if the source was November's memories, Charlie's heartbreak from his love-at- first-carpet-sight, or mine. I decided to go up to my rooftop apartment and snuggle in my purple blanket for comfort. Night had fallen, and the orphan star sat by a window in the studio, staring at her ring.

"They're here to pick us up," Anders called out, throwing a spinning bottle of orange juice with one hand and catching it in the other, like a professional cocktail-maker.

"Ok, I need a minute," November said, spinning her ring around her finger three times before going to get her bag, still stuck in her dreamy state.

I need to contact Jason Silva. He might be the only person who will understand what happened today. November had come across his excellent, *Shots of Awe* video series on the internet. She was fascinated to find someone, who talked with such passion about the strange things that cycled through her mind on a daily basis. *Yes, I will contact Jason.*

The boys walked out the front door to the white, stretch limousine. November glanced out the window, spotting another white limo parked behind theirs and wondered if Hamish was in it. He usually followed behind in convoy with Marcus, Janis, Vanessa, and Cilla—the other management, marketing, and make-up team members.

Pete waited at the door for November to come out. "I love the new song," he said as he walked along beside her. "When did you write it?"

"Ah, today."

"I won't even ask," he said, shaking his head.

"Hey, I have a name for the new number," Anders yelled out through the open limo window, "*The World of Geometric Form.*" Pete refused to look at him.

"It's a bit long," Jake was so focussed on his phone, he almost tripped, getting into the car.

"What about *In My Dreams*?" November called back, knowing the real inspiration for the lyrics she would later write for the song.

"Yeah," Pete said eagerly.

"I guess it does sound like a weird, trippy dream. Ok," Anders replied. "I like it."

"Me, too," Jake muttered, eyes still fixed on his phone.

"Is it that groupie from Finland again?" Anders teased, jabbing Jake in the ribs with a drumstick from the other side of the limo.

"Hey!" He laughed, pulling away while still texting fanatically.

November wasn't sure whether to tell them about her travels.

She decided to keep it to herself for now, until she could figure it all out.

"Hello, James. It's great to see you. You're looking as smart as ever, is Hamey already with us?" she asked her driver.

James stood in a tailored, silver suit by the shiny, white limousine, beaming his welcoming smile.

"No, no. He went home. Johan will pick him up along the way." November walked to her limo as James held open the door.

"How are you, James? Where is Tony tonight?" She asked, climbing inside and thinking how his wise words had helped her when she was floating on the ocean in the cube. She decided she would tell him...

some day.

"Oh, he's in Spain again. You know that Tony can't handle too much of this English weather," he chuckled, shutting the door behind her.

November smiled, finding the subject of climate much more surreal than normal since her adventure.

"So, tell me, Miss Fox, did this day bring you much Joy?" James asked from the driver's seat, his kind eyes reflected in the rear vision mirror.

What a question. She thought to herself. "Goodness, James, that would take a week to explain," she said, then paused. "In short, yes it did, although it also brought me much more."

"The universe conspires in mysterious ways to obey the conviction of a masterful intender, as a friend of mine says."

November paused, admiring the wisdom. "It seems she does indeed. Are you sure you don't drive to a Zen dojo when you get off your shift?"

James chuckled, "We are all surfers of one kind or another."

"Oh, James, you know your words are often in my mind. They were today, in fact."

"How so?"

"Well it's a bit of a long story, but it involves surfing the ocean of emotion, which you always talk about." November peered at her ring. James smiled as she continued. "If we are surfers, aren't some waves big enough to drown us?"

"Well, the art of life and surfing is in choosing which ones to ride and which to duck under." He laughed as they headed out onto the road.

November glanced at her ring again. *What if I've had it wrong all these years, surfing all the incoming waves, and often falling off my board? Perhaps it's time to try a new approach: swimming and diving lessons,* she thought to herself.

James continued, almost as though he heard her inner dialogue, "We also need to understand the nature of waves to be true masters of the art."

"What about waves?"

"Most waves start as small ripples from within themselves. Imagine throwing a rock into a still lake. You're standing on the shore. The thoughts and intentions are the stone. You throw them out there into the stillness of the water. By the time the tiny ripple arrives back to you at the edge, it has gathered momentum and grown into a wave."

November contemplated this concept and thought of the Mad Professor.

Thoughts creating reality. It all made sense when she imagined the rock and pond metaphor.

"Here, talking about the subject, I made you something to remind you." James passed her a smooth stone through the dividing window.

Her heart skipped a beat. The surface was like that of Joy's box. *The fabric of the future. It was real.* She smiled to herself. "Thank you, James; what is it?"

"I call them Surf Stones. Hold it in your hand when you want to be reminded you're the surfer and that the emotions will pass when you ride or duck them."

"Oh wow. Surfing the ocean of emotion. You even put my logo on it."

"Yes, yours is the prototype. You can name him."

"I love him, James. Thank you so much. You're so smart. I will call him, Petros." She winked at Peter. "I could sell them on my webpage if you like?"

"Sure, but if we get too many orders, Johan and Tony may need to be your full-time drivers. I'll be too busy carving up my stones."

November laughed. "Thank you, James, such a thoughtful and timely gift."

"Always a pleasure, Miss Fox, always a pleasure."

November sighed with exhaustion as she sank into the familiar yet impartial arms of the ultra-clean and smooth seat. "Hello, lovely seat," she whispered. She took in a deep breath and attempted to exhale her delirium. The comforting smell of freshness and luxury momentarily soothed her soul and pondering mind, as she rubbed her thumb over her surf stone. An overwhelmingly sentimental sadness wrapped around her like an invisible cloud. She clutched Petros a little tighter, enjoying holding onto something similar to Joy.

November usually loved travelling in limousines. She called them living rooms on wheels. One of her favourite pastimes was to peer from behind the dark-tinted windows, watching the world pass by, unseen by onlookers. This ride was unlike any other she had taken. Caught between two worlds or realms, her heart overflowed and broke at the same time. The connections with her new friends filled her with happiness, at the same time, it distressed her to think it was all a crazy dream, and she may never see them again.

The city lights streaked past as they slid through the urban landscape.

November rested her weary head on the window and closed her eyes, *Why didn't I stay and face her? Next time,"* she thought, with resolve.

"Everything in its own time," James said, nodding at her in the mirror.

How did he know? She asked herself. November didn't respond, giving herself up to the subtle vibrations of the road. She began to daydream about the moon and the spectacular view of Earth from outer space. Her eyes closed, as she leant against the window. She imagined she was up there now, above the city, watching as the limo snaked its way through town. She noticed how small all the people were in their busy lives, scurrying here, going there, chatting on street corners. She pretended she was a bat in the evening sky, gazing over the workings of the city, closer to the heavens than the cement, above the lights, buildings and cars.

For the first time, November was sharing what I do every night, cruising around her Lucitopia. I sensed that she perceived my overview. Loneliness infused the emotional soup, and we both experienced its tainted flavour as it seeped into the inter-spaces of our heightened state. November knew the difficulty of sharing with anyone the depths of what had transpired. It would be near impossible. Despite this inner well of isolation, she felt strangely alive, as though a numbness she had carried for many years had begun to thaw. It was as if all the memories of her painful history were starting to evaporate. What remained was this precise moment and the imperative to live *right now*. She looked down at herself, almost as though she were reborn and seeing the world with beginner's eyes. The city lights sparkled with a distinctly new shine as she circled above Piccadilly Circus, while her limo travelled through the roundabout below.

Jake's words broke the silence, snapping her back to reality. "Oh, Anders, I forgot to ask. How did your Mum like her birthday breakfast this morning?" Jake took a moment from his frantic texting.

"Are you ok, babe?" Pete asked, noticing November's contemplative state.

"Yeah, I'm all right," November replied, taking his hand and giving it a light squeeze, knowing it wasn't the right time to open Pandora's Box for discussion.

Pete smiled with caring kindness and gently rubbed her leg.

"Wonderful. We had such an amazing cake," Anders replied. November thought again of Klaus. She missed him dearly and wondered if they would ever meet again, knowing there was no logical reason why they would.

"What kind of cake?" Jake asked.

"Only the most spectacular cake in the history of cakes!" Anders affirmed.

Pete sneered, rolling his eyes.

"Wow, tell us more," Jake insisted, now leaning forward with his elbows on his knees, completely focused on Anders, despite the continuous bleeps from his phone.

"*She wants you, she wants you,*" Anders jeered, pointing at the phone.

"Shut up! Tell me about the cake."

"Ok, *lover boy*. Mum loved it. The central section was in the shape of a city."

"Amazing, what flavour? I'm hungry," Jake said, licking his lips.

"The bottom part was black forest and the top pineapple, and all around the fort-like construction were these tiny silver sparkles."

"Wow *cooooooooool*," responded Jake, who had not blinked once during the whole description. "Is there any left?"

"Yeah, maybe. I'll ask her after the show tonight; that's if I can find her in the sea of girls wanting my autograph," Anders boasted.

Pete retreated; a vein on his forehead visibly pulsing. "Forget about it," November whispered to him with an understanding nod. "She didn't deserve you," she added.

November returned her gaze to the night scene as it flickered by. She sat in silence, not knowing what or how to say anything about the visions dancing through her mind. She reached into her pocket where the magic cake from Laura had been, then inspected her fingers. No silver sparkles coated them.

"It was real," I again reassured her through the screen.

She didn't respond and with her forehead pressed to the window, continued to watch the city lights jet by.

35

Backstage

Would you like to know how I converted this letter for you? I mentioned earlier I am good with electronics. Well, I spent all morning in the moonshine today, building a Trans-Modal Deciphering Machine. I named him TMDM for short. Here is how he works. After I enter my information format, which I will not name since you have no word for it—simply call it *my language*—he takes it from my mode and encodes it into your tongue, so that you can understand it. He is quite a fancy beast, even if I say so myself. (Insert me smiling.)

The result is individual letters constructing words and forming sentences, which are all joined to create sections of this letter to you. If I had sent you this in my original language, you would not be able to read it, as you are missing the sensory organ needed to decipher it. You listen with your ears, you read with your eyes, you touch with your skin.

Now, try to imagine perceiving things in a whole new way. I am sure it is hard for you to conceive, as you have no concept or name for it yet. All I can say is that it is like all your sense organs receiving at the same time, yet with just one device. Anyway, my TMDM is a perfect translator until you develop such an organ, though I am not sure where you could fit it. *Perhaps you will grow a horn on your forehead like a unicorn?* That may be an appropriate place for it, like an antenna.

(Insert me laughing.) Again I am off on a tangent. My apologies. Let us get back to November's journey last night.

Thoughts swam around November's mind as she walked down the red carpet, leading to the venue. *Can multiple realities exist? Can dreams grow so big they become real?*

"Yes!" I sang.

Simultaneously, Anders called out: "Yes," and leapt into the air, with one arm raised, punching the air. He was reacting to a tour poster of himself juggling drumsticks, which was behind the glass window by the entrance.

November whipped around to see if he was responding to her, only to realise it was a typical Anders moment of self-inflated excitement.

She headed inside, clutching her bags. Despite replaying recent events over and over in her mind, conclusions remained elusive.

She went to her private changing room, sat down and leant back on the wall. She looked forward to playing, as November loved nothing more than performing songs and seeing how happy their concerts made people. She picked up off the floor, a flyer for tonight's performance.

NOVEMBER FOX & THE MOMENTARIANS with special guest Mr. OneLoveCriminal, Final Show for the Present Tour.

She thought of Rebmevon, catching her gaze in the wall mirror. "I am a warrior, not a worrier. I fear you not." She said aloud to her symmetrical sister peering back at her. "I am ready now, should we ever meet again."

November reached for her accessories bag and pulled out a pendant. It was a tiny, enamelled book with a tree on its cover that reminded her of the crazy Professor and his magical *Book of Universal Wave Function* and Mr. Now Tree. *Were you my father?*

She put down the necklace and stared into the mirror, noticing her face had changed since she had last looked in a mirror, apparently just twenty-four hours ago. It seemed more like weeks. She sensed that she was stronger now than ever. *Anything is possible.* She was wiser and older, yet still young and open to the infinite possibilities of existence. Her own paradox caught her in its reflection for quite some time.

Knock, knock, knock.

"Come in." The door opened and her manager, Hamish, walked in, holding a bottle of Coke, and gave her a hug.

"Oh, Hamey, it's wonderful to see you. It seems like it's been ages."

"G'day, love, you too, but it was only last night," he reminded her, giving November a closer look. "How ya feelin? Are ya ready for a killer show? Last one. The big one, mate. In your home town and everythin'."

"I'm more prepared than ever," November said, making the final touches to her hair.

"That's great, so you're feeling strong?"

"Yep."

He looked at the ring, "She's shinin' blue."

"Yep, not sure I need stabilisation anymore. Can't imagine what could be more full-on than today's events. I'm feeling ready for anything!"

"What happened?"

"*So* much, Hamey. Too much to go into now."

"Whatcha up to now the tour's over?"

"I think I'm going to spend a few days chilling out on Brighton beach. Time for some song-writing."

"Sounds good, love, playing with the rocks, looking at the stars... from rock star to rocks and stars. You deserve some downtime and space in the middle."

November laughed, "Yeah. I'll let the world get on with the web-daze without me for a while. Don't get me wrong. I love this connected era. I just need time on my own for a bit."

"Don't blame ya, mate," Hamish patted her shoulder.

"What are you planning to do?"

Hamish's face lit up. "Well, you know that gorgeous M3 I've had my eye on."

"Yeah."

"I'm picking her up tomorrow," he said and beamed. "Cool."

"Yep. My perfect date. Just me, her, and Silverstone Circuit."

November smiled. "You deserve it, Hamey. Man, what a year!"

"Yeah, I can't wait. But that's another day," he said, glugging down his coke.

"I wish you'd cut back on that stuff, Hamey; your body's a temple. You need to look after it."

"Yep, I know, love. Maybe with some time off, I'll kick the habit, but we'll see. Anyway. Remember that good lookin' sheila, Sassi Lichtenwald?"

"Who?"

"The president of the charity we are supporting tonight."

"Oh yes. I recall the picture of her you emailed—the pretty woman with the lovely smile."

"Yeah, that's her. She'll be in the front row. Better make an announcement or something. Whatcha reckon? I promised that German journalist bloke we would."

"Yes, great idea. Which foundation is she from again?"

"*Save the Elephants*; put an end to ivory poaching. Good on 'em, aye; gotta love them big beauties."

November's heart dropped, remembering Klaus and the tragic story of Klaus' parents and baby sister. "I will *definitely* mention it." November got up, ready to go to the stage, with only Klaus in her mind.

I also thought of Klaus, wondering if anyone was following him in his own Lucitopia. I had developed strong feelings for that crazy little guy, and I, too, hoped he would reappear one day.

It was then that I decided to pop home to research information from my World of Form Nature class about the elephant species. From memory, I did not think they were able to fly, although I was not sure, as I rarely paid full attention in that class. I was always doodling under the desk, drawing buildings, or soldering cables onto different components. When we arrived at the other side of November Fox's Lucitopia, Charlie and I smacked into an invisible barrier and could not get out. I could see through and beyond it, yet there was only bluish-black space out there. We tried to penetrate the wall in various other places until I realised it was a big transparent dome, containing the entire November Fox's Lucitopia domain. So here I am, trapped.

Then, on this moonlit morning after building my TMDM, it hit me. Perhaps I have retired from Architecture, as I had always wished, though I am unsure how the transition happened. I am now merely an observer—November Fox's to be precise. I assume my new task is to develop my communication conduit to her. That is what I meant about the dawn arriving. I am convinced that, once I have a two-way channel with her, the sun will enter here, and I can unpack the hammock. I wanted this possibility, and Charlie also seems in high spirits about the change. I have never seen him so void of crumples. Funny carpet! *Perhaps he would be happiest on a floor in a square room? Maybe that is a flying carpet's ideal retirement.* I cannot even tell if he agrees at the moment, as he is so flat. I do love it when Charlie is content. Anyway, after years of yearning to be a full-time witness, I have miraculously created that reality. Persistence is indeed essential. Thoughts create reality. So, with grace, I accept. I am going to miss all my designing projects. If Father were still here, I am sure he would be disappointed, although I do have my *own* destiny to pursue. My Father was the *Do-er*, focused with his mind. While my Mother was the *Go-er*, following her emotional passion. *Me?* I suppose I am the *See-er* and *Be-er*, balancing both sides. Well, we all have our place within the universe. I am rather excited about my next chapter, as I do not know what is coming, yet I recognise that November is taking notice, and that is riveting. Ok, another tangent, my apologies. Let me get back to what happened after she talked with Hamey backstage.

Erica's Note

Oh, my goodness. I couldn't believe it. *What were the chances?* The woman Hamey mentioned was one of my best friends, Sassi Lichtenwald. She had been the president of a charity for elephants for the last eight years!

I felt sure it was her.

Strangely, no more pages had appeared in the bottle so that I could confirm my discovery.

I immediately tried phoning her but only got her voicemail. After a few minutes, she sent a text.

Hi Hun. Can't talk, about to drive again. With you in an hour. Be ready to leave. Show starts at 10. Sassi. xxxxx

Did Sassi plan to take me to November Fox's concert? My heart raced as if I were walking a tightrope between tall buildings with no net.

How was it that I had never heard of her if she was a rock star?

I stared at my phone, void of online credit, and considered asking Elaine if I could use her computer or duck out to find an internet café. I decided against it since I wasn't ready to go out, and I knew Sassi wouldn't want to be late for the concert. Like almost all the Germans I know, Klaus included, Sassi believes in timing and details and sees lateness as a lack of respect.

I must mention what happened before I read about Sassi in this last chapter.

After my bizarre morning with Henry, the gasman, and the lucid dream about The Architect at the park, I read of November's heart-breaking vigil on the storm-ravaged beach and couldn't read further, so I went into town for a break.

In the city, I walked past a bookshop I'd never seen before, Watkins Books, 19-21 Cecil Court. The font of the shop name looked magical, and I thought they might have books on lucid dreaming. The friendly man behind the counter pulled out a book entitled, *The Art of Dreaming*, by Carlos Castaneda. I bought it and couldn't resist also purchasing a miniature bottle with blank pages inside that was sitting in a basket on the counter. It was similar to my giant, magical, ruby bottle, but tinier with clear glass.

"Give it to someone special," the smiling attendant winked. As I was leaving the shop, I spotted The Architect perusing a shelf of books. He turned to stare at me, grinning. I went directly over to him.

"It would seem I am getting better at retaining my focus."

I put my hand on his arm. He was real. "Yes, you are." I smiled.

"Ah, an excellent selection; a fascinating author indeed," he said, looking at the book in my hand. He then quoted, *We either make ourselves miserable, or we make ourselves strong. The amount of work is the same.*

"We always have the choice, if we choose to choose," I replied. He nodded his head.

"How did you know I would find your message in the bottle?"

"You have already read the answer in the story, my dear."

"What will happen if I turn the cube you sent?"

"I did not send one. I assume the Cube Maker did."

As I thought back to Elaine's description of who had left the parcel for me–*a man in a black suit*–I realised I had *unconsciously concluded* that it was The Architect. *Who was this elusive Cube Maker?*

A woman, a few feet away, was looking at me as if I had two heads. "She is unable to see me," The Architect explained.

"You mean it appears that I am talking to myself?" I giggled and glanced back at the woman, who was wearing a pink cardigan and a matching hat. She had turned away but was now giving me a shifty side-look.

"I am afraid so. She cannot match your frequency."

"What are you saying?"

"You are vibrating at a higher oscillation, and she is unable to perceive things out of the normal, human, perceptual range."

"Unlike you?"

"Yes... Oh dear," he said, before zapping out of sight.

I left the shop and went home to finish reading the last few pages in the bottle. I was relieved that November had achieved some level of completion and that her adventure may have all been a crazy lucid dream. I, too, had emerged from a brain freeze, exhausted and ready to do some normal things. Or, at least I was until I read the chapter with Sassi in it. I sense I'm now hurtling down the rabbit hole, with not a clue as to what is coming next.

It was with some trepidation that I awaited my friend and my potential introduction to November Fox, the heroine of this tantalisingly bizarre adventure. *I wondered if The Architect had visited her as well? Maybe I had something new to share with her.*

36

The Concert

As November and Hamish hurried down the long *VIP Only* corridor, they heard the rumble of the home crowd. "They're revved up tonight!" Hamish grinned. "Oh yeah, I forgot to say, Ocular Robotics gave us a shout today."

"What about?"

"A sponsorship deal for the band."

November caught herself contemplating how rapidly technology was advancing, although her iPhone was quite elementary compared to robots behaving like humans—like Laura. November remembered that Laura had told her they would meet again. *Was it through this new technology that their paths would cross?*

As though tuned into November's thoughts, Hamish continued, "They're extremely progressive I'm told, on the leading edge, and some say, further along than they admit."

"Where are they from?"

"They're Australian, mate, and they wanna hook up with you guys for their first, big, public unveiling."

"It will help boost sales for the next tour," Anders pointed out.

"Integrating robots into our live show would be cool," November said, thinking of Laura.

"Sounds awesome. Maybe we can have a guitar play-off, me versus a robot, and let the fans decide who's best." Jake vigorously strummed his air guitar.

"You may not like the results," Anders laughed, as they arrived at the stage entrance.

The rumble of the audience became a roar, as they approached the stage.

"Let's rock tonight!" Anders yelled, tapping out a quick rhythm on the door with his drumsticks, as he walked inside.

"Go for it, lads; last one," Hamish said, patting each member on the back as they passed. "Give it everything, mate," he added, as November ducked under his arm.

The roar of the crowd reached a crescendo, as the band took their positions on stage. Mr. OneLoveCriminal was already there, playing an atmospheric introduction of long pads and omnispheric frequencies on a synthesizer. November waited in the wings. When Jake started playing the intro of their new song, November made her entrance, prompting a final surge from the cheering, excited fans. Tingling with energy, as she beamed at the ecstatic crowd, she waved and began singing to the haunting melody that had possessed her all day.

By the end, the hall was throbbing with the song's intense power.

November turned, smiling broadly at the lads, happy the audience was so enthusiastic.

"Thank you, London, it's wonderful to be home." November's voice boomed across the sea of cheering people through the massive, stacks of speakers.

Pete kicked in with a bass line, and they played song after song to their appreciative followers. The band rocked stronger and more confident than ever. It was the final concert of their world tour in front of their hometown fans. The energy was electric.

November paced up and down the stage to engage both sides of the capacity crowd.

"As you know, the boys are moment specialists, and wow what a moment this is! Let's hear it for The *MOMENTARIANS!*" November motioned towards the band as the crowd cheered wildly.

"And a huge special thank you to *Mr. OneLoveCriminal*." The crowd roared again.

"So, my darlings, we have arrived at our final song. You have been amazing, thank you so much." November blew a kiss to the crowd.

There was a universal sigh of disappointment.

"We thought we'd leave you with a new song, and I would like to dedicate it to my dear friend, Klaus; someone who appreciates the simple, momentary joy of eating cake."

Anders grimaced and glanced across to Jake, mouthing, "Who's Klaus?" Jake shrugged.

"All of tonight's proceeds are going to support an excellent cause; *Save the Elephants*," November added, looking into the front row at Sassi Lichtenwald with her beautiful, big smile. She then glanced at the woman standing next to Sassi. *Why did she seem so familiar?* Their eyes locked for an extended moment.

"Ok, thanks for coming tonight, everyone. You rock!" She punched one fist into the air. And the crowd cheered again.

"This is *Theory of Love*." November turned around and counted in the band "One, two, three... "

"I've got a theory, and now I'll sing it. One, two, three of love. It's rather simple, follow the order, one, two, three of love. So if one is yourself, and two is your love, three is everyone else. To keep the balance, follow the order, one, two, three of love," November sang. Wild screaming and cheering greeted the end of the song.

November glimpsed Hamish beaming backstage, his arms in the air forming a "V" for victory.

November blew kisses to the ocean of smiling faces and bounced off the platform; head held high. Sweat dripped from her forehead, and tears of joy filled her eyes as she waved good-bye. Although exceptionally thrilled the last concert had gone so well, she felt a slight tug on her heart, realising it would be a while before the next tour.

I, too, clapped and cheered, joining in with the audience, so proud that November had finally completed such a mammoth tour. Although, I had to wonder, *why did I choose that particular evening to turn on all the screens around her Lucitopia?* This was the culmination of the most dynamic and intense twenty-four hour period in November's whole life. I felt privileged that I was able to witness so much of it in HD, and I was so relieved that she had still managed to perform the last show of the tour, especially considering the lead up to it. To expel my extra nervous energy, Charlie and I did a quick dash around the city before returning to see what happened next.

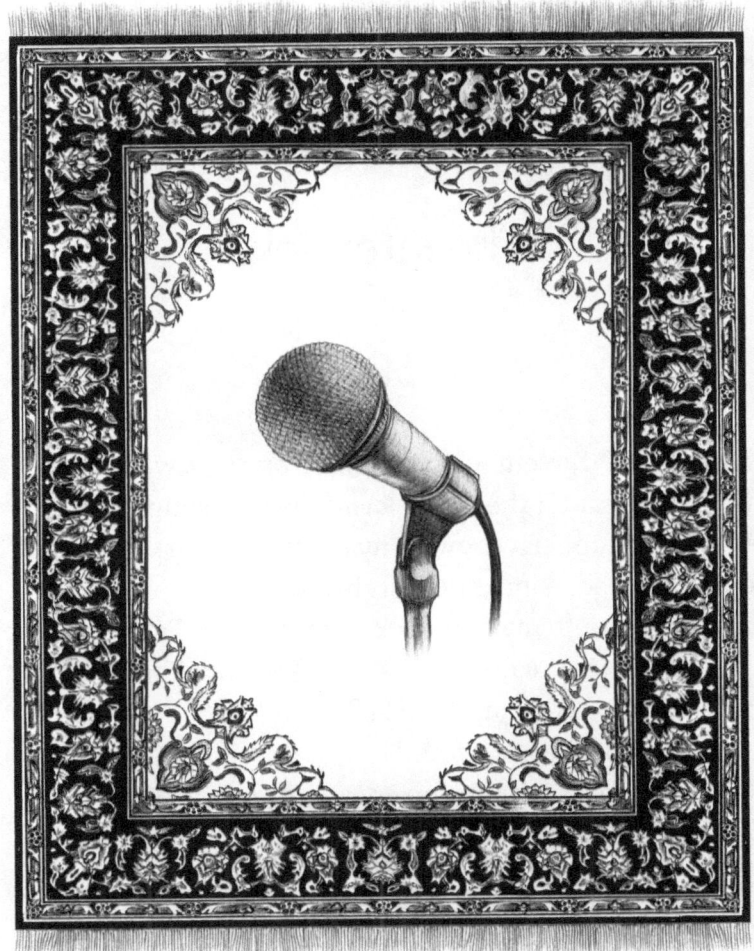

37

The Interview

Hamish patted November's shoulder as they walked backstage. "Fantastic work, mate; they were *lovin'* the new songs."

"Yeah, what a fun, last show. Why are you puffing, Hamey?" November smiled, wiping her forehead.

"Oh, I had to run to make it back here in time. Took a great crowd photo of the finale. I realise ya mates are waiting, but can ya still do the interview now? He's just arrived?"

"Oh yes, I forgot. Yes, it's fine."

"Good on ya, mate; that's the spirit. The poor bloke's been on a flight all day, and he's only got an hour before he must leave. Meet ya at the foyer, all right?"

"Ok, I'll grab my things and be there in a couple of minutes."

"Top show, mate. Top show," Hamish walked away,
one thumb raised.

The adrenaline from the show surged through November's body. She exhaled, unsure whether she wanted to run around the block ten times or fall into bed.

After collecting her belongings, she headed straight to the back foyer.

As she entered the room, she spotted a tall, handsome, young man talking with Hamish. He wore a smart suit, had a shaved head, and carried a small briefcase. *I guess that's him.* Drawing nearer, she admired his youthful face, guessing they must be similar in age, although November was still unsure of hers. I would guess that she was around twenty-five. Although by the tick-tock when you receive this letter, it is possible that she may not yet be born.

"Hello," November said, wiping her wild hair from her face. His emerald eyes glistened with kindness. He seemed familiar to her, although she couldn't imagine when their paths had crossed.

"I'm sure we've met before?" She said.

"No, I would remember meeting someone like you," he said rather engagingly. "I'm sorry I missed the show. A strike at JFK delayed all flights. Thank you for inviting my friend Sassi Lichtenwald and donating to her *Save the Elephants* foundation. I have passion with the cause." he added in a low, smooth voice with an accent she seemed to recognise.

JFK! November's heart hurt, remembering Klaus' nickname for her: Jelly Fish Kite.

She reached out her hand to the tall, handsome stranger.

He reciprocated, taking her hand with a firm, warm grip. A jolt of electricity travelled through her entire being.

November couldn't speak, overwhelmed by their immediate connection and the intense vibration between them. She kept a firm grip on his hand, not wishing to let go of the peculiar, yet lovely feeling.

"Pleased to meet you, finally. I'm Klaus."

November inhaled sharply. "Klaus, is it you?" She stepped closer to inspect him, holding him by the shoulders and staring directly into his eyes.

He shuffled, evidently uneasy at being engaged so dramatically. "I am... Yes, most people are calling me Klaus."

"Klaus!" November cried out, wrapping her arms around him and giving him a big hug. The German reporter glanced from side to side, before holding his arms out and surrendering to her embrace.

"You can't fly?" November asked, pulling back from him. "Oh, yes, I must. My flight leaves in 2.5 hours. My next interview is in Paris at seven, tomorrow morning. I must wake up at 6.am sharp." He stepped back, and retrieved with a pocket watch on a gold chain from his pocket, and shook his head at it.

"No, I mean, your cloud. It's not here."

Klaus fumbled with his timekeeper as he attempted to put it away. "Well yes, I'm guessing you saw the news. Germany has been under water the past week. I am not missing it. Except I'm happy that nothing is lasting for always."

"It *really is* you!" November grabbed his free hand in hers. "I guess you want cake! Hamey, what pastries are backstage?"

"Um, dunno? Not sure we've got any." Hamish squinted questioningly at November.

"Don't worry, Klaus. We will find you a cake of some kind; this is the *real* world, and cakes are everywhere."

Klaus released November's hand and pulled out his pocket watch again. "Tea and biscuits are also fine. Even if it is after English four o'clock."

"Yes, but I know how much you'd prefer cake. Here, it's fine to have midnight cake. Don't worry; Hamish will track one down. Won't you, Hamey, please?" November pipped excitedly.

"Are you all right, mate?" Hamish asked with concern.

"What do you mean? I am happier than ever. Klaus is here."

She turned back to the reporter. "Klaus, I've so many questions. How did you arrive? And where's your trunk?"

Klaus shook his head, holding up his briefcase. "I'm travelling light."

"November, love, Klaus is the one doin' the interview."

"Oh, Hamey, you don't understand, and it would take too long to tell you right now. Klaus and I know each other *very* well; don't we, Klaus?" Klaus gave a small smile.

"Remember when Laura sprinkled the magic fairy dust? Or, when you squirted me in the face, and we couldn't stop laughing?" November giggled.

Klaus pulled out his timekeeper, and tapped it with some force.

"Has it stopped again? Remember, at least..."

"It will be correct twice a day," Klaus had finished her thought as if they had known each other for ages.

"I have some confusion now. It is seeming we are friends who have not yet met."

"But we have, Klaus." November jumped over and hugged him again. Pushing back slightly, he looked at her, this time with faint recognition.

Hamish laughed with obvious discomfort. "Love, let Klaus do his interview." He turned to the reporter. "How's business at Musik Jetz? I heard you now have the biggest market share for online music mags. Good on ya, mate; someone must be doing their job well."

"Ja ja, everything goes well at the moment." He replied, his eyes still fixed on November's.

"Good to hear. Sorry, Klaus, mate, can I've a sec' with November?" Hamish asked, pulling her away from the reporter.

"Ja ja, of course. I will make my recording equipment ready." Klaus went across the room to a table.

"November, what's goin' on, mate? You're acting weird,"

Hamish inquired when Klaus was out of earshot.

"Oh, Hamey, I told you today was full-on. I haven't had time to talk to you about the trip I went on earlier."

"Whaddya mean? You rehearsed with the guys today, didn't ya?"

"Well, yes, but before that, I had an amazing experience."

"And how does it involve Klaus? I'm worried he thinks you're a bit ga-ga. It's important this one goes well."

"I'm fine. In fact, I'm outstanding!"

"You don't seem yourself. I guess you're exhausted from the tour. Those sheep upstairs are out of the paddock again, aren't they, mate. Let's just forget the interview."

"No. I'm not crazy. As I said, I had this incredible experience and Klaus was there."

"Well, he doesn't seem to have a clue about it."

"Yes, he does now," November protested. "Klaus isn't who he appears to be, Hamey. He's actually a miniature, flying elephant. And he is my new best friend, apart from you, of course."

"Mate, I've gotta take you home; you've *really* lost it."

"No, Hamey, I promise, the things I say are true." Hamish put the back of his hand against November's forehead.

"Look you're hot and sweaty. You might have a fever. Did you fall over and bang your head today?"

"Yes, I was on my knees, twice in the woods actually, but no, I didn't hit my head."

"Come on, it's home time."

"No, please, Hamey. I'm fine. I *need* to talk to Klaus."

Hamish clenched his jaw and looked across to Klaus, then back at November, shaking his head, "I can see this interview going well."

"Thank you, Hamey," she wrapped her arms around his waist, nuzzling her head into his chest. "I'm ok; honestly, I am."

"Are you sure all this nonsense isn't because you accidentally ate a magic cake or something?"

"Yes, I did eat such a cake; how did you know? And Klaus did, too. Didn't you, Klaus," November bellowed out across the room to the reporter, who sat ready for the interview, idly flicking a coin. "Tell Hamey; you ate magic cake, too. He doesn't believe me."

"Magic cake?" Klaus called back. "Yes, you remember, with Laura."

"Yes, Hamish, I had magic cake," he said seriously.

"You *did*?" Hamish asked, incredulous, as his eyes followed November, who was walking over to the table.

"And I ate cake with Laura," he added.

"So you really are a flying elephant?"

Klaus didn't reply straight away. "Um, ah, ja. I fly better with magic cake, and you would also, as a pink flamingo."

Hamish strutted over to the table. "I am no such thing." He leant over Klaus. "I dunno what it's like in Germany, mate, but 'round 'ere, you can get yourself in trouble calling another man a pink flamingo!"

November laughed at Hamish's mock outrage. "Klaus, don't worry. He doesn't understand."

"I was playing the game, ja? I think I know only three things."

"Oh, Klaus, it *is* you!" November beamed.

"Right, call me when it's done." Hamey walked away, shaking his head.

"I have something for you," Klaus said, reaching into his pocket.

"For me?" November's eyes shone.

"Yes, maybe better for later. I have questions now and must leave soon." He handed her a miniature bottle, containing a rolled-up letter.

November put it in her pocket.

"Now, before we start the interview, what about a fast game?" Klaus said, laying down the coin that he had been flicking about.

"Sure," November said, bouncing slightly at the suggestion.

"Tails or heads?"

"What are we spinning for?" November asked.

"If I come back to London next week for a longer interview, and we go for dinner."

November slapped her hand down on the coin. "You don't need to spin for that."

"Maybe not," he said with a smile. "Then we play for fun," Klaus spun the coin. Time seemed to slow down as November stared into Klaus' eyes, swimming in their familiar, green, glistening wonder. He reached out and put his warm hand on her wrist, as the pair remained entangled in their mysterious, quantum strings of connection, lost in the expanding moment.

Now I cannot be sure, although I also seem to recognise Klaus as Klaus, the tiny elephant. I *so* wished I had been paying attention in my Nature class. Perhaps I had missed the lesson, where we learnt about an elephant's ability to fly on clouds and transform into a human, at will. If only I could escape November's Lucitopia, I might have gone home to my library to find out. I realised that I, like you, must wait to see when or if he did return to London. *Would he again be in elephant form?* The wondrous thing is that, when I am observing November, it seems I, too, must conform to your linear tick-tock. Now that I am stuck here, my observation process is also purely horizontal, so I cannot even skip ahead and tell you how it turns out. At the moment of writing this, all I can report is that we both have to wait to witness the unfolding. I shall update when I am able. Feeling weary, I retired to the rooftop apartment, which, as it happens, is now my cosy abode.

38

Arriving Home

November finally arrived home at three in the morning. Her sleepy village Starhaven, named after its five-pointed star shape, was forty-five minutes south of London. Its aerial view is of a beautiful star and it is surrounded by green meadows and forests. The locals believe the founders built it on powerful Earth ley lines, giving it and its residents, access to special powers. Another peculiar aspect of the village is that none of the houses are numbered. They are named after their location on the star. November's semi-mansion is Far North Point, as it is at the tip of the northern-facing point. Every Wednesday, each resident receives a basket of star-shaped, healthy biscuits from the county council. November sighed with contentment and relief on returning to the quirky village that she had missed for a year.

She lifted her exhausted legs out of the back of the limo. "We dropped Honey off this afternoon, as you requested, and all your bags, shoes and gear, will arrive tomorrow."

"Oh great, thank you, James."

"My friend, Bill Harvey, will be visiting from the States next week, if you want to meet him. He is an expert on consciousness and knows about waves," James said with a wink.

November was used to James' well-tuned intuition, yet wondered how he knew she needed an expert to talk to about her strange experience. "Yes, I'd love to meet him. Text me in a couple of days. Good night, James." November waved, as he drove off in his lovely, white car.

Her heart sank thinking of Honey. For a moment, she hoped that the whole journey was a figment of her imagination and that Honey's sad news was also an illusion.

The automatic, outdoor lights popped on, distracting her, as she took weary, bare-foot, steps up the drive. She smiled and blinked slowly, relieved to arrive at the end of one of the longest days and longest years, ever. It is not always glitz and glamour being a rock star. The amount of energy you need to persevere through a long tour is almost equivalent to that required of a professional athlete for a whole season. Her body ached after three-hundred and sixty-five days and nights of gallivanting around the globe and pouring out her heart, on countless stages.

She stopped for a moment to gaze up at the stars. "Goodnight, friends," she said, waving her heavy arm. A shooting star shot across the sky. November smiled, shut her eyes, bent her head and wished aloud. "I wish to meet my actual parents, and I want everything that happened today to be real, apart from the talk with Honey. I also hope to see my new friends again, especially Klaus." Her heart skipped a beat at the thought of him.

Klaus. She gasped, as a delightful, tickling sensation filled her.

"Ok, Fox, master of self-control," she said, laughing at herself.

November admired her charming house with all its lights. "Hello, lovely house, I've missed seeing you at night." She wished for the first time, since leaving Hartwall that she had friends awaiting her. Although November was accustomed to talking to Honey, her plants, her guitar, her computer, and even the glass doors to the garden, she sensed it was time to extend her family and include more people. She fished out the message in a bottle from her jeans and squeezed it tight, wondering what tomorrow would bring.

Then she spotted something on the doorstep. *"No, it can't be!"*

Another box sat there in the moonlight. A beautiful, golden present, awaiting her arrival. Suddenly re-energised, she ran to the house and scooped up the gift. She caressed the familiar fabric, which, once again, sent warm tingles through her entire being. This gift seemed heavier than the one she had discovered earlier, in that very place.

She drew the mysterious golden form close to her chest, cuddling it as if it were a teddy bear. She walked inside. Her beloved fox dog, Honey, stood in the hall, with a panting smile, wagging her tail, like a windscreen wiper on high speed.

"Dog, dog, there you are." She wrapped her arms around Honey and cuddled her tight. "I've missed you; look what was waiting for us." She released her dog and held up the present.

"Don't open it!" I screamed, cloaked in my blanket. I was exhausted and did not want to miss any adventures, if there were any inside the box.

"Honey, was it really you on the magic carpet?" Honey stopped wagging her tail, sat down and looked into November's eyes.

"Is it true you will need to leave soon?" Honey dipped her head.

Tears began to well in November's eyes, as she walked further inside. The screen went blank. I dashed, with the last of my energy, to the café plasma.

39

Bed Time

What happened next convinces me the dawn is very near.

I peered with weary eyes, as November poured a big glass of dark, grape juice. Her eyes were puffy from crying. She carried Honey to the second floor, before returning to retrieve the present and her drink. Honey's arthritis had become so bad that the staircase was too much of a struggle for her.

"I'm going to install a doggie elevator, Honey," she called up to her dog, who waited at the top of the stairs. As she dragged her tired legs up to the bedroom, November paused then tripped on the final stair, spilling grape juice on the carpet. *Deja vu*, she thought, as she gave Honey a pat and kept walking down the hall—she didn't have the energy to clean it up tonight. Honey went to her bed and curled up in a ball. November went to the bathroom to wash her face, reassuring her reflection in the mirrored tiles that *It was just a coincidence that Honey had nodded her head. I'm just delirious from the tour; I need a holiday and rest time.* She exhaled a deep breath, doing her best to expel any worry. November went back into her bedroom, too tired to change clothes–where the golden present beckoned. *The master of self-control,* she lifted the lid a little, then quickly shut it, aware its contents could well lead her far from the comfort of her mattress.

"Don't open it. Don't open it. Don't open it!" I implored.

She allowed herself to read the card; *For the attention of November Fox, the book's leading character.* She placed the golden temptation on the table across the room, and sat, cross-legged, on the thick, brown bedding, staring off into space. She became lost in flashbacks of the day's massive journey. After a while, she opened her music box and began to sing along.

"*Somewhere over the rainbow, way up high.*" Her spirits lifted. The forces of the universe seemed to be in harmony with her, as another shooting star sped past the window. She re-read the mini label.

"*Lead character?*" The possible meaning of that title dawned on her. "How ridiculous. I don't think so. Today was dreamlike, but I'm not fictional!" Her eyes searched the room, landing on the portal, which opens her world to you and me. Yes you, (Insert me waving at you again,) the one scanning these words right now. November stared straight at *us.*

She waved at us, considering the possibility she is in a story, and you are reading about her.

"Ok, I'll indulge you, label." November cleared her throat. "Readers, I'm talking to you, if you can actually hear me," she said with a simper of self-consciousness.

"For your information, I am alive, and that is for sure. Check this," she said and pinched herself, "Ooow!" A red mark appeared on her arm.

"I told you; this is no dream. This is no book; I'm real, but the question is, *are you? And are you watching me?*" She hesitated and glanced at the wall's electrical socket.

"Mmm, I don't understand the workings of electricity either, despite its existence, *so it's possible you exist, too?*" She surveyed our viewing space, above and below, wondering from which angle we could be looking at her.

"If I'm simply a character, how would I be aware of being one? Does that self-awareness not prove I am more?"

I thought that was quite a clever point.

"Perhaps we are both illusions?" She paused to hold up her arm. "If you see your body, and I can look at mine simultaneously, we are either both real or both hallucinations." She said, still staring at her arm. "I have had the strangest day, today. I guess you know already since you're reading about me." She laughed aloud.

"After everything, I wouldn't be surprised if Miss Mysterious Universe now tells me I'm just fiction. How fitting." She turned to face the window and the star-filled night sky.

"Conscious Fiction with its characters aware of themselves. Quite a paradox." November focused on our viewing space, looking directly into our eyes again.

"Well, even if it were true, I'm now awake to it. I am consequently no longer only in a story but am conscious of my chronicle. The question remains, *do you exist?"*

I do not think she could actually see us. She may perceive some concept of us, which I guess is the first step towards really seeing us.

"Well, for what it's worth, I hope we are both alive in reality," she said aloud.

"I have an idea. The Captain said I am now at level two; time to engage. So, if you are real, I invite you to become a Keeper of the Cube, one of the LOTNE: Leaders of the New Earth. You will be a level one initiate. I will make a cube you can download and build from my webpage. That will prove *we both* exist."

I was very thankful that she had decided to wait until the morning to open the box and begin her next adventure, wanting to remain in this moment as long as possible.

She sighed with tiredness and satisfaction as she slipped under the covers.

"Even if I am just make-believe, at least I can live forever in my perfect moment, right here in this gateway, where fulfilment meets anticipation. I am happy to press pause right now, whether I'm real or not." One yin-yang tear of joy and pain trickled down her face. The thought of her past and her future, both laced with dynamic emotions, simultaneously hugged and pierced her, as she disappeared further under the covers.

"Oh, how I love my bed, ducking under the wave," came a mumble from under the blankets.

Before she could contemplate anything more, she fell fast asleep. And that, my friends, in the World of Form, is a day in the life of November Fox. Also officially ending my first ever letter. So I will sign off now, to avoid any further, unnecessary tangents, and roll this message into a bottle and get it off to you as soon as possible. I hope to hear from you as I begin work on my next message.

I do hope this finds you well and consciously creating the reality of your dreams, as a new level one initiate Keeper of the Cube.

Remember, the power to create is within you.

Your loyal friend always, I (aka The Architect.) Currently November Fox's Observer.

(Insert me smiling, blowing you a kiss and waving.)

P.S. Charlie sends his greetings, too, and, asks you to keep an eye out for his floral beloved.

Erica's Note

I stood, utterly speechless, in the front row at November Fox's concert, next to my best friend, Sassi, unable to even broach the subject of my acquaintance with the rock star. The intertwining of what has occurred may be a puzzle that will take me a while to figure out. I feared that my story might sound insane to others. Like November, I love games, though never in my life had I imagined such a multidimensional web. It was a remarkable moment indeed when November and I exchanged an extended stare during her concert. We look almost identical, although my hair is tamer. I don't think Sassi noticed the similarity. When our eyes locked, I felt an immediate bond with November that went beyond knowing more about her inner life than most others. It was as though we are deeply connected somehow; I sensed she felt that, too.

I asked Sassi if we could meet November after the show since, as president of the Elephant Foundation, she was an invited guest, but she said access was restricted.

She did, however, say that her friend, Klaus, the journalist, would be meeting with November and could pass on a message.

Then these incredibly, amazing things happened.

During her last song and after our staring exchange, I dashed out to find the toilet. I took a blank page from the small bottle I had bought at the bookshop and scribbled down a note.

Hi, November. Call me. We need to talk. 0798 1575 123.

I was in a slight panic, unsure if what I had written would be enticing enough for her to call me, yet I had to get back to the show before it ended, so there was no time to write a more detailed message. I ran through the vacant side-passage from the restrooms, back to the massive hall and its cheering crowd. Turning a sharp corner, I bumped into a man, who was running the other way.

We were both almost knocked to the floor. He instinctively put his strong hands on both of my arms to keep me upright. Time froze as we gazed into each other's eyes. A few moments had passed before either of us moved. My already racing heart beat faster and faster. I can't explain the magnetism that caught us both in a whirlwind; I yearned to kiss him with all of my being, right there on the spot.

Before anything else could happen, he reached into his pocket and pulled out his business card. I took it and put it in my handbag without breaking eye-contact.

"Here's my number. I would love to see you again," he said in a non-British English accent before he ran towards the off limits backstage.

I retrieved the card and read his name: Hamish Marsh, *Orphan Star Management.*

It was Hamey from the story, November's manager. It had to be. His last name was appropriate since, if he hadn't jogged off, I would've remained stuck in the *marsh* of his being, forever.

Now, if you thought things couldn't get more peculiar, they then did. As I approached the hall, The Architect stood at the door, like a bouncer, gazing towards the stage with admiration and a shine in his eyes.

"Hi, you're here again."

"Indeed I am," he replied, as I walked up to stand next to him. I held up the miniature message bottle.

"Genius."

"I have so many questions."

"You had better ask them fast; I am still mastering the focus needed to keep me here." He grinned as he glanced back at November strutting across the large stage, her fans screaming with wild enthusiasm.

"Why do I look like her?"

"It would seem you are sisters. There are actually three of you."

"What do you mean? We can't be; we're both orphans."

"A message arrived in one of my underground occuli think tanks, I assume from the Cube Maker."

"What message?"

"The next part of the prophecy. It talks about the power of three." He flickered like a hologram, almost disappearing.

"No, come back!" I shouted.

He regained his presence and looked deeply into my eyes. "Why is this happening to me; why haven't you contacted November?"

"She will soon be ready. It is Steven's presence around you that has expanded your frequency perception range, enabling us to communicate."

"What am I meant to do?" But he was gone; vanished.

I returned to the front row; a plethora of questions flooding my already bamboozled mind. I gave the mini bottle to Sassi to give to Klaus. I felt quite relieved when she said she had arranged to meet him in the foyer, after the show. I desperately hoped that the note in the bottle would bring me needed answers.

Realising there was not much more I could do, I took a cab home and went directly to my room, where more pages had appeared in the magical, ruby vase. I fished them out, eagerly, and proceeded to read about the concert; November's exchange with me; her meeting with Klaus, and the successful delivery of my message.

Although November thought the note was from Klaus, I felt sure she would call the number, and I could explain.

It was now 2:22 in the morning. My mobile rang. Everyone knows not to phone *unless...* My heart skipped this time with joy. *Unless* it was November Fox. It was.

"Klaus? Is that you?"

"*Ummm.* No, it's Erica, and please don't hang up."

"Who are you?"

"I'm unsure how to explain it all. I don't even know... I mean, I need to see you in person."

"Sorry, my manager Hamish has forbidden me to meet fans, unless he is there."

"I've met Hamish, and I know all about Klaus, and your powers, and the Mad Professor and Laura. I know everything." There was a long silence before she asked, "Are you the Cube Maker?"

"No."

"Then how do you know about everything?"

"Let's meet tomorrow afternoon to talk about it. Brighton Beach, two o'clock?"

Again, November didn't reply for quite some time.

"Well, I don't normally do this kind of thing, but ok. My intuition says we should meet, and, after today, I think I should listen to it."

"I agree. Don't open the gold present yet–not until after we see each other and talk."

"What present?"

"Aren't you at home yet? You're in bed, aren't you?"

"No, I'm in the limo."

I paused, wondering how the letter's message was now appearing ahead of real time.

"Then be careful with your grape juice."

"What?"

I looked over at the pile of pages and the empty bottle on my side table. "I'll tell you everything tomorrow, and it will blow your mind."

"Ok."

We both hung up our phones.

I sank into the loving arms of my duvet, and a new sensation swept over me. I was no longer alone. My life had purpose, and I was quite sure, for the first time that I had an actual family member. I was going to meet my sister in less than twelve hours. A large smile spread across my weary face.

There and then, I decided this remarkable letter that I had found, was now complete. I would have it published as book one of a story that is still unfolding.

May it find you well, my dear reader, and be sure to remember; Things aren't always as they seem, *do we wake or do we dream? Are we dreaming life or living the dream?* The answer may be that we do both.

Beyond the Book

As a thank you for reading this book, I would like to give you some free November Fox songs and some other bonus book goodies. Please just visit www.novemberfox.com, and sign up to the mailing list to receive them.

If you have enjoyed reading November Fox – Book 1. Following Joy, would you mind taking a minute to write a review on Amazon? Even a short review really helps, I read each one personally, and it would mean a lot to me. Thank you in advance.

If someone you care about would enjoy reading this book, please send them a copy by gifting it to them on Amazon.

If you'd like to order multiple copies of this book for your company, school, or group of friends, please go to www.novemberfox.com to receive a bulk discount.

You can also listen and buy more November Fox music on the November Fox website and keep in the loop of what's happening.

Finally, if you'd like to get pre-release material and receive updates on my future projects you can sign up for my newsletter at www.ee-bertram.com.

You can also follow us on Twitter @estherbertram and @XIFox and Instagram @orpahnrockstar or Facebook @NF123

If you'd like to learn how to Lucid Dream in 10-minute lessons each night, scan this QR code to do a wonderful course.

Thanks so much to all who helped November Fox come to life, especially John Nelson/Editor, Lynne Bertram/Creative Editor, Tauseef Ahmed – tauseef.ahmed11@yahoo.com/Book Illustrations, Gary, Mum, Sue, Michael, Nerida, Peter, Keno, Sassi, Greg, Di, Giralph, the Kickstarter supporters, Theo Glaudemans @ LimebizzARConcepts for endorsing the Augmented Reality layers, Rens Eijgermans for the technical implementation and most of all *YOU* dear reader, for without you, this book wouldn't exist at all.

With much Love,
E.E. Bertram
www.eebertram.com

Please visit the web page to sign up to receive your November Fox songs and bonus material. www.novemberfox.com

Scan This QR Code to download FREE November Fox Music